Praise for *Overdrive*:

"As perceptive and vivid a portrayal of the business world and its ramifications as *The Crack in the Teacup* was of the political maelstrom."—*Library Journal*

"Gilbert is as vigorously readable as ever."—*New York Times*

"Mr. Gilbert is a gifted writer of thrillers and he hustles the reader into a more than willing suspension of disbelief."—*New Yorker*

"Mr. Gilbert goes from strength to strength with each new book."—*Springfield News*

Also by Michael Gilbert from Carroll & Graf:

Game without Rules

MICHAEL GILBERT

OVER-DRIVE

Carroll & Graf Publishers, Inc
New York

Reprinted by arrangement with Curtis Brown Associates

First Carroll & Graf edition 1988

Carroll & Graf Publishers, Inc.
260 Fifth Avenue
New York, NY 10001

ISBN: 0-88184-402-0

Manufactured in the United States of America

Contents

POSTSCRIPT

A FOLDED ribbon of dusty track zigzagged up the side of the hill, twisting itself into a final loop around the shoulder on which the Villa Korngold was perched.

Three of us were sitting at a late breakfast on the veranda. Dr. Hartfeldt was looking tired, as a man might who had been called out at midnight and had been working, on and off, ever since. Herr Professor Lindt, with his patrician face and small imperial beard, was serious but composed. As for me, I was wondering how Oliver had ever persuaded his architects and builders to put the Villa Korngold where it was. Even to the Swiss, who are used to solving curious problems of this sort, the blasting of the foundations, the laying of the drains, and the pumping up of the water supply must have presented almost insoluble difficulties.

But that was a trait in Oliver's character which had to be reckoned with. All his life he had been seeing ends without bothering too much about the means.

The view compensated for everything. The remote and peaceful valley was spread, as a map, at your feet; from the high peaks in the south it fell in a broad sweep downward, to the point where the little village of Aronschildt nestled on its shelf of rock, then made a second dip down to the river, at Oberthal, and the railway and the civilization which lay beyond it.

Dr. Hartfeldt said, "One has the impression, sitting here, of looking down, as a spectator, on the struggles of one's fellows, but being happily above them for oneself."

"I'd rather be sitting here," I said, "than sweating up that track with a bicycle."

At the farthest turning, just above the village, the figure of a man had appeared. As we watched, he gave up the struggle against the gradient, dismounted, and started to push his bicycle. A thin tail of chalky white dust blew out behind him.

"He must be coming here," said the Professor. "The track leads only to the villa. I wonder who it can be."

"He'll be pretty hot by the time he gets here," I said.

I had been up most of the night, too, and I was in that mood of relaxed fantasy which fatigue sometimes brings. The white twisting road, the hot sunshine, and the fact that I was thinking of Oliver chimed together.

It is the summer of 1944 and I am in a Sherman tank, with my eyes just above the level of the turret, and I am trundling forward into one of the sweetest deathtraps of the Italian campaign.

The Germans had had two months to prepare for our advance up the Adriatic side, and two months for those mole-like masters of defensive warfare was a hell of a long time. All the easy lines of approach had been cratered. The remaining ones were covered by anti-tank guns sited in depth, and worse—we suspected—by the turrets of German Tiger tanks dismounted and dug in, hull down, behind successive crests. It was a position which could have been taken easily enough by infantry, preferably at night. But the available infantry were all busy on the other side of the peninsula. Our own Brigadier had already refused to make this particular attack, and had been Stellenbosched by a Divisional Commander who had one eye on a K.B.E. and a Corps, and wasn't going to let a few damned tank casualties stop him. We knew all about this before the attack started, and it had done nothing to raise our morale.

Oliver was commanding A Troop at the time. I had B. Dumbo Nicholson had C, and D was—I've forgotten his name, but can remember what he looked like. A little dark chap, with bow legs like an ostler. Oliver got us together the night before, and when we had finished speaking our minds about our commanders, he had said, "There's only one thing for it, chaps. We've got to go into that bloody valley like gangsters walking into an enemy headquarters. It doesn't matter *what* the orders say. One troop moves at a time, and the other three cover him. Agreed?"

The fact that we *did* agree was the clearest proof of the confidence we had in his judgment. This confidence had been a plant of four years' growth.

The day we had arrived together at the Regimental Depot of the 22nd Lancers at Weybridge, Oliver said to me, "How did you get into a crowd like this?" I said, with a touch of youthful hauteur, "As a matter of fact, my father was in the Poms in the last war, and he knows the Adjutant." And then, since it seemed a natural question, "How did you?"

"Oh, one of my racing pals wangled it," said Oliver. "He thought it might be up my street."

"If you're keen on riding, you ought to have joined the King's Troop. The Poms lost their horses six months ago. They're armored cars now."

Oliver looked at me in blank surprise, "My dear old boy," he said. "You don't think I'd have come within a mile of them if they'd had horses, do you? Smelly archaic quadrupeds. When I said racing, I was talking about cars."

"Well, you'd better not say that when you get there," I said. "There are still a lot of senior officers who wouldn't appreciate it. You'd better be careful."

"Oh, discretion itself," said Oliver, with a grin. "To tell you the truth, this war cropped up in the nick of time. Three months later and I'd have been in Carey Street. I'd just spent the last penny of the family money."

But it was I who was out of step, not Oliver. Cars were in, horses were out. And cars were things Oliver understood. Being without a nerve in his pudgy body, he could drive any mechanically propelled contrivance, from a motorcycle to a tank, at least ten miles an hour faster than its makers had thought it could be driven, and his reflexes were quick enough to get him out of the trouble he created. He had other talents and peculiarities. He was a fine shot; was opposed to unnecessary exercise in any form; had a remarkable capacity for absorbing alcohol; and had an endless repertoire of dirty songs and recitations. Nature had constructed him to specifications precisely apt for a modern cavalry regiment.

It wasn't until we got to North Africa that we discovered something more: that he had a natural tactical sense. It was something between an eye for ground and an instinct for what an opponent was going to do, and it made him a natural tank fighter. His troop called him lucky. It was a high compliment. And it was the reason three troop commanders, all senior to him in age and appointment, were listening to him now.

"Willie's orders say something about advancing by bounds, two troops up," said Dumbo Nicholson, looking at the mimeographed sheet of paper clipped to his map board.

"And why do you suppose Willie gave us orders in writing?" said Oliver. "It's to cover himself. He knows we'll interpret them sensibly."

"What about the timings? If *we* move one troop at a time, and all the other squadrons advance two up, we're going to be a bit late on all our check lines."

"When I was learning to drive," said Oliver, "my instructor said to me, 'Better ten minutes late in this world, young man, than ten years early into the next.'"

The D Troop Commander said, "Pipe down, Dumbo. Oliver's talking sense. We can tune in to each other on our intercoms. Cut out the squadron net altogether. Once we're out of sight, we can take it in our own time."

And that was how I reached that particular point in my history, going very slowly forward in bottom gear, up a narrow re-entrant in the foothills of the Apennines, with the practical certainty that I was a sitting duck for the first German who bothered to pull the trigger.

Better ten minutes late in this world than ten years early into the next. Ten years? I was only twenty-five at the time. On normal expectations I had another fifty years to live. Or maybe fifty seconds?

I turned my head slowly, from left to right and back again, trying to pick out the danger spots. In theory this was something you could do through a periscope, but it was much more difficult that way, and not a lot safer. Anything that was fired at a tank was designed to go through the tank, as well as the people inside it.

The No. 19 set behind me crackled. This was the set

which connected me to the Squadron Leader. He had a second set in his tank back to the Colonel, the Colonel to the Brigadier, and the Brigadier to the Divisional Commander in his caravan, tucked away somewhere down by the blue Adriatic. It was a system which gave the higher command an illusion that they were directing a tank battle.

I said to the operator, "Roger and out." I wasn't listening. All my attention was concentrated on the other set.

"Able to Baker," said Oliver's voice in my ear. "Keep a bit left, then you'll be out of sight of that nasty line of bushes ahead of you."

"I didn't much like the look of them myself," I said. "Keep them covered while I see if we can get down into the bottom of the valley."

"There's a pimple up on your right," said Oliver. "It doesn't look entirely natural. Can you see it? Half right, two o'clock—look out!"

A pencil of yellow flame, a shuddering thump, as if a giant had slugged the side of my tank with an enormous sledge hammer, and, much later, the sound of the shot. The armor-piercing shell, fired from the Tiger on the crest ahead of me, had hit the front end of my right-hand track, deflected, and sliced through the driving compartment, taking off my driver's head and my right foot. As the German gunner was traversing for the shots which would finish me off, stationary and helpless, Oliver finished *him* off instead.

It was a fantastically skillful and fantastically lucky shot. Bear in mind that all Oliver had to aim at was an armored slit, roughly eighteen inches wide and four inches deep, formed like the mouth of an undershot bulldog, with the lower lip protruding and partly blocking the upper lip. On a range, with plenty of time to lay, a good shot might have done it once in twenty times. Oliver put his first shell slap through the letter box. It killed all four Germans inside the Tiger. A bit later he came up, got me and the two unwounded members of my crew out, put a tourniquet on my leg, and wirelessed for the M.O. After that he got on with the battle.

We lost one more tank, knocked out two anti-tank guns, and were the only squadron to get onto our final objective at all. Oliver might reasonably have expected a gong for what he did. Actually what he got was a bollocking from the Squadron Commander, who had heard of his unofficial order party.

I finished up in Caserta General Hospital, had the remains of my right foot snipped off, went back to England, and was fitted out with one of the new two-way stretch artificial feet. In lots of ways they're an improvement on the natural article. If you get osteoarthritis, you can cure it with a grease gun.

I kept in touch with the 22nd by writing to friends in it. I knew that they had taken part in the crossing of the Senio in the spring, and had landed up in Austria, nearly getting into a fight with Tito, and finishing up doing guard duty while the odds and sods of the Germany Army trickled in from Hitler's inner fortress, some truculent still, but mostly so fed up they gave no trouble to anyone.

I got only one letter from Oliver. He wasn't a great letter writer.

On a Saturday morning, three years later, I was sitting in the snack bar of the pub near Bucklersbury known to young City men as the Royal Nob, trying to decide between tinned crab and tinned salmon as a filling between tired pieces of brown bread calling itself a sandwich. In those days, believe it or not, a lot of people in the City worked on Saturday mornings. I had finished the half pint of beer which I had carried across with me, and was debating whether, if I tried to order a second drink, I should get back to my place at the lunch counter when a hand came over my shoulder, holding a large gin-and-tonic, and put it down beside me.

"I seem to remember," said Oliver, "that you have a weakness for this nauseating mixture. How's the foot?"

"Terrific," I said. "I played five games of squash on it yesterday. No trouble at all. How are things with you?"

"Fair to middling. The last two years have been a bit of a grind. By and large it's been great fun, really."

We were both taking stock of each other, in the way people did when they met again for the first time after the war. We'd all heard stories of ex-officers of the 1914-18 war who met their company commanders selling boot laces off a tray on Victoria Street. Oliver was fatter than when I had seen him last. He looked prosperous. Clothes rationing had leveled people off, but his suit and shirt had cost at least twice as much as mine, and the shoes were the sort which came off a last, not out of a box on a shelf. He had a scar down one side of his jaw which looked too recent to be a war wound.

"I suppose you're a qualified accountant now?"

"I qualified in autumn, 1945. That was the very first exam after the war. They let you through if you could multiply up to five in your head. They tell me it's more difficult now. What about you?"

"I'm a manufacturing chemist," said Oliver. "I don't mind you drinking my gin, but I do draw the line at your depositing your cigarette ash in it." This was to a stout man standing next to him. The man muttered an apology and squeezed out of the crowd. "Are you fixed up in a firm yet?"

"I've got a job," I said. "I'm not a partner."

"Let's move over to the other bar. There's a bit more room there."

We had two more drinks, and I was brought up to date with the doings of the 22nd Lancers and the fates of a number of my friends, but I could sense that Oliver was only going through the motions. He had never been very interested in the past.

He was drinking double gins with single Frenches in them. The girl behind the counter seemed to know what he wanted without being told. She had dark-black hair, an Irish accent, and a sweater so tight it must have been knitted on her.

"It's no use getting ideas about Maureen," said Oliver. "She's married to an all-in wrestler. If you haven't got anything better to do, why not come down and spend the weekend with me?"

"Well—"

"I've rented a revolting little furnished house at Radlett. But the beds are comfortable and Mrs. Comrie cooks the rations beautifully, with a little help from the black market. All you'll need is your pajamas and a toothbrush. What about it?"

What about it? If I didn't, I should spend the afternoon at a soccer match, and the evening either drinking beer or sitting at home with my mother, listening to her blitz stories. I sometimes thought she'd had a more exciting war than I had.

"Besides," said Oliver, "I've got a proposition I'd like to put to you. While we drive down, I'll tell you what I've been up to during the last two years. It's had its moments."

He had already assumed I would come.

(The little man, pushing his bicycle, had reached the first elbow bend in the road. I watched him out of sight.)

PART I

Skirmishing in Elsfield Wood

IN THE early part of that year, the Minister of Food aroused great indignation amongst housewives by proposing to discontinue the bulk purchase of dried egg from America; the expenditure of nine million pounds on films was also criticized, but the Chancellor of the Exchequer said that American films were better for morale than dried egg. The British Union of Fascists held a meeting in the Albert Hall which was attended by two hundred members; since three hundred Communists also attended, few speeches were made. Sir Hartley Shawcross, introducing the Trades Disputes Bill, said that the trade unions had been victimized and intimidated long enough. The 2-pound loaf was reduced to 1¾ pounds, but, in order to overcome the objection of bakers, was sold at the same price. Mr. Bevan, introducing the National Health Service Bill, said that it would mean happy doctors and efficient hospitals. A puma escaped from a private zoo in Kent. Mr. Laski said that the age of Socialist planning had arrived, and twenty thousand people squatted in abandoned Army camps.

Later that summer, Oliver Nugent accompanied Dumbo Nicholson on a visit to Elsfield Wood.

(ii)

Dumbo spent most of the journey apologizing for Quinn & Nicholson. In the end Oliver said, "I expect it's a bloody shambles, Dumbo. But if you go on about it, I shall begin to feel sorry I put my gratuity into it."

Dumbo, big, pink, and serious, like a grown-up Wolf Cub, said, "You won't lose your money, old boy. I guarantee that. If the worst comes to the worst, I'll buy you out myself."

"You'll do nothing of the sort," said Oliver. "I'm not buying preference shares in your outfit. I've got a slice of the equity. It's sink or swim, on this trip. Just at the moment, I feel rather buoyant. It must be the weather."

The September sun was beaming down out of a sky of implausible blue. Its smile warmed even the battered North London suburb, and the rows of prefabs which were beginning to show among the rubble of the blitz like mushrooms in a devastated field.

Dumbo said, "I joined the firm as soon as I left Bedford. I don't suppose I was much help to the old man. You know what it was like in 1937. I was already in the T.A. and doing two parades a week, and I played a lot of rugger."

"A typical product of the decadent thirties," said Oliver. "You realize that if you'd taken life more seriously— gone to the London School of Economics and read *Time and Tide*—Hitler would never have dared to attack us. *You* were responsible for the war, Dumbo. I wonder if that girl knows we can see straight into her bedroom? Yes, I think she does."

The train started again with a jerk.

"I ought to have helped the old man more," agreed Dumbo. "I realize that. We had quite a nice little business. In theory, we were prepared to make anything for anyone, from talcum powder to tummy pills. Actually we made the mistake of getting too involved with one outfit. The people who made San-Fine."

"Isn't that what every nice girl rolls on under the armpits or the stuff you scour out neglected lavatories with?"

"It's a skin cream. Or it was. When United Druggists bought up the San-Fine boys, they suppressed it. It conflicted with one of their own products."

"That seems to be one of the troubles of this business," said Oliver. "Too many products chasing the same market.

Why did you say it was a mistake getting invovled with the San-Finers? Couldn't they pay their bills?"

"It wasn't that. But by the time I came along, about sixty per cent of our business was making their products. So, you see, if they'd walked out on us, we should have had to sack half our staff. They used their position to squeeze us on costs."

"They had you by the short and curlies," said Oliver. He was leaning forward, really interested now. (It was like an orders party. Information about own troops. Information about enemy. Intention. Method. Plan of attack.) "So what happened next?"

"We clung to them like grim death. We cut prices to the lowest possible, and then cut them again. In the end I'm pretty sure we were producing for them at a loss, but the old man couldn't face the idea of closing down half the works, even temporarily. Then, one morning, we read in the papers that they'd been taken over by U.D. Of course, they do all their own production."

"So you *had* to sack half the staff?"

"Actually, no. That was August, 1939. As soon as war broke out, the government took us over."

"What for? Cough mixture for the troops?"

"They converted us into manufacturing filter ingredients for gas masks."

"Flexible," said Oliver. He smoked in silence for a few minutes, staring at the rows of miniature gardens, each with its own air-raid shelter. It was a new idea to him that a factory could be converted, almost overnight, from face cream to gas masks, and he was examining its implications.

"When your old man died, who kept the place going?"

"Len Williams. A good type. He was works foreman when I was there before the war. Father put him on the Board in 1941. He kept it going."

"I suppose turning out standard fitments for gas masks wasn't a very exacting job."

"Gas masks finished in 1943," said Dumbo. "Either they'd made enough or the powers that be realized we were never going to use them anyway, so we switched again, to first-aid kits for bomber crews. Antiseptic dressings. Antiburn ointments and morphia syrettes."

"Anti-burn? Made of what?"

"I don't really know. Yellow jelly. Acro-flavin, wasn't it?"

"Not proto-mycil?"

"Never heard of it. What is it?"

"Something I picked up in Switzerland," said Oliver. He seemed to have lost interest in the subject. "What a ghastly train this is. Think of it in the rush hour. When the carriage is full of steaming commuters."

"What are you doing about it?"

"I've rented a house near Radlett. It's a beastly little place, but it'll do for the time being. I shall come to work by car. As soon as I can find one."

The train had been rattling along for some minutes between green fields and now plunged into another zone of bricks and mortar: yards, back gardens, and the gable ends of barn-like structures which might have been factories or film studios; then it slowed and halted.

"When you think," said Oliver, "of all the attractive, historical, and desirable places that the Luftwaffe *did* drop bombs on, one wonders why they had to overlook this."

"We had three misses," said the ticket collector. "One of them just missed the Public Convenience."

"A horrifying thought," said Oliver. "Is there anywhere here I could buy a motorcar?"

"Snyder's, over the bridge on the right."

"And have lunch?"

"Duke of Cumberland. Over the bridge on the left."

"It looks as if we'd better go over the bridge, then."

Elsfield Wood was undergoing a change of life. For eight hundred years it had nestled round its flint-towered church, a community of farmers, market gardeners, and pig-breeders, selling produce to the ready markets of London. And then, almost overnight—no one could quite say when or how it had happened—London had opened its mouth and swallowed them. They had become part of the great sprawling beast they had been helping to feed.

The war had accelerated the processes of digestion.

Abandoned film studios were converted into factories. A steady flow of troops had stimulated all forms of local production. The illegitimacy rate had trebled. Now, by the summer of 1946, the last of the troops had departed, the wartime factories were closing down, and the speculative builders were closing in.

("If you listened hard," Oliver maintained, "you could hear the springs creaking as it got ready to stretch. It was tattered and battered and it wanted a coat of paint, but its streets were paved with gold. If I'd had any capital, I'd have gone into property dealing on the spot, and I'd have been a millionaire ten years later. Unfortunately, all I had was my gratuity, which I'd already invested in Dumbo's joint, and a sympathetic bank manager.")

While Dumbo went into the Duke to order lunch, Oliver had a look at Snyder's. It was a big, rambling outfit, with garage and workshops at the back and a forecourt full of prewar cars in the front, labeled, like slave girls in the market at Fez with a list of their alleged attractions, but with the price carefully concealed.

He hesitated in front of "Two-Cylinder Jowett 1926 Model. Still in Remarkable Condition," and "Standard Coventry. Reliable Little Runabout. Recently Entirely Overhauled," and came to rest between a neat Wolseley ("12 H.P. 1938 Model, One Owner, in Holy Orders") and a vast, sleek Lagonda ("Drophead Coupé, 1933/4 Model: 26 H.P. Seat Eight in Comfort").

Oliver poked his head inside the Wolseley. The speedometer showed a reading of just under nine thousand miles. Its owner must have had a very small parish, or done most of his visiting on foot. He saw that the accelerator and brake pedals had brand-new rubber pads on them, too.

He laid his folded newspaper on the ground, knelt on it, and looked under the edges of the mudguards. The rust had been sandpapered off, and they had been carefully repainted.

"Smart operator, this parson," said Oliver.

"Lost something?"

He got up and saw a mountain of a man, a human elephant in corduroy trousers and khaki pullover, leaning against the Lagonda, watching him. He was wearing plimsolls, and must have come up very quietly.

Oliver said, "Would you, by any chance, be Mr. Snyder?"

"I would."

"How much are you asking for this heap?"

"Two fifty."

"The list price, new, was a hundred and eighty pounds."

"Ah! That was 1938. You buy a new car by writing out a check then. Two-year waiting list now. A bargain at the price."

"*If* what the speedometer says is true," said Oliver, "it might be."

"And just what might you mean by that?"

"I've got a horrible feeling," said Oliver, "that the reverend gentleman who owns this car has been fiddling the speedometer. It's not difficult, given patience and a strong pair of pliers, but it's not the sort of thing one expects from the Establish Church, is it? Has it got a starting handle?"

"There's a self-starter."

"I'd prefer to start it on the handle. Easier to judge the compression that way."

Mr. Snyder gave Oliver a long hard look. Then, finding this wasn't making a great deal of impression, he opened the trunk and produced a starting handle.

Oliver switched on and swung the handle slowly. It went round easily, twice, before the engine kicked into life. He listened to it for a few moments.

"Perhaps you thought there wasn't an engine in it at all," said Mr. Snyder.

Oliver went round to the back, put the sole of his shoe against the exhaust pipe to check the running, took it away again, and repeated the operation. Finally he kept it there long enough to stop the engine altogether, came back to the front of the car, and switched on again.

"I should say that engine's done about twenty-five thousand miles, give or take a mile, wouldn't you?" he said.

"I believe what I'm told," said Mr. Snyder, wooden-faced.

"We could easily get an expert opinion," said Oliver. "The makers would know at once if the speedo had been tampered with." He let the thought hang for a moment, and then said, "Of course, I wouldn't want to get a clergyman into trouble. I'll give you a hundred and seventy pounds for her as she stands."

"Two hundred," said Mr. Snyder, in a choked voice.

"A hundred and eighty," said Oliver, and got out his

checkbook. "I see the license has got three months to run. And I'll tell you what, I'll buy all my gas from you. In fact, you can fill her up now."

When the deal had been completed, Mr. Snyder said, "Are you living down here, do I gather? Or is it business?"

"It's business," said Oliver.

"You ought to do well in business," said Mr. Snyder.

The Duke of Cumberland was the illegitimate offspring of a respectable coaching inn and the modern licensed catering establishment which is playfully known as a roadhouse. It had enjoyed the war and was now reluctantly getting used to the idea that customers might object to watery beer, uneatable food, and grudging service.

"The alternative luncheons," said Dumbo, "would appear to be boiled sole of boot with spring carrots or cold spam and plastic lettuce. And this is Len Williams."

"Good morning, Mr. Williams," said Oliver. "Mr. Nicholson was telling me all about you."

"Nothing to my discredit, I hope," said Mr. Williams.

"On the contrary," said Oliver. "He tells me you have been the mainstay of the firm since his father died. What's that you're drinking—Scotch?"

"If you want whiskey, I'd better do the ordering. They still like to keep it under the counter."

"Then you'd better get three doubles while you're at it," said Oliver. "I don't want much to eat. Perhaps a couple of pork pies."

He watched Len Williams fighting his way through the lunchtime crowd at the snack bar, and said, "He doesn't look too fit, Dumbo."

"He's had a hard war."

"Not like you and me," agreed Oliver.

Three-quarters of an hour later the middle-aged lady behind the bar started to intone, "Last orders, please," and the two barmen started collecting empty mugs.

"Your credit seems to be good, Len," said Oliver. "See if you can get us one more."

"Not for me," said Dumbo.

"You'll have one, Len?"

"If you insist," said Mr. Williams. A pink flush, starting round his jowls and moving upward like a sunset in reverse, was now enveloping the bald expanses of his head.

"Make it two big ones if you can," said Oliver.

As Mr. Williams pushed his way through the crowd round the bar, Dumbo said, "If he's going to show us round the works this afternoon, we don't want him stinko."

"Len's all right."

"Not everyone's got your remarkable capacity for whiskey."

"I'm conducting a scientific experiment. Watch his hands, and his chin. Particularly his chin."

When Mr. Williams came back, he was carrying a glass in each hand. He placed them carefully on the table, one at a time. Oliver topped them both well up with water, raised his, and said, "Prosperity to Quinn & Nicholson."

As Mr. Williams picked up his glass, some of the drink slopped out of it onto the table top.

"I'll drink to that," he said.

Dumbo could see that his left hand was gripping the side of his chair so tightly that his knuckles showed white.

"Time, gentlemen, *if* you please. Act of Parliament."

Dumbo was watching Mr. Williams. His head kept jerking round, as if he were trying to scratch the top of his left shoulder with his chin but just missing it each time.

Oliver said, "Well, now. Hadn't we better be starting our tour of the works? There's a lot to look at."

Mr. Williams put down his glass. The drink in it was almost untouched.

"If you'll excuse me for a moment," he said, speaking each word as if it hurt. "I've got to go home and pick up some papers. I'll see you at the works in half an hour."

"Fine," said Oliver. He sat back in his chair, his eyes dreamy, swirling the whiskey lovingly round in the glass. As an afterthought, he added the remains of Mr. Williams' abandoned drink to his own.

"What's it all about?" said Dumbo.

"I'm afraid we shall have to be looking for another managing director," said Oliver.

"Because he can't drink level with you?"

"Not only that. Let's go and look at the works."

The crowd round the bar was still thick. As they pushed through it, a character in a light-gray flannel suit with a Clark Gable mustache was saying, "Now that all those pansy soldier boys have stopped playing games and gone home, perhaps we can get on with some real work."

Oliver stopped and swung round.

"I expect you had a good war, didn't you?"

"Eh?"

"Made a lot of money, too?"

"What are you talking about?"

"While the soldier boys were keeping you nice and safe."

"Look here—" said the man, and stopped. There was something about the way Oliver was holding himself that he didn't like. He said, "I wasn't talking to you."

"Quite so," said Oliver. "But I'm talking to you. I'm one of those pansy soldier boys."

There was a fringe of babble going on all round, but the circle in which they stood was quiet.

The man said, "You're tight. I don't want any trouble with you."

"That's one way out of your difficulties," said Oliver and went out, followed by Dumbo.

(iii)

To get to the Quinn & Nicholson works, you turned left in Elsfield Wood High Street, went for thirty yards down a side street, crossed a small waterway, turned left again into an unmade road, proceeded along that for fifty or sixty yards, recrossed the waterway again by a concrete slab bridge, and found yourself at the main entrance.

"Is this the only way in?" said Oliver.

"Access has always been a snag," said Mr. Williams. He had met them at the bridge, and seemed to be himself again. "We've got a right of way through the Strickland Engineering Works—that's the big building there—and out on to the High Street, but we can't load lorries that way. They have to come down here."

"Pretty difficult in winter."

"They do get bogged sometimes. If it's really wet, we carry the cartons on hand trolleys to the corner and load there."

"Quite an operation," said Oliver, and led the way in.

The works was a roomy, one-story construction, with a

double row of skylights, partitioned down the middle.

"The offices are at the far end," said Mr. Williams. "We go through the packing to get to them. It isn't a very convenient arrangement—"

He found he had lost his audience. Oliver had stopped to talk to the little girl operating the carton-stapling machine.

"I seem to have seen you before," he said.

The girl grinned. "We had a dance together," she said.

She had a nose like a little boot and hair like a kitchen mop but, in spite of these drawbacks, or possibly because of them, looked just about as sexy as it is possible for a girl to look when she is wearing a utility smock and flannel trousers.

Oliver perched himself on the corner of the packing bench, and the other girls within earshot abandoned all pretense of work.

"The only dance I've been to in the last five years," he said, "was the Christmas Eve sergeants' mess dance at Thetford in 1942."

"That's right. I was fifteen, and it was my first dance. I thought you danced beautifully."

"I don't expect your standards were so high then," said Oliver. "Let me guess. You must be Sergeant Taylor's daughter."

"Ten out of ten," said the girl.

"What's he doing now?"

"Dad? He's doing a lorry run up to Covent Garden."

"Does he like that?"

"It's good money. But it means getting up at two o'clock in the morning."

"Mmm," said Oliver.

"Through here," said Mr. Williams, "we've got the distillation plant, and the refrigerators."

"Be with you in a moment," said Oliver. He turned back to the girl. "Let's have your father's address, will you? Telephone number, too, if he's got one. Jot it down here."

"Most of the raw material we use has to be kept under refrigeration," said Mr. Williams.

When they had finished with the refrigeration plant and the sterilizers and the various mixing and pounding and cooking and steaming machines—"Like a witches' kitchen," said Oliver—they repaired to the office. This was a jumble of filing cabinets, cupboards, box files, crates, and cartons surrounding and threatening at any moment to engulf an old wooden roll-top desk, all squashed together in a partitioned corner of the packing-room floor. A padlocked door led off it into a further and apparently even smaller apartment.

"That's where we keep the restricted drugs," said Mr. Williams. "Morphine, cocaine."

"Who's got the keys?"

"There's only one key," said Mr. Williams, "and I've got it."

Oliver held out his hand. There was a moment's hesitation before Mr. Williams said, "Actually it's a bit difficult. I have to sign an undertaking to the local Inspector not to let the key out of my possession."

"What's his number?"

"Number?"

"The local Inspector. Where does he hang out? What's his telephone number?"

"Why?"

"If you feel any scruples about handing over the key, I'll ring him up and fix it quickly enough."

"I shouldn't think that'd be really necessary. I was just explaining the regulations. If you're prepared to take the responsibility—"

"It won't keep me awake at night," said Oliver with a smile, and held out his hand. Mr. Williams passed across the key. "Now, let's have a look at some of these records. Can you find a chair for Mr. Nicholson?"

The little office was like an oven. The afternoon sun shone directly through the skylight. A single electric fan barely disturbed the heat-laden air.

Oliver and Dumbo took off their jackets and rolled up their sleeves. "Make yourself comfortable, Mr. Williams," said Oliver. "We've got a lot to do."

"Fine," said Mr. Williams. "Where would you like to start?"

"You'd better start by explaining the filing system."

By half past six, the last of the workers had departed. Dumbo had gone off on some errand of his own. Oliver was still asking questions.

"Do we have a night watchman?"

"We haven't got one of our own," said Mr. Williams. The perspiration was running down his white forehead in great drops. He dabbed at them from time to time with a handkerchief. But he still hadn't taken off his coat.

"Then what do we do about security?"

"Strickland's man looks in on us from time to time. We pay a small part of his wages."

"Which means he keeps a careful eye on their stuff, but doesn't bother about ours. Who locks up at night?"

"Whoever's last away. Usually me."

"Has there been much pilfering?"

"There isn't a lot here that anyone would want to steal, really."

Oliver looked down the silent bays of the packing shop and the works: at the row of machines, each tucked up for the night in its canvas jacket; at the piles of cartons and containers, the boxes of labels, the row of bottles and tins stacked ready for the morning.

"I suppose not," he said. "I shall be here for some time yet. There's no need for you to hang on if you don't want to."

"What about locking up?"

"I expect I can manage. Are those the keys on that hook?"

"That's right. There's a Yale on the outer door, and the big key's the padlock on the gate over the bridge. Strickland's man comes through the communicating door. He's got his own key."

"Fine," said Oliver. "I'll finish looking through these duplicate invoices before I go."

Oliver was still there when Dumbo came back at half past seven. His heels were on the desk, and his chair was tilted back at an extreme angle. There was a faraway look in his eyes.

"Directors don't get paid for overtime," said Dumbo. "Come and have a drink. There's a decent little local round the corner. Not like that ghastly roadhouse we had lunch in."

"It's fascinating," said Oliver. He made no attempt to move. "So nearly dead, but not quite. Heart hardly fluttering, yet still alive. Like an old, old elephant, lying on its back in a jungle thicket. The vultures drop in and have a look at it. Is it all over? No! The tip of the trunk gives a tiny twitch. There's life in the old pachyderm yet. Tomorrow, perhaps—"

"What *are* you talking about?"

"I'm talking about this firm." Dumbo sat down. He said, looking rather white, "Is it as bad as that?"

"You remember, on the train coming down, telling me how you got into a spot in 1939 by giving too much of your business to one outlet?" Oliver turned the pages of the ledger in front of him. "Do you realize how much of our turnover last year was War Office work? I haven't worked it out accurately, but over ninety per cent. And the war's over, Dumbo. It's been over for a year. As soon as Stalin stops making faces, we'll go back to a peacetime Army. And a peacetime Army isn't going to have its medical supplies manufactured in a dump like this."

"It is a bit disorganized at the moment."

"You've got a gift for understatement. It isn't disorganized, it's a bloody shambles. No proper security arrangements. No quality control. Old man Williams talks about keeping his drugs in refrigerators. One of them wasn't working, and another one looked as if someone had been keeping his lunch in it. And as for the transport arrangements. Did you ever see anything so daft? The stuff has to be carried by hand out of that door. Then taken in job lots in a small handcart over the bridge."

"It has to be a small cart. It's a small bridge."

"Naturally," said Oliver. "And if the bridge wasn't there at all, they could swim over with it in their mouths. After it gets across it has to be loaded onto a van, in an apology for a service road, which is so narrow that the van can't even turn round, and so badly surfaced that the first shower of rain turns it into a quagmire and the vans can't get down it at all. What they do then, I haven't found out. Put it on pack mules, I expect."

"Loading has always been a problem," said Dumbo. "We've managed to get through in the past, and I expect we shall do it again."

"You got through in the past because man power wasn't a problem. You could get a loader for thirty bob a week. Not now."

"What do you suggest?"

"What we need is two big trolleys—preferably power-operated. Machines which will carry up to half a van load at a time."

"And how do you suggest we get them across the river?"

"We don't. We take them out the front way and load in the High Street."

"That means going through Strickland's. They'd never let us."

"We go through Strickland's already. Most of the staff walked out that way tonight. I saw them. We must have some sort of right."

"Now you mention it," said Dumbo, "I seem to remember that there is some sort of right of way. But I doubt if it entitles us to load stuff through it."

"It might be a good idea to find out," said Oliver. "It's a minor part of the problem anyway." He swung his chair and pivoted forward onto his feet. "Let's go and look at that pub of yours."

He sounded remarkably cheerful for someone who was in danger of losing a gratuity earned by six years of military service.

Over their second drink Dumbo said to Oliver, "What do you make of Williams?"

"It's too soon to be quite sure," said Oliver.

"Quite sure about what?"

"About what's wrong with him," said Oliver. "Drink up. There's time for another one. Then we're going to sample the night life of Elsfield Wood. One long round of uninhibited debauchery, I shouldn't wonder. He pointed to the hand-printed notice on the wall beside the bar, which said, "Elsfield Wood Social Club. Partnership Bridge Evening in Aid of the Club Restoration Fund. Entrance Fee 2/—. Handsome Prizes, Best Ladies' Pair. Best Gentlemen's Pair. Best Mixed Pair and Lowest Score. Refreshments."

Dumbo shuddered. "I can imagine it," he said.

"Why leave it to your imagination? Come and watch the mixed pairs of Elsfield Wood lock in internecine struggle for a handsome prize."

"You can't be serious."

"A game of bridge would be the perfect ending to the day."

"I'm going home," said Dumbo.

A faded notice on the front of the Elsfield Wood Social Club said, "Warden's Post," and an arrow pointing down the passageway beside the building promised a W.V.S. Canteen, a First-Aid Post, and a Gas-Mask Distribution Centre, but these were mere fragments of old battle dress. The club was reverting to its peacetime function. As soon as sufficient Partnership Bridge Evenings, Whist Drives, Bring and Buy Sales, and Informal Dances had been held, the decorators would come in and paint out these last scars of war.

A strongly constructed woman, with gray hair cut *en brosse*, accepted Oliver's two shillings and said, "Are you alone?"

"I'm afraid so, yes."

"Bit of luck. Serena!"

"Hullo?"

"I've got a partner for you."

"Are you sure—" said Oliver.

"You needn't worry. She's a good player."

Serena was, Oliver judged, under thirty, but not by more than a year or two. She had brown eyes, a pleasant serious brown face, and thick wiry hair of that shade of jet which looks plain black most of the time but can change, in certain crosslights, to chestnut brown. She had a good body, which she carried well. "Show ring, dressage, first class," said Oliver to himself. "Wonder what she's like over the jumps." And to Serena, "It looks as if you've got lumbered with me. I hope you don't mind."

"It's very kind of you to take me on. Francis—that's my husband—was going to partner me, but he ratted at the last moment."

"Better get cracking," said the gray-haired woman. "There's a table to make up in the corner. Mr. and Mrs. Stackpool. He's our Chairman, incidentally. You play one rubber at each table. Losers go on. Winners stay put."

Mr. Stackpool was a stout, cheerful, talkative solicitor. He wore a pair of horn-rimmed glasses which were so thick and heavy that they constantly threatened to pull his face down into his collar. Mrs. Stackpool was smaller all round. She had a worried expression. It could easily have been caused by her husband's bidding and play.

The last game of bridge that Oliver had played had been a week before. He had gone as a guest to the Portland Club and had lost exactly four pounds, which he had considered a moderate price for a very good evening's entertainment.

"One spade," said Mr. Stackpool. Oliver passed. Mrs. Stackpool announced a poor spade fit by sighing audibly, and ventured two diamonds. Serena doubled. Mr. Stackpool looked at her with loathing and said three diamonds.

Oliver pondered. If Serena was a reasonably good player, her double almost certainly meant that she had a heart suit. Since he himself had four hearts to the ace, a single-ton spade, and the ace and queen of diamonds, a game was odds-on. He said, "Four hearts." Mrs. Stackpool said, "No bid," with the air of one who has done her duty in a difficult situation, and Serena said, "Six hearts."

Mr. Stackpool was deeply offended. It was unheard of. He himself had opened the bidding. His partner had supported him, and then his opponents had not only contested the auction and bid a game but had now reached a slam. He weighed against each other the considerations that, as newcomers to the Social Club, they should be treated kindly and that such irregular bidding must be punished. The bridge player came out on top. He doubled. Mrs. Stackpool, completely unnerved, led away from her king of diamonds, and Oliver made the slam without further difficulty.

Mr. Stackpool was so busy telling his wife what he thought of her play that he allowed them to bid and make three no trumps on the next game.

"Poor woman," said Serena as they removed themselves to the next table. "He'll give her hell tonight."

Oliver raised his left eyebrow very slightly, and saw the blood rushing up into her face. "Dr. and Mrs. Gwynn," she said hastily. "This is— I'm afraid I didn't catch your name."

"Nugent," said Oliver. "Oliver Nugent."

As the evening progressed, he was interested to discover two things. The first was that everyone was cheating. No one actually looked at his opponent's cards, but every nuance of voice, gesture, mannerism, hesitation, soliloquy, and riposte was employed to assist one's partner and deceive the opposition. Most of the pairs were husbands and wives, who had long learned to detect the precise tone of voice which their spouse employed when telling a lie, their exact manner when bluffing, and the reliability or otherwise of their assertions.

The second thing was that Serena was a good player. She wasn't equipped with all the latest conventions, but she had a sound grasp of technique and an intuitive card sense. He found it agreeable to hand her a difficult contract and watch her play it.

He could feel her interest in him, too.

Neither of them had much thought to spare for the score card and were agreeably surprised to be presented with a bottle of English sherry (Mixed Pairs, Second Prize).

"You can keep it," said Oliver as they walked back to the main road. "It'll be useful for staining the floors with."

"I'll put it in a decanter," said Serena. "Francis never notices what he drinks. It's been a lovely evening."

"We've been so busy," said Oliver, "that I never got as far as asking you your name."

"It's Strickland. Serena Strickland."

"Would that be anything to do with the Strickland Engineering Works?"

"That's right. My brother-in-law and my husband run it. They're both keen bridge players. Would you care to come along and have a game one evening? This is the house."

Oliver held the gate open for her.

"I'd like to very much," he said.

As he walked back to Snyder's garage to pick up his car, he thought that it had been a promising evening.

(iv)

"For God's sake," said Dumbo, "can't I go away for a fortnight to get married without coming back to find that you've sacked half the staff?"

"I've sacked two men and a girl," said Oliver. "One man because he seemed to think this was a rest home and the girl because she was impertinent once too often."

"I'm not talking about the man and the girl. I'm talking about Len Williams."

"Yes," said Oliver thoughtfully.

"Well, I mean to say, he was Managing Director. It was a pretty important decision. Couldn't it have waited till I got back?"

"I thought about that," said Oliver. "And I came to the conclusion that it'd be easier all round if I did it while you were away."

"Easier," said Dumbo. "Easier for you, you mean." He was really angry.

"Another thing," said Oliver. "It isn't strictly accurate that I sacked him. He resigned, although it's true that I don't think he had much option."

"That's not what Mrs. Williams said."

"What did she say?"

"She was waiting on the doorstep when I got back last night. According to her, you started picking on her husband as soon as I'd left, wouldn't let him give any orders to the staff—took over his job, in fact."

"And did you believe Mrs. Williams?"

"Not entirely, but I'd like to hear your version."

"I haven't got a version," said Oliver. He was leaning back in his favorite position, relaxed, but with his soft brown eyes watchful. "I just told Williams that unless he resigned I'd have to report him to the police."

"For what?"

"Larceny. Or maybe it was embezzlement. I don't know. I knew there was something wrong when he was so reluctant to hand over the key of the dangerous drug store. I can quite see why. He's been helping himself to morphine syrettes out of the tank kits. I thought he might be an addict the first time I saw him—that odd chin jerk they get, as if they're trying to unscrew their heads at the neck. Do you remember that quartermaster sergeant in North Africa?"

Dumbo said, "For God's sake," and sat down quickly as if his knees had been cut from under him.

"You noticed I filled him up with whiskey a bit at lunchtime that day. It's always fatal for a real addict. The more drink he takes, the more he wants the other stuff. That's why he had to dash home and give himself a quick booster before he could show us round the works."

"Did he admit it?"

"When I showed him the indents and sales records, he couldn't very well deny it. He was the only person who had the key. He'd told me so himself."

"What's he going to do?"

"I gave him the name of a doctor at Wàtford who deals

with that sort of thing. I don't know if he'll go to him or not."

"Come to that," said Dumbo, whose mind was beginning to grapple with the problem, "what are we going to do? You can't do Williams' job permanently as well as your own. Nor can I."

"I've tackled that one, too," said Oliver. "I haven't finalized because I didn't want to take an important decision without consulting you."

He said this with a grin and was relieved to see Dumbo grin, too.

"You're a bloody liar," he said. "You only consult other people about things that don't really matter. What have you done?"

"I contacted Miss Taylor's father, Sergeant Taylor. He wasn't too happy in his lorry-driving job, and I told him that *if* you agreed, he could have a shot at smartening up this place. I also threw out the suggestion that if he could get hold of one or two other useful types—particularly in R.E.M.E. or Signals—we might be able to use them."

"For God's sake," said Dumbo for the third time that morning. "What is this? A factory or a private army?"

"A private army may be just what we need," said Oliver. "I'll tell you more when I've seen brother Stackpool. I'm having audience with him this afternoon."

Mr. Stackpool removed his glasses with every appearance of relief, ran a hand upward and backward over the smooth summit of his head, and said that he was very glad to see Mr. Nugent again—splendid début he had made at the Social Club—carried off the Second Prize—do even better next time, probably. What could he do for him? Was it a personal problem or was it a company matter? Quinn & Nicholson—fine old firm—used to play a lot of golf with old Mr. Nicholson before the war.

"There's one preliminary point I'd like to clear up," said Oliver. "Do you happen to act for the Strickland Engineering Company?"

"Afraid not," said Mr. Stackpool. "I'd very much like to. Another fine old company, but they use London solicitors."

"I'm glad of that," said Oliver, "because if they were your clients you couldn't have acted for us."

Mr. Stackpool sat up in his chair, picked up his glasses,

weighed them in his hand, and said, "You having a fight with them?"

"I'm not sure. It depends on whether we can win it or not. I never start a fight unless I'm sure I can win it."

Mr. Stackpool smiled a little uncertainly and said, "Sound principle, of course. What are you proposing to fight over?"

"It's a right of way." Oliver extracted a fat envelope from his briefcase. "These are the deeds of the property. I borrowed them from the bank, who were pretty unwilling to let them go, I may say. We seem to owe them rather a lot of money. This is the deed that transferred the property to Mr. Nicholson, Senior."

"The conveyance, yes."

"Right. There's another one handing it over to the company, but that's not so important. The first conveyance was signed—"

"Executed," said Mr. Stackpool mechanically.

"At a time when there was nothing there but a couple of fields between the canal and the road. The back field—that's the one we're built on—had a right of way through the front one onto the road. It's still there, too, only it's no longer a path. It's a concrete passage with a glass roof over it separating the two Strickland factory blocks, if you follow me."

"Perfectly," said Mr. Stackpool. He had his glasses back on his nose by now and was following the fifty-year-old law script with one pink finger. "Here's the bit we want: 'Together with a free right of ingress, egress and regress over and across the land colored pink between the points marked AB on the front boundary and CD on the rear boundary of the said land colored pink'—this was drawn up in the days when we got paid for our conveyancing by the yard, ha-ha—'at all hours of the day or night, with or without horses, carts or other vehicles for the benefit of the messuage delineated on the same plan and thereon colored blue.' Well, that's all right, as far as it goes."

"As far as it goes?"

"Even a legal right of way can be lost if you don't use it."

"We use it all right. Every night. The chaps go out that way."

"With vehicles?"

"Some of them were wheeling bicycles."

Mr. Stackpool considered the implications of this.

"The best way to test it would be to have someone drive a vehicle over it. Could that be done?"

"It'd cause a considerable sensation," said Oliver. "The trouble is I doubt if you'd actually get a car through the communicating door. Suppose someone rode a horse through it?"

"Better still," said Mr. Stackpool, "if you used it for some business purpose. I expect you have those little hand-powered trolleys. They'd certainly be classed as vehicles."

"Curiously enough, we were discussing the question of buying some only the other day."

They talked for a bit about other matters. Mr. Stackpool behind his desk was a different and shrewder person than Mr. Stackpool at the bridge table.

"Most of your insurances need doubling," he said, "particularly the fire and third-party. They're both at prewar levels. Perfectly satisfactory in 1939, ridiculous now. Half the property in Elsfield Wood is underinsured. I act for one large garage and motor-repair shop which hasn't increased its insurance since it was built in 1930—and won't do it."

"Snyder's?"

"No names, no pack drill," said Mr. Stackpool hastily. As Oliver was going, he added, "You realize that this quite certainly means a fight, don't you?"

"Over the right of way."

"Yes, I've heard a rumor that Strickland's is putting in for permission to rebuild. If you establish your right of way and they did want to build, they'd have to buy you out. Would you sell?"

"At a price," said Oliver.

It was a fortnight later that Squadron Sergeant Taylor, released from his Covent Garden duties, appeared at Quinn & Nicholson. Skin the color of a medlar and the texture of sandpaper, deceptively candid blue eyes, hair now grizzled but still cut in a pudding-basin ring, as it had been since he was a recruit, he contrived somehow to look even more formidable in mufti than he had in uniform.

"It's a bit of a shaky do at the moment," admitted Oliver.

"So my daughter tells me," said Taylor.

"What did she say?"

"She said the place had gone to pot under old Williams but that you and Mr. Nicholson were going to make things hum."

"She's an intelligent girl," said Oliver with a grin. "We must promote her."

"Trouble with her is she wants to get an office job up in London. Doesn't like getting her hands dirty." Sergeant Taylor spoke of his only daughter in exactly the tones he had used in speaking of recalcitrant troopers.

"We'll see about that," said Oliver. "First things first. What we want here is new work, so that when we lose our Army contract, we've got something else to get on with."

"What sort of work?"

"Anything, provided it's got a profit margin or is in short supply. What about film developing? We could do it in our sleep with the equipment we've got. Undercut the chemists and bag all the work that's going. And what about battery-charging?"

"Chicken feed," said Taylor.

"Maybe," said Oliver, "but it's chicken feed that keeps the chickens alive and laying. Then, I thought we might have a shot at radio spare parts. We could buy Army spares and adapt them, and what price the up-and-coming television market. I'm no technical expert, but I believe that most radar parts are interchangeable with television sets. They work on the same principle."

"If we could get hold of someone like Corporal Fisher," said Taylor, "or young Everton—you remember him, he used to be Number One operator on the Command set. They said he could take it to pieces and put it together again blindfolded."

"Get both of them," said Oliver, "and anyone else who's going. They're going to be a lot cheaper to pick up now than they will be in a couple of years' time. I wouldn't mind having a few R.E.M.E. chaps, too. Who was that enormous Scotsman?"

"R.E.M.E.?" said Taylor, looking dazed. "This isn't a garage."

"No reason we shouldn't run a garage as a side line,"

said Oliver. "It'll be six or seven years before the motor trade catches up with the new car orders. During that time every spare part and every reconditioned engine is going to be salable at twice its market price. There's an empty bay at the end of the packing shed that'll make a good workshop. It's already got overhead block and tackle."

"You're assuming, I suppose," said Taylor, "that we lose our present Army contract."

"As a matter of fact," said Oliver, "I wasn't assuming anything of the sort. I had an idea about that, too, but I don't see why we shouldn't have two legs on the ground."

"Two hearts," said Serena.

Her husband peered at his hand in a shortsighted way, extracted a card which had strayed from the fold and restored it to its right suit, and finally said, "Two spades." Oliver doubled.

Arthur Strickland said, "Really, Francis, if you can't do any better than that you'd better not call at all."

"I can't call cards I haven't got."

"I agree, but if you look at your hand as though it was an unexpected surtax demand and call 'two spades' in tones appropriate to a funeral on a wet Wednesday in Hull, you're bound to give Mr. Nugent ideas."

"Actually," said Oliver, "I doubled on my own cards, not on Francis's tone of voice, which, to tell you the truth, I took to be a cunning subterfuge."

Arthur Strickland said "Hmm" and looked down at his own cards. Twenty years ago, thought Oliver, he must have been quite an arresting figure: tall, broad-shouldered, and thick-necked. Now the brown of his skin was beginning to roughen off into the red of burst capillaries, the shoulders were dropping, and little pouches of flesh were beginning to spoil the firm outline of his jaw. It was difficult to imagine two brothers more different than were Arthur and the thin, pale, intellectual Francis. All the same, if he had been an insurance actuary, Oliver knew which one he would have backed.

"Redouble," said Arthur.

"You're bluffing," said Serena. "I pass."

Francis looked more unhappy than ever. He started to

count something up on his fingers, caught Arthur looking at him, and put his hand in his pocket. Then he said defiantly, "I pass, too."

"Three hearts," said Oliver.

"Scared 'em," said Arthur. "I pass."

"Four hearts," said Serena, and Oliver looked at her with approval—an approval which increased when they made game and rubber, and broke off for refreshments.

"We might as well face it," said Arthur, inserting an egg sandwich into his mouth, "we're in for a beating."

"You're only fifteen points down so far," said Serena. "Cheer up."

"I'm not talking about bridge," said Arthur. "I'm talking about something that matters. Economics and politics. It won't take those bloody Huns long to climb back into the world market again. Or the Eyeties. The war's been over less than eighteen months, and they're already starting to flood the market with cheap typewriters. It's a critical position. Anyone with eyes in his head can see that, and what do we do about it? What do the bloody marvelous electorate of this country *do?* They turn out the man who won the war for them, the one man who could take a grip of things now, and they elect a paralytic bunch of parlor pinks, most of whom didn't see a week of war service, and *they* start telling *us* what to do."

"Arthur doesn't like this Town Planning Bill," said Francis.

"Have some more coffee," said Serena.

"Don't you agree with me, Nugent?"

Oliver said, "I entirely agree with you. I'd go further. I dislike and distrust *all* politicians. I'd abolish the lot."

"That's all very well," said Serena. "If you abolish all politicians, who's going to run the country?"

"I'd elect a board of directors," said Oliver. "Solid, experienced businessmen with no ideals, no platform, and no political axes to grind. Their sole job would be to make money for the country. If your'e rich, you're happy. It's as simple as that."

Arthur said "Hmm" and looked at Oliver suspiciously, but he seemed sincere. Francis said, "It sounds all right but would it work?"

Serena said, "Of course it wouldn't. I've never heard such nonsense in all my life."

"I don't know so much," said Arthur. "It sounds quite sensible to me. What we've lost is our old buccaneering business drive. We've gone soft. We spend half our time trying not to tread on other people's toes and the other half saying sorry because we think we've hurt their feelings. American businessmen don't behave like that, I can tell you. That's why they're leading the world."

Oliver said, "I concur entirely. Shall we cut or go on as we were?"

They cut, and Arthur, in partnership with Oliver, was further mollified by winning the next two rubbers, after which he announced that he—unlike some people, perhaps —had a hard day's work ahead of him. When he had taken himself off, Oliver accepted a nightcap.

"You can't mean what you said about businessmen," said Francis. "They always make the most hopeless politicians. Look at Baldwin's first government, or the French between the wars."

"Of course he didn't mean it," said Serena. "He was pulling Arthur's leg."

"I wouldn't dare," said Oliver, sipping the excellent malt whiskey, savoring the sharp tang as it slipped down his throat, the warmth in his stomach. The flames of the log fire were drawing unexpected lights from Serena's hair.

"Do *you* enjoy business?" said Francis.

"It's early days to say. But, yes, I think I'm going to enjoy it. It's a lot like war, really, and I certainly enjoyed most of that."

"Francis hates it," said Serena. "He'd rather live in a cottage in Devonshire and write books."

"What about you?"

"I'd like that, too. I'd look after the garden and be secretary of the Women's Institute and make Devonshire cream, and we'd send all our children to the village school."

Oliver nearly said, "How many children do you propose to have?" but stopped himself in time. If ever he had seen a body made for love and childbearing, it was Serena's. There must be some trouble there. He said, "If both of you want to go, why don't you?"

"The usual reason," said Francis. "Money. Any capital I've got is tied up in this business. It brings in a good return but I can't get it out. So I'm stuck."

As Oliver walked back to pick up his car from Mr. Snyder's forecourt, he wasn't thinking about Francis and his financial troubles. He was thinking about Serena. He was wondering if it was only her face that was brown or if she was brown all over.

(v)

As Oliver looked round the tiny, cluttered office, he felt a glow of satisfaction. Taylor had cast his net and had drawn in three good fish.

There was Man Mountain McGlashan, eighteen stone of imperturbability. Oliver had once seen McGlashan lift the back end of a jeep singlehanded in deep mud and hold it up while runnels were put under the wheels. There was Tom Everton, who looked like a stable lad and was the only man in the Army who knew how to operate an electric razor off a No. 19 wireless set. And there—the pick of the lot—was Fred Fisher, a thin, sad Cockney with a face like a long list of home-and-away defeats.

As some men understand women and as other men understand horses, so—and with the same mixture of passion and precision—did Fred understand the internal combustion engine. Oliver thought of him as he had seen him once, sitting cross-legged beside a track in North Africa. A few feet behind him an armored regiment was smashing past. White with dust where he wasn't black with grease, Fred was busy counting the ball bearings from a dismantled clutchrace, passing them from one hand to the other with the dispassionate absorption of a Buddhist monk counting his beads during an earthquake.

"I gather you're all willing to give it a try," Oliver said, "and I'm very glad to have you here. We've got a roof over our heads and a certain amount of gear. What we want now is work. The more work we can do, the more money we can make, and the more money we can make, the more I can pay you. It's as simple as that."

"I've had a look at the local motorcar situation," said

Taylor. "There's plenty of work going. No doubt about it. Everything from battery-charging to putting in complete reconditioned engines. The trouble is we'll be muscling in on an existing market. Most of the local work goes to Snyder. He's charging fancy prices and getting away with them, too, because there isn't any competition."

"Fine," said Oliver. "Now there *is* some competition. We'll put advertisements in all the local papers and see what happens. If Snyder keeps his customers waiting, they'll come to us."

Everton said, "I've got a friend—he was a signaler with the gunners, actually—he's got a job in the Q.M.'s department at Woolwich. He says there's mountains of stuff there. A lot of it's not actually being issued any more. Well, you remember those old Number Thirteen sets we had in the first year of the war?"

"The ones that never worked unless you could actually see the person you were talking to?"

"They weren't a lot of use but they had good parts in them. Get hold of a few dozen of them and you'd be laughing."

"I take it you're not suggesting we send off a van and just help ourselves?"

Everton said, "Not quite, but they have auctions from time to time. Give me a lorry and a bit of cash and I'll get all you want."

McGlashan said, "What about sweets, eh?"

They all stared at him.

"You've got a chemical works here. I was told by a man in a chemist's shop they were selling all sorts of things—cough drops and lozenges and pastilles they call them, but they're sweets, really. People buy them on account of all the real sweets are rationed. You call these medical supplies—people can buy them without coupons."

Oliver said, "I'm not sure that isn't the best suggestion yet. It's just the sort of thing we *are* geared for. We'll have a look at the regulations. You've probably got to make them without using sugar, but that shouldn't be impossible. Come in."

A girl put her head round the door and said, "Mr. Noogent?"

"That's me," said Oliver. "What can I do for you?"

"It's Mr. Strickland," said the girl. "He'd like a word with you."

"Would he, though," said Oliver. "You work for Mr. Strickland, do you?"

"I'm his secretary."

"He has excellent taste," said Oliver lazily.

The girl blushed. She was disconcerted at finding five men in the room.

"If you'd care to come with me," she said.

"There's nothing I'd like more, in a general way," said Oliver, unmoving, "but this happens to be a very busy morning. Would you convey my apologies to Mr. Strickland—that'd be Mr. Arthur Strickland, I take it?"

The girl nodded. When anyone in that firm said Mr. Strickland, they naturally meant Mr. Arthur Strickland.

"And tell him that if he wants a word with me I shall be here for the next twenty minutes. After that I've got a date with my lawyer."

The girl looked as if she would have liked to say something, swallowed it, and disappeared.

"That'll be about the right of way, I take it," said Taylor. "I had three truckloads go through this morning. I took the first one myself. I thought they looked a bit old-fashioned about it. Do you think they're going to make a fuss?"

"I'm quite sure they are," said Oliver, "and I think you'd all better clear out. We can't have quarreling in front of the children."

Ten minutes later Arthur Strickland walked into Oliver's office. He closed the door carefully behind him and said, "I won't waste a lot of your time. I understand you're a very busy man."

"Won't you sit down?" said Oliver.

"This can be said quite quickly. I can't have you using our passageway for loading. It interferes with our people Both buildings have their own separate exits."

"Both *have* separate exits. Ours is over a narrow bridge onto a cart track. Yours is direct onto the main road."

"That's the way it happens to be."

"That's the way it isn't going to be in future," said Oliver.

There was a moment of silence. Arthur Strickland's already red face had turned a shade darker. He said, "I'm giving orders that the intervening door is to be bolted—on our side."

"If you do that," said Oliver, "you'll be obstructing a legal right of way. I'm told I could sue you for damages and get an injunction to stop you, but that would all take time. So I'd better warn you that if you try to bolt the door I shall have it removed altogether, together with any other obstruction you may put up. I've got people here quite capable of doing it. And then I shall leave *you* to sue *me*, if you can."

Strickland took two quick steps forward. Oliver wondered if he was going to be silly enough to hit him, but all he said, quite quietly, was "Where is Mr. Nicholson?"

"My partner's in London at the moment, but he's given me full authority to conduct these negotiations. We should get on much better, I'm sure, if you'd sit down."

"There are not going to be any negotiations," said Strickland. As his color rose, his voice got thicker. "I don't care a row of brass buttons if you've got some legal right over that passageway. If you try to use it I'm going to stop you, and if it causes trouble you'll have brought it on your own head."

He swung round, and as he did so Oliver leaned forward and clicked off a switch. Strickland stopped.

"What's that you've got there?"

"Actually," said Oliver, "it's a tape recorder. As I gathered you'd finished, I was switching it off. Of course, I'll turn it on again if you've got anything more to say."

"Why—you—"

"*If* the matter comes to court, the judge should be particularly interested in that last bit. Where you admit that we've got a legal right of way and threaten to obstruct it by violence."

Strickland, as white now as he had been red before, turned on his heel and went out without another word.

"You hadn't really got a tape recorder, had you?" said Dumbo.

"Don't be silly," said Oliver. "Of course I hadn't. It was the switch on the cord of the desk lamp. I noticed the other day what a loud click it made. How did you get on up in London?"

"Not too well. The man I saw at the War Office couldn't promise anything. He'd had no complaints about our stuff, but they're cutting down on suppliers. The general feeling is that the small ones like us will be the first to go. I don't see that there's much we can do about it."

"I'm not sure," said Oliver. "I ran into Blackett at my club the other day."

"The C.R.A.?"

"That's right. He wasn't too happy about his prospects. They're cutting down on brigadiers, too."

"What's he doing now?"

"He's tucked away in some corner of the War House on a desk job. Not the sort of thing an active and ambitious man like Blackett really fancies."

"Blackett's a career man all right," said Dumbo. He remembered Bill Blackett, a dark, dry, efficient man, a modern soldier, the antithesis of the traditional Blimp. "What department have they shunted him into?"

"Oddly enough," said Oliver, "it's the department that deals with contracts and supplies."

Dumbo stared at him for a moment, then burst out laughing. "Cough it up," he said. "I can see you're mulling up something really filthy."

"It's common sense. Bill Blackett wants to get out of the Army and into business. He as good as told me so. We've got the sort of up-and-coming business that would suit him very well."

"Up-and-coming?" said Dumbo, looking dubiously at the small, cluttered room and beyond it at the jumble of the workshop, the chemical kitchen, and the packing department.

"Cheer up," said Oliver. "Nuffield started in a bicycle shed. We'd have to give Bill a seat on the Board and a good salary, but if he can use his last few months in the War Office steering a long-term contract in our direction, he'll be worth it ten times over."

Taylor put his head round the door and said, "Sorry to disturb you, gentlemen, but we've had a bit of trouble."

"Strickland's again?"

"Not this time. It's Snyder. Some of his garage men cornered Tommy Everton when he was minding his own business in the Duke at lunchtime."

"Did they rough him up?"

"Not this time, but they made it pretty clear they weren't going to stand much more from us."

"We're doing nothing illegal," said Oliver. He looked relaxed and happy, as always, when a fight was in prospect. "All the same, you'd better warn the chaps. The main point is they're not to start anything. If Snyder's chaps turn nasty, we'll have the police in fast. Understood?"

"I'll tell 'em," said Taylor. "I hope they don't start anything with McGlashan. You remember that jamboree we had with the U.S. Navy at Bari?"

Oliver found Mr. Stackpool reading a letter and smiling.

"It's from Headingly, Hewson & Company," he said. "A very well-known City firm." He sounded like the manager of a works team that had drawn Manchester United in the fourth round of the Cup. "Judging from the reference on the letter, we're dealing with young Mr. Headingly."

"And what has young Mr. Headingly got to say for himself?"

"It isn't what he says, it's what he doesn't say. If he was sure of his position, he wouldn't still be arguing. He'd have instituted proceedings long ago. You'll notice that the letter starts 'We are surprised . . .' When a solicitor starts a letter like that, it usually means that he doesn't know what to do next."

"Do you think he'd compromise?"

"I've a feeling he'd be very glad to if Strickland's would agree, but I'm afraid that pride is involved here." Mr. Stackpool rubbed his hands together gently. The pride of clients, as he well knew, lined the pockets of the law.

"There's a suggestion in this letter that you might share this access on an agreed basis. Do you think that'd work?"

"It might," said Oliver, "with good will on both sides. Unfortunately that's a commodity we're a bit short on. I don't think sharing's the answer here."

"There's another point," said Mr. Stackpool. "I told you I'd heard Strickland's was planning to build. Well, I've been doing a little research for you at the offices of the local authority. And it's true. They've put in an application for development. It's only in outline at the moment, but it's clear that they need to pull down most of the existing buildings and erect a single new block fronting on the main road. The way things are going here at the moment, a site developed like that could be very valuable. Very valuable indeed."

"But he couldn't do it without settling our right of way."

"No, certainly not. It would come right across it."

"Then his only course would be to make us an offer and buy out our rights."

"It would certainly be one solution of his difficulties. If such an offer were to be made, had you any particular price in mind?"

"I should start by asking for ten thousand pounds. We could always settle for a bit less."

Mr. Stackpool beamed. Oliver was a client after his own heart.

"You're setting the Thames on fire," said Serena.

"We've been having quite a lively time these last few months," agreed Oliver.

For the second time since he had been there, spring had come to Elsfield Wood. Its few remaining open spaces were putting on a show of green, a brave but hopeless resistance movement in the teeth of the army of brick, cement, and asphalt which was engulfing them.

"I believe you like trouble."

"Nonsense," said Oliver. "I'm too lazy to go looking for trouble. My ideal life would be to lie in a deck chair under a willow tree in the warm sun and have a beautiful woman bring me a succession of dry Martinis. Omar Khayyám had much the same idea."

"He wanted a book of verse, too."

"Reading's such a bore. One might, perhaps, have an L.P. of modern verse bubbling away somewhere in the background."

"You don't fool me," said Serena. "You like work. You enjoy every minute of it. Dumbo says you sometimes stay in the office until nine and ten o'clock at night."

They were sitting together in the front of Oliver's car.

They had driven Francis up to London. He was off on a selling trip to Sheffield, a trip which he had been putting off for weeks but had at last been dragooned by Arthur into making. Now, on the way back, Oliver had stopped the car on the crest of the hill overlooking Elsfield Wood. A few lights were beginning to appear in windows as the spring evening closed in.

"Francis does hate it so, poor lamb. He's not a bit like you—about work I mean." She shifted slightly in her seat, very conscious of Oliver beside her.

Oliver said, quite seriously, "I'm not mad about work for its own sake. I like it for what it can bring in. I've got plans. If they come off, I'm going to make a lot of money. And I'm not aiming to save it, either. That's a mug's game. Can you think of anyone more pitiable than a rich man on his deathbed? It's not dying he minds about so much. What makes him hopping mad is the thought that all the money he's made by his sweat and blood is slipping out of his fingers. A lot of it going to the state—horrid little civil servants who've been teasing him and taxing him all his life—and the rest to relatives who can scarcely wait for the last breath to go out of his body before they dip their fingers into the boodle. You know what the emperors of Byzantium did? When they died, they had all their wives and family and household killed and stacked on the same funeral pyre. Even the dogs and horses."

"Horrible," said Serena. "The dogs, I mean. They were probably the only ones who really cared."

"So I decided long ago that anything I make I'm going to spend."

"What on?" said Serena. It was the first time in the whole of their acquaintance that he had ever said anything as if he really meant it, and she was warmed and excited by the confidence.

"On myself," said Oliver. "On soft lying and hard liquor. On French cooking and Havana cigars, and on all the vices I've been warned against."

He slid his left arm under her back. There was a moment of resistance; then he felt her body lifting to accommodate him. He kissed her slowly. She tasted like toast and butter and honey.

When they got back to the house, a good deal later, Serena said, "You'd better not come in." Somehow she managed to make it sound like a question.

Oliver pondered. Discretion said no. Desire said yes. Desire seemed to be mustering the more cogent arguments. In the silence they could hear the telephone ringing in the house.

Serena slipped quickly out of the car, opened the door of the house, and went inside. Oliver sat on in the darkness. If he had been a cat, he would have been purring.

The front door of the house opened suddenly, letting out a shaft of light. Serena pattered across the pavement, opened the car door, and said, "It's for you."

"For me?"

"They've been looking for you all over the place. It's Mr. Taylor. He says there's been trouble with Snyder's men. Smithy's been hurt. They've taken him to hospital."

(vi)

Oliver found the lights on at the works and Taylor, with McGlashan, Fisher, and Everton, in the office. They looked serious but excited.

"It was definitely deliberate," said Taylor. "Not a shadow of doubt of it, sir."

The fact that he said "sir" for the first time since the armistice gave Oliver an accurate summary of his feelings. It was war.

"All right," he said. "Just tell me what happened."

"About six o'clock this evening. It was getting a bit dark. Smithy was bringing one of our delivery vans back from London. You know that nasty corner right opposite Snyder's? There was a transporter, with some heavy machinery on it, coming the other way. Smithy pulls into the entrance of Snyder's place to let it get past. Well, Palmer was backing out, you see."

"Wait a minute," said Oliver. "Who's Palmer?"

"Big chap with a red face," said Fisher. "Drives Snyder's breakdown van. He was very likely backing it out to go on a job."

"He came straight out of the shed," said Taylor. "Didn't stop. Put the crane arm through Smithy's cab. Smashed in the door and smashed Smithy's arm, too."

"Could it have been an accident?"

"It could have been, but it wasn't. Smithy says he could see him grinning at him in the driving mirror. Besides, he's an experienced driver. He wouldn't back out without looking, would he?"

"What he'll *say*," said Oliver, "is that he thought the entrance was clear, and anyway Smithy was on their property, where, strictly speaking, he hadn't any right to be."

"That's what he'll say tomorrow," agreed Taylor. "He'll be very sorry about it, too, I expect. Tonight he and the other boys are laughing their heads off about it."

There was a growl from the other three.

"Where do they do all this laughing?" said Oliver.

Fred Fisher said, "Mostly after work they go to a caffay on the corner of Station Approach, Sam Shorter's Snack Bar. Quite a nice place for a cuppa. Easy on the rations, too. I been there myself."

"Fine," said Oliver. "I could just do with a nice cuppa. Why don't we look in on Sam?" He thought for a moment while the others watched him, wondering how far he was prepared to go. "If they see the lot of us, they won't start anything. It'll just turn into a slanging match. So I suggest we don't all go in together. Only Taylor and me. You three can happen to be passing by. You can join in when things warm up."

"How'll we know when things are warming up?" said Fred.

"You'll know, all right."

Sam Shorter's Snack Bar was a one-story brick building with a counter across the far end, some tables and chairs in the open part, and not much else. Sam was sitting behind the counter, keeping one eye on the tea urn and the other on his evening paper. He could do this because he had a marked squint. He was a tired-looking man with a white face and bilious pouches under the eyes. He didn't trouble to look up when two new customers walked in.

Oliver was sizing up the opposition. There were five of them, he noted with satisfaction, and no strangers present. It could hardly have been better arranged. Three of them were sitting at one table and Palmer, with one man, at another. When they came in, there had been a clatter of conversation and laughter. Now there was a complete silence, broken only by the hissing of the tea urn and the crunching of Taylor's feet as he walked through some spilt sugar on his way to the counter.

It was the silence which made Sam look up. He said, "What can I do for you, gentlemen?"

Oliver rested one elbow on the counter, looked round the room, and said, "For a start you might open one of the windows. There's a nasty sort of smell in here. Can't you smell it?"

"Horrid," said Taylor. "Do you think perhaps something's died under the floor boards?"

"Might be a rat," said Oliver.

Sam blinked at them. He could feel trouble coming. The nearest telephone was the box outside the station. There was no way out through the kitchen.

Palmer got up, walked across, and said, "You don't like it in here, why don't you buzz off?"

"Well," said Oliver, "if it isn't Mr. Palmer. Been breaking any more arms lately, Mr. Palmer?"

He was resting comfortably on the balls of his feet, as taught by his boxing instructor at school.

"Any more of your vans come on our premises they'll get the same treatment."

"So—you admit you did it on purpose."

"I'm admitting nothing. I'm just warning you."

"You've got it all wrong," said Oliver. "You're not warning me about anything. I'm warning you, you big yellow bag of gas and wind, that if you touch one of my men again—"

He was halfway through this carefully constructed sentence when Palmer started to swing at him. Oliver shifted his weight back, came forward again as Palmer tried to recover, and hit him very hard and very low. Palmer made a noise which was halfway between a gasp and a scream and folded forward, clasping the bottom of his stomach. Oliver picked up a bottle of tomato sauce from the counter and cracked it over his head. The bottle broke, and the sauce ran down over Palmer's head and neck and down inside his collar in a thick brownish-red stream.

By this time there was a lot more action going on. The other four men had pushed back their chairs and closed in

on the group by the counter. Sam, who had slipped under
the counter and scuttled toward the street door, was un-
lucky enough to meet the reinforcements coming in. He
was knocked down and trodden on by McGlashan.

It was an interesting fight. Though reduced to four by
the early elimination of Palmer, Snyder's men showed
themselves no mean exponents of the art of roughhousing.
One of them knocked Tom Everton down with a sweeping blow with a chair, and was in turn felled by Taylor
with a backhand blow with a cake-stand. Oliver, grappling
with another man, tried to remember the principles of the
Harai Goshi, or sweeping loin throw, to be followed by
the Jigoku Jime, or hell-strangle. The first was reasonably
successful, and they went down onto the floor together. In
executing the second he got his left hand in the wrong
place and was bitten in the wrist. At this point someone
kicked him in the face, and he rolled under the counter
to recover.

The decisive blow was struck by McGlashan. He picked
up the hissing tea urn, twisted it off its gas pipe, and threw
it at the two of Snyder's men who were still on their feet.
One of them, trying to get out of the way, slipped and
cracked his head on the corner of the table and went
down. The other caught the urn, screamed, and dropped it.
It fell on the man on the floor.

The smell of escaping gas was overpowering.

"Time we left," said Oliver.

"You're quite clear," said Mr. Stackpool, "that it was
Snyder's men who started it?"

"Absolutely," said Oliver. "In front of witnesses. He
swung at me. I had to defend myself."

"Of course," said Mr. Stackpool. "Certainly you had to.
I should say that the state of your own face is a clear case
of *res ipsa loquitur*."

"I don't know what that means," said Oliver, "but it's
damned sore."

He had a puffy eye, and below it a purple laceration turning yellow at the edges, reaching to the corner of his jaw.
His left wrist was bandaged.

"You went into the café to inquire about the accident,
and they set on you?"

"That's right."

"And you defended yourself?"

"To the best of my ability," said Oliver.

"And some of your employees happened to be passing by and came to your rescue?"

"They certainly did."

"I don't *think*," said Mr. Stackpool, who had been carefully writing down Oliver's replies in longhand, "I don't think that we need fear any charge which Mr. Snyder's men may bring. Indeed, I was wondering whether it might not be good tactics for us to bring some charge against them."

"Certainly not," said Oliver. "We're very good friends now. I didn't tell you what happened afterward. Both parties bolted when the gas started escaping, and by coincidence we bolted to the same pub. There didn't seem to be much point in starting fighting all over again, so we started drinking and had a hell of a party. Luckily no one had been badly hurt. I was the worst, and really it was nothing compared to a guest night in our mess."

Mr. Stackpool gaped at him and said, "If that is so—"

"We soon found out what I'd suspected all along, that it was old Snyder who was egging them on. Incidentally, if he's prepared to go to those extremes, we must be worrying him more than I thought. No, the person I want you to square is the café proprietor. We did a bit of damage there."

"Yes, indeed," said Mr. Stackpool. "When I got your telephone message, I went straight round to see him. Luckily he hadn't made any specific complaint to the police, although I think he might have done if I'd been half an hour later."

"Good for you," said Oliver. "How much did he want?"

"I pointed out that it must be better for him to be paid promptly for the damage than to go in for two lots of court proceedings. He'd have to bring a criminal charge, you see, before he could hope to recover damages."

"I bet you sounded convincing," said Oliver, "How much?"

"He suggested fifty pounds."

"That means the real damage is twenty-five. Offer him thirty, in notes, and he'll jump at it."

"Bis dat qui cito dat," said Mr. Stackpool. He was having a good morning with the classics. "Talking of offers, a rather interesting one arrived on my desk this morning. It's from Headingly, Hewson. They say that they are authorized to offer the sum of"—he paused for a moment to let the full effect sink in—"two thousand pounds for a surrender of your right of way over their client's property, provided that they can have a definite answer, yes or no, by the end of the month. That is in two weeks' time."

"Naturally we say no to that."

"You say—"

"Of course."

"It seemed to me," said Mr. Stackpool faintly, "to be a very substantial figure."

"They'll go a lot higher than that. Time's on our side. They're worried about all this new planning legislation. If they don't clear the thing and start building soon, they mayn't be able to start at all."

"You think they'll go higher than two thousand?"

"That's just the ante. It's not the real bid at all."

"I wish I could share your confidence," said Mr. Stackpool sadly. He had already worked out the negotiating fee and the legal costs payable on the surrender of a right of way for two thousand pounds, and it had brightened his morning for him.

"Don't you worry," said Oliver. "I may know next to nothing about the law, but I've played a lot of poker."

"You ought to see his face," said Taylor to Dumbo Nicholson. "It looks as if a tank ran over it. It was a lovely scrap, though."

"What he's got to realize," said Dumbo severely, "is that the war's over. He can't go round behaving like that. Sooner or later he's going to get into bad trouble."

"We shan't have any more trouble from Snyder's people. By the time we all got slung out of the Duke last night, we were blood brothers."

"I don't mean that sort of trouble, but Snyder's a vindictive man. He's not going to sit down under this."

"Sit under it or sit on it," said Taylor. "I don't see what he can do."

Dumbo ignored this. He said very seriously, "Someone's

got to put the brakes on. You've got to help."

"I'll do what I can, of course, but if he won't listen to you I don't suppose he'll listen to me."

Dumbo said, "I remember him once, in the mess, after one of our wilder guest nights, putting four little tables one on top of the other. He started a game of follow-my-leader. First we all crawled under the bottom table. Then we went through the gap between the first and second tables. Then he did a sort of flying dive between the second and third tables. A lot of people fell out at this point because it was bloody dangerous, but quite a few did it. One man broke his glasses and another split his blue patrols. Then, before we could stop him, Oliver did a terrific sort of salmon leap over the third table and under the fourth. He slid down the other side in a heap, rolled over, and got up laughing. Only one other person was stupid enough to try it and he broke both wrists."

"He's a whole-hogger," agreed Taylor. "You remember that night at Wolfsberg? When he shot those three Germans?"

"That's different. They were trying to rescue a prisoner."

"True enough," said Taylor. "All the same, as you said, the war was over. I'd have fired at their legs."

Oliver came in, and said, "Who's shooting at who?"

"Taylor's shooting a line," said Dumbo. "What have you been up to?"

Oliver told them.

"You turned down two thousand. That was pretty cool. We could have used it for that extension shed we're planning. If Blackett lands us the N.A.A.F.I. contract for hair cream, we shall need a lot more space. They eat hair cream in the Air Force."

"He'll get us the contract all right," said Oliver. "As soon as it's signed, he's leaving the Army and joining us. All the same, I suggest we back-pedal a bit over the idea of building this extension. I've got other ideas."

"Such as?"

"Too early to say," said Oliver. "I'll let you know as soon as I've worked it out a bit more."

"You'll let me know," said Dumbo, "just as soon as you've committed us to a point where we can't possibly turn back."

"Admit that we've done all right so far," said Oliver. In spite of the livid bruise down one side of his face, he was looking remarkably cheerful. "The first year we made a small loss. Nothing crippling, and we shouldn't have been in the red if we hadn't spent so much on new equipment. The first six months of this year we're well on the right side. Now's the time to start planning for the big money. I've got a feeling that the tide's running in our favor. I feel that sometimes when I'm playing cards. That's the time to stake big."

"Last time you felt like that, if I remember rightly, you had a full house and the man on your left had four queens, and you had to borrow from me to pay your next two mess bills."

"We all make mistakes," said Oliver. "But I'm not wrong about this. I feel strong enough to take on I.C.I. and Unilever together with Boots thrown in."

"I'm glad you're feeling strong," said Dumbo, "because there's a job to be done right now. Someone's got to see Mrs. Williams."

"Mrs. Williams?"

"Len Williams' wife. She wants us to give Len a job. Not the job he had before. Any job. On the packing line or the dispatch. Something to keep him busy. She says that if he doesn't get something soon he'll go mad. Literally."

"You can't be serious," said Oliver. "Williams is damn lucky not to be in prison. You know what our auditors told us. He'd not only been taking drugs out of our stock for himself, he'd been fiddling the petty cash as well—probably to buy more of the stuff outside."

"I know," said Dumbo. "I know, but if we gave him a job where he couldn't get his hands on anything—"

"He can't work as a packer in a place where he's been boss. It's psychologically impossible. Anyway, if he wants a job, there are lots of other places. Why should he come to us?"

"I suppose," said Dumbo slowly, "that he feels we owe him something for the work he did keeping the place going during the war when there was no one else to do it."

"Anything we owed him," said Oliver, "was paid back, with interest, when we kept him out of jug. Now, let's have a look at those indents."

(vii)

"The man's a crook," said Arthur Strickland.

"He's clever," said Francis.

"He's too clever by half." Arthur swirled the remains of his whiskey a little pointedly round in the heavy cut-glass tumbler and swallowed it.

Francis said, "The decanter's on the sideboard. Help yourself. While you're up, you might put another log on the fire. I told Serena I'd sit up for her."

"Five thousand pounds," said Arthur as he reseated himself. His face was a reddish purple, and the heat of the fire was combining with the whiskey to make him sweat. "Five thousand pounds, all for nothing."

Francis said, "It wasn't nothing as far as we're concerned, was it? What figure did the Pru put on the completed building?"

"Two hundred thousand," said Arthur. A measure of complacency had crept back into his voice. "They'll put up three-quarters of it, in installments of course, as the building goes up."

"It seems to me," said Francis, "although everyone knows, of course, that I've got no head for business, but it does seem to me that when you're doing a deal involving nearly a quarter of a million, all told, five thousand pounds isn't a lot to pay for something that can make or break the whole thing."

"It's a lot to pay for a pathway. That's all it was. The right to drive cows across someone else's field."

"Come to that," said Francis, "two hundred thousand pounds is a lot to pay for a field. Even when it has got a factory on it."

Arthur Strickland stared at him curiously. His brother had been in rather an odd mood lately. Francis was, of course, intellectual. When he said the word, even to himself, Arthur managed to import a sneer into it. But in matters of business Francis had usually been content to play second fiddle, leaving the decisions to him. Arthur wondered if this odd mood might be connected in some way with his friendship with Oliver, which had been growing more marked in the last six months, a friendship which, Arthur noticed, he had not been invited to share.

There was a possible motive for Oliver's buttering up of Francis which salvaged his self-esteem.

"Where *is* Serena?" he said abruptly.

"She's been to a Pony Club committee meeting over at St. Albans. Oliver offered to fetch her. It was kind of him. He knows I hate driving at night."

"Hmm," said Arthur.

"You know," said Francis, "the real trouble with you is you're jealous."

Arthur, whose mind was on Serena, said, "What the hell do you mean?"

"You're jealous of Oliver. He does all the sort of things you do, but he does them better. When he pinched a lot of that man Snyder's business, you laughed and said, 'Jolly good show. There's an example of free enterprise for you!' When he takes five thousand pounds off you, he's a crook."

"Oh, balderdash."

"You've both got exactly the same outlook on business. Devil take the hindmost and the weakest to the wall. Instead of fighting each other, you ought to amalgamate."

Arthur looked up sharply. There was something here he didn't understand. Something which needed probing.

"Is this your bright idea? Or did Oliver suggest it to you, by any chance?"

"It cropped up in conversation. It was just an idea. We didn't go into details."

"It's a damned silly idea. It wouldn't work at all. We're engineers. They're cough-drop merchants."

"They do a bit of engineering."

"They do repair work. That's not engineering. Their money's in cough mixture and hair cream."

"They seem to be doing quite well at it."

"They're doing all right," agreed Arthur. "I've never denied that he's clever. After all, he's turned a loss on the first year into something damned near a five-figure profit this year."

"How do you know that?"

"I hear things," said Arthur.

"Figures like that aren't published. How can you possibly be sure? You're only guessing."

"If you want to know," said Arthur, "one of the young

chaps who does his audit is a pal of the accountant who does ours. I believe they were articled together. I suggested to our chap he might get the figure out of his friend."

"In confidence, of course."

"Well, yes," said Arthur uncomfortably. "In confidence."

"A confidence he immediately broke by disclosing the figure to you."

"Everyone in business always wants to know other people's profit figures. If *his* accountant was stupid enough to talk to mine, that was his bad luck."

"I seem to recollect," said Francis, "that at one stage in our discussion you were calling Oliver a crook."

Arthur's face went darker still.

"I suppose," he said, "that if you'd wanted to know, being so friendly lately, you simply would have asked him."

"Why not? He'd probably have told me."

"Or perhaps," said Arthur, "you'd have got Serena to put the question."

Immediately he had said it, he saw that he had made a bad mistake. Francis got up, his face white, and said, "Do you mind explaining what you mean by that?"

"I didn't mean anything."

"Then why did you say it?"

"Good heavens," said Arthur, "it was just a comment. They see a good deal of each other—go out a lot. They're pretty friendly."

"You mean you think they're lovers."

"You're putting words into my mouth."

"They were there already. Filthy words. If you knew the first thing about Serena, you wouldn't have dared to say it. It's laughable. Now apologize and go home."

Arthur was also on his feet by now. He said, "I've said nothing to apologize for. If your conscience is so tender that you read something into a perfectly innocent remark—"

"If you don't apologize, I promise you you'll be sorry."

"You can go to hell."

"Thank you very much," said Francis. His voice was as brittle as the first ice of autumn. "You're too stupid to realize it, but you've done me a very good turn." When Arthur stared at him in surprise, he added, "You've helped me to make up my mind."

Oliver and Serena were sitting together in the private bar of the Woodman, which is a nice little public house where the beer is still properly cellared and run up through wooden pipes to the old beer engines on the bar. The bar had a half crown countersunk into its wooden surface. The coin was worn as smooth as the bar top itself, and you had to look closely to see that it was a crude forgery. Someone had passed it off, late at night, thirty years before on the landlord's predecessor.

"Do you think," said Serena, "that you and Arthur could work together?"

"It depends on him," said Oliver. "He's a bit bossy, isn't he?"

"He bosses Francis about in everything to do with the business," agreed Serena. "It isn't that Francis is afraid of him. In anything that really matters, he's probably got more guts than Arthur. It's just that there are some things he doesn't think are worth arguing about, and business happens to be one of them."

"Do *you* think business is important?"

Serena considered the matter seriously. She said, "I think I feel rather like you about it. It's important for the money it produces, but I don't really see why someone like Francis should make himself unhappy for the best part of fifty years so that he can make enough to live happily for the next ten, if he survives that long—do you?"

"It's quite daft." Oliver wandered across to the bar and ordered two more whiskies. When Serena protested, he said, "I'll finish yours for you if you don't want it."

"You drink a lot."

"I drink an enormous amount," said Oliver. "I hope you're not going to try to reform me."

"That would be a labor of Sisyphus. What you want's a good wife."

"Actually, it's the last thing I want. If she really was good, she'd try to reform me. If she failed, *she'd* be unhappy. And if she succeeded, *I'd* be miserable."

"That's the most cynical thing I've ever heard."

"It isn't really," said Oliver. "The only logical reason for marriage is to produce children. And the only reason to produce children is if you happen to like them. Some people do. Same as horses and dogs and budgerigars. I don't.

I think they're boring little nuisances. You—"

He stopped, and Serena said, "That's the third time you've nearly asked me why Francis and I haven't got any children, isn't it?"

"Well, I did wonder."

"Without going into details," said Serena, "I can assure you it's not for want of trying."

Oliver finished his own whiskey, took charge of Serena's, and changed the subject with cheerful brutality.

He said, "If you're not interested in business, why did they give you a share in it?"

"The solicitors worked it all out. It was something clever, to do with estate duty. They didn't want Arthur and Francis to have exactly half the shares each, so they gave me a few. If Arthur had been married, they'd have given some to his wife as well."

"Solicitors always get their priorities wrong. They work out elaborate schemes to save estate duty in forty years' time without thinking about what's going to happen the day after tomorrow."

"What do you mean?"

"I was just thinking aloud," said Oliver. "What would Francis do if he retired?"

"He'd write."

"Has he any idea what?"

"Articles for newspapers to start with. He's done quite a lot of reviewing already. One of his friends has promised him a regular column for one of the Sunday papers."

"I'm told that reviewers sell the books they review to bookshops at half price, and the bookshops add them to their stock as new. If you review enough books, you can make as much as an extra fiver a week that way."

"He's writing a novel, too."

"He won't get rich on that. If he sells two thousand copies—and that's good for a first novel—he'll make just over two hundred and ten pounds."

"They get bought for the films sometimes."

"Zero turned up seven times running, once, at Monte Carlo. It was in 1913 and the croupiers haven't stopped talking about it yet."

"The trouble with you," said Serena, "is that you think

of everything in terms of money. And if you drink any more, I'm not going to let you drive me home."

"How are you going to get there, then?"

"I'd rather walk then end up in a ditch."

"It's a popular fallacy to imagine that alcohol in anything short of stupefying quantities will always make a man drive badly. With the average bad driver it may be so. The safety element in his case is his lack of confidence in his own skill. When he's sober, he realizes what a bad driver he really is and that keeps him driving safely. When he's had a few drinks, he forgets it and then he's heading for trouble."

"Alcohol slows your reactions."

"My reactions are normally so fast," said Oliver, "that a little slowing down does them no harm at all."

As he drove home, his mind was still running on the problem of Serena. He was thinking that she and Francis were perfectly suited to each other. Basically they were both intellectuals. Where any other girl would have said "Trying to reform you would be a waste of time," she had talked about a labor of Sisyphus. (Who was Sisyphus? Some relative of Hercules?) The other thing he was thinking was whether he would ever get her into bed with him. It wasn't that he underrated his own powers of seduction or even Serena's essential willingness. What stood between them was the stupid confidence and trust which Francis seemed to have in her. It was this that was locking her up more securely than any chastity belt. "Anyway," said Oliver to himself as he swung the car deftly round the corner and changed down for the climb up to Elsfield Hill, "she wouldn't really enjoy it. She'd be visualizing the whole thing in terms of *News of the World* headlines. And after it was over she'd be so remorseful that she'd feel bound to confess to Francis. And Francis would be round the next morning with pistols for two. And anyway it's a great mistake to mix business and pleasure." Here he started to laugh at himself, and said, "Sour grapes, old boy. Sour grapes."

"What's that?" said Serena sleepily.

"Nothing," said Oliver.

"This last downhill bit always terrifies me," said Serena. "Please take it slowly."

"Slow as you like," said Oliver and realized as he said it that his brakes had stopped working.

The road they were on was a country lane which made a short cut over the top of Elsfield Hill and back to the Watford by-pass. They were on the final run down to the point where it emerged into the A road. Oliver's hands and brain worked in unison. While he was thinking, "If I let her run out onto the by-pass, I'll never turn her. We'll go through the center barricade and be hit for certain," his hand was slamming the car down through the gears. It wasn't enough. The gears alone wouldn't check it. One thing for it. He smashed the gear lever into reverse. There was a tortured scream as the engine fought for an instant against the wheels and the teeth stripped on the mesh of the gear. Then the gear lever jumped out into neutral. Oliver jammed it back with a shock which nearly broke his wrist. The car went into a back-wheel sliding skid. Oliver got both arms round Serena as the car hit the bank, rolled over sideways into the ditch, rolled right over again, and came to rest on its left-hand side. The engine was roaring. Oliver felt for the ignition key, found it, and switched off. Then he switched off the petrol. Then he lifted himself off Serena, who was lying underneath him against the near-side door.

The offside door was jammed, but the window winder still worked. He turned the glass down, climbed through, leant down, and lifted Serena out.

She said, "I told you we'd finish up in the ditch."

Oliver started to laugh, then said, "Excuse me a moment," and turned away as he saw that she was about to be sick.

His head was full of bees, the blood was running down his face from a long cut on the side, and he had cracked his right kneecap against the steering column when they went over. It was stiffening up painfully but he could still hobble. There was a telephone kiosk, he remembered, on the main road about a hundred yards from the turning. Serena was sitting with her head in her hands. He wondered if she was going to be sick again. He held a handkerchief against his face to check the bleeding and hobbled slowly off.

Half an hour later Taylor and Fred Fisher were on the

spot with the breakdown van and a first-aid kit. As Oliver strapped up his knee, they set about righting the car and extracting it from the ditch. Serena was on her feet now and looked more or less all right. She had fallen off too many horses to take the bruises seriously.

"We'll take Mrs. Strickland home first," said Oliver. "Then we'll take the car to the works. There's something I want to look at."

"Tonight?" said Taylor.

"Yes, right away," said Oliver.

It took an hour to get the car back to the works, up onto the hoist, and stripped down. After that Oliver and Taylor sat smoking and watching Fred Fisher at work. He was the surgeon. They were only the nurses and assistants. Occasionally he asked for one of the inspection lamps to be shifted or for another spanner or wrench. Otherwise he worked in silence. Finally he climbed out of the pit and wiped his hands on a rag.

"What's the verdict?" said Oliver.

"Well, it's a neat job," said Fisher.

"Not accidental?"

"It didn't just happen," said Fisher. "It was helped. I'll get the parts out, you can see for yourself." He disappeared into the inspection pit again and there was some more hammering and wrenching. He reappeared with two pieces of rod and what looked like a short section of bright steel tubing.

Fred said, "Mind you, it's been done real clever. If you weren't a bit suspicious to start with and looking for trouble, you'd pass it up every time as an accidental break —a flaw in the metal, see."

He placed the two jagged ends of the rod together, and it did indeed look like a fracture.

"He didn't use a hacksaw or a file. That'd have been dead obvious. What he did, he clipped it away a bit this side and a bit that side with a Size One cold chisel. If you look close, you can see the marks. See what I mean? What's more, he done it *inside* this sleeve—" Fred indicated the metal tube. "It's a sleeve that slides down when the rods are straight to give it a bit of extra strength at the joint. Doing it that way, no one would spot it supposing they happened to be underneath greasing the car."

"A job like that," said Oliver, "would take a bit of time, I suppose."

"You could do it in about an hour if you had the car properly jacked up."

"I see," said Oliver.

He thought of fat Mr. Snyder lying on his back under the car late at night with the door of the workshop locked against casual intruders, the sweat running down his cheeks in the heat from the inspection lamp, busy chiseling away his life.

"I never dreamed he had it in him," he said at last. "If I had, I wouldn't have left the car where he could get at it. My mistake." He turned matters over in his mind for a few seconds. Taylor thought he had never seen him looking so ugly, six years of war included.

"I'll have to report this to the insurance company," he said, "and the police, I suppose, though since no one else was involved, there's no hurry about that. If you put those two bits of rod back just as they were, will the insurance people tumble to what happened?"

Fred Fisher snuffled through the back of his nose. It was the nearest he ever came to laughing. "Those insurance jockeys," he said. "They won't notice a thing. They don't bother about *why* an accident happened. It's what it's going to cost to put it right."

"Fine," said Oliver. "Then, as far as we're concerned, this was a straight accident. A fractured brake rod. Understood? And thank you very much, Fred. You'd better get home now or your wife'll be wondering what you're up to."

When Fred had gone, Oliver said to Taylor, "I seem to remember that those S.A.S. boys had a toy. It was a thermite bomb with a time fuse operated by acid eating through wire. It was a favorite with the sabotage teams because it was self-destroying and no one could really tell whether the fire was accidental or not. Do you think you could get hold of a couple for me?"

(viii)

"Two hearts," said Oliver.

Serena, on his left, said, "No bid." Dumbo took a second and third look at his cards, counted under his breath, and then said, "Six hearts. After all, it's only a penny a hundred."

"Your husband's in fighting form this evening," said Serena. Sylvia Nicholson, who was knitting a shapeless garment in two shades of wool with four needles, said, "What's that?" She looked up, dropped a stitch, and said "Damn."

Francis said, "No bid. I hear you got a total write-off out of the insurance people for that car."

"They couldn't do anything else," said Oliver. "The chassis was twisted like a corkscrew. No bid."

"Lucky *you* weren't twisted like a corkscrew, too."

Serena said, "Oliver was all right. He landed on me. Double."

"Now you've given the game away," said Oliver. "I shall finesse through you for all the missing trumps."

Serena said "Humph" and shifted on her seat. "It was more than a month ago but I still can't sit comfortably."

"It must have been such a terrible shock for Francis," said Sylvia.

"We argued about it at the time," said Oliver. "Whether it would have been more of a shock if Serena had rung up and said quickly, 'We've had an accident, darling, but it's quite all right,' or whether it was better to turn up on the doorstep as she did and start explaining her appearance before he could get a word in edgeways."

"I have a slight preference for the second way," said Francis to Serena. "That is, if you're thinking of doing it again."

"I shall never again in my life drive or be driven at more than fifteen miles an hour," said Serena.

"That resolution will fade away when the last bruise fades," said Oliver. "I'm running the ten of hearts—see? I told you you shouldn't have doubled."

"Pig," said Serena. "Where were all those men going in that bus?"

"What men?"

"Mr. Taylor and the gorgeous big Scotsman—what's his name—McGlashan? And the tall, sad one who looks after your cars for you."

"That's the Quinn & Nicholson Works Darts Team.

They're hot stuff. They're playing the Watford Police this evening. It's the semi-finals of the North London Section of the *News of the World* Championship."

"Darts matches," said Francis, "are just an excuse for beer drinking. Two spades."

Serena said, "Most of them looked as if they'd drunk a good deal already."

"You play darts better with a bit of beer inside you," said Oliver. "No bid."

Serena said, "Like driving, I seem to remember you telling me. Four spades."

No one contested this. Serena became dummy and went over to talk to Sylvia, who had recovered her lost stitch and was rattling merrily away like a one-man band on all four needles.

"If it fits into that," said Serena, "it's going to be an enormous baby. Or are you planning to have triplets and fit them all into it together like birds in a nest?"

Sylvia looked worried. "It *is* rather big, isn't it? The pattern distinctly says, 'P15 K15 follow with P and K alternating times 15, reducing one each row.' That's sixty rows alone. By the way, I hear you got that cottage in Devonshire you were after."

Serena looked startled. "How on earth did you hear about that?" she said. "It's meant to be the most deadly secret. Francis only signed the contract yesterday."

"Sorry if I've been indiscreet," said Sylvia. "Our char's daughter goes to the same hairdresser as your *au-pair* girl."

"And the Africans were supposed to have invented the bush telegraph. Well, it's true."

"Does that mean you'll be—" Sylvia broke off. The players were all listening, too. Something was happening.

"It's a fire engine," said Serena. "And another one."

They looked across to the window.

"It isn't far off, either," said Oliver. "You can see the glow. It's somewhere just over the bridge."

"It must be the Duke or Snyder's garage," said Dumbo.

"Not the Duke, I hope," said Oliver. "They're just beginning to turn back into a decent pub. Only yesterday one of the barmen—"

No one was listening to him.

"Let's go and watch," said Serena. "I love fires if they aren't me."

"Wouldn't that happen," said Oliver, "when I've just been dealt the best hand I've held for years?"

"A total loss," said Mr. Stackpool. "When a fire starts in a garage, you can't expect to salvage much. If the wind had been blowing the other way, it might have spread half-way down the High Street."

"Bit of luck, that," said Oliver.

"It's the only thing about the whole business that was lucky. Snyder's miserably underinsured. If I warned him once, I warned him twenty times."

"I remember you mentioned it to me," said Oliver. "Do I gather that he'll be broke?"

"With what he can hope to get for the site, plus the insurance money, he'll just about clear his mortgage and his trade debts."

"What will he get for the site?"

"Five hundred pounds—seven fifty if he's lucky. The person who bought it would have to do a lot of clearance before he started building, and he might have to wait a long time for the licenses."

"Offer him a thousand," said Oliver.

Mr. Stackpool looked sharply at him and said, "I take it you're serious."

"Never more so," said Oliver. "I'm well placed to buy it, you see. After last year's trading, my bank manager looks on me as his favorite son. He'll advance the money, and I can afford to wait for the licenses. I don't mind if it takes a year to get them. What's the position about planning?"

Mr. Stackpool hesitated. That masterpiece of Socialist legislation, the new Town and Country Planning Act, had just reared its craggy head, looming over the legal horizon like an unchartered mountain range. No lawyer was anxious to prognosticate what precipices and chasms it might contain.

"I *think* it'll be all right," he said, "provided, that is, you intend to put up a garage or a motor workshop. Anything different would be what's called a Change of User."

"Well, that's fine," said Oliver, "for it's exactly what I

had in mind. When our new plans get under way, we shall want all the space we've got in the existing building for our own production. That would involve moving the transport section out, in any event. And Snyder's site will do very well for it. Of course, a lot depends on how the new plans work out."

"Yes," said Mr. Stackpool.

"Have you heard anything yet?"

"I sent the transfers in to the secretary yesterday. Lucky that the articles give founder members a free right of transfer. Otherwise they'd have taken steps to block them, I don't doubt."

"But in this case they can't?"

"No."

"You're sure about that?"

"Quite sure," said Mr. Stackpool. He might be hazy about planning, but he understood his company law.

"Good," said Oliver. "I expect we shall hear something today. By the way, I could use one or two of Snyder's men. They'll be out of a job now. There's one called Palmer. I'd like him particularly. And two or three other drivers. Could you sound them out for me?"

"Certainly," said Mr. Stackpool. "A public-spirited gesture, if I might say so."

But after Oliver had gone he rotated silently in his chair for some seconds, trying to pin down an elusive thought. The whole operation was like—yes, that was it—it was very like a pirate, capturing a ship, disposing of the officers, and then offering the men a chance of joining his own piratical crew. But there was a flaw in it. To make the analogy a true one, Nugent must somehow have been responsible for burning down Snyder's garage, which was clearly unthinkable. After a preliminary inspection the insurance assessors had been unable to attribute any specific origin for the fire. They suspected that it might have been caused by a cigarette end dropped into oily cotton waste—a suspicion fortified by the fact that Snyder had been notoriously slack about discipline, and had himself more than once been observed smoking while actually serving petrol.

"Like master, like man," said Mr. Stackpool. "If they join Nugent, he'll smarten them up."

Oliver, walking through the packing department on his way back to the office, missed a familiar figure.

"Where's your daughter?" he said to Taylor.

"We're not good enough for that young princess," said Taylor. He sounded huffed about it. "She's been taking evening classes in shorthand and typing, and now she's gone off to the great metropolis to make her fortune."

"Enterprising," said Oliver.

"It's daft," said Taylor, "but a lot of girls are doing it. I'm told she can get four and five pounds a week in the City. That was a man's wage before the war. If it goes on, we shan't be able to get any girls in the works at all. Did you see Mr. Nicholson?"

"Not this morning."

"He's looking for you. He's in a lather about something. I think he's in the office now."

Dumbo was in more than a lather. He was angry. He said, "Look, we're in this thing as equal partners, aren't we?"

"Right," said Oliver.

"Then, for a start, when you make plans for the business you might tell me about them. And if those plans include putting yourself into control of the show behind my back——"

"If you'll preserve absolute calm," said Oliver, "I'll deal with all your questions, but I can't do it if you froth. Sit down. Relax. Undo the bottom three buttons of your waistcoat. That's better. Now, do I gather that you've been talking to Arthur Strickland?"

"He's been talking to me. Is it true that you've gone and bought Francis and Serena's shares? And that you now hold more than half?"

"It's completely and absolutely untrue," said Oliver. "If I had done any such thing, I should deserve anything you could say about me."

"But Arthur said he'd just seen the transfers."

"He was obviously too agitated to look at them properly. The shares have not been transferred to me. They've been transferred to Quinn & Nicholson. They are now the property of this company. Half owned by you and half by me."

"Oh," said Dumbo blankly. "I see. Well, of course, that does make a bit of difference."

"I'm sorry I had to be so cagey about it, but if a word of

it had got out, Arthur would have gone to Francis and talked him out of it."

"Is it true you paid fifteen thousand for the shares?"

"Quite true. Five thousand in cash—that came from the sale of the right of way—and ten thousand to be put up by our bank of the security of the shares themselves. And pretty adequate security at that, when you think that they represent a controlling interest in a company which owns a site and building valued at two hundred thousand, even if three-quarters of it is mortgaged."

"Then," said Dumbo, "actually, what it boils down to is that you—we, I mean—get Strickland's without having to find a penny for it."

"We've only got fifty-one per cent of it," said Oliver, "but I'm told that under various provisions of the new Companies Act, which are much too complicated for a simple chap like me to understand, if you own fifty-one per cent of the shares, you control the company. For instance, we could remove Arthur Strickland from the Board if he didn't do what he was told. I wonder whether he realizes that."

"Judging from his expression when I saw him, I should guess that his own solicitor has been talking to him."

"He didn't look pleased?"

"He looked as if he was going to have a fit."

The telephone rang and Dumbo took off the receiver, listened and said, "Yes, yes, all right. Eleven o'clock. We'll do that," and rang off. "That, as you may have guessed, was Arthur Strickland's secretary. He'd be ever so glad if we could both go round and see him in about a quarter of an hour. I said we would."

"On this occasion the mountain shall go to Mohammed. There's a lot to be said for getting these things over quickly."

"But, look here." Dumbo sounded upset. "You're not suggesting we just barge in and tell him he's sacked. This business is something he's been building up for forty years. It's his life."

"Certainly not," said Oliver. "Arthur is, in many ways, a businessman after my own heart. We shall get on excellently together, once he realizes that if it comes to the pinch, he's got to do what he's told."

Dumbo still looked doubtful.

"He's been boss so long," he said. "Do you think he could ever?"

"We'll have a little talk and find out."

When they reached Arthur Strickland's outer office, it was not the secretary who came from the inner office but a grizzled man in a fawn raincoat whom neither Oliver nor Dumbo remembered seeing before.

"I'm afraid that no one can see Mr. Strickland," he said. "I'm Dr. Frewen, by the way. He's just had a heart attack. The ambulance should be here any moment now."

Dumbo said, "He isn't—"

The Doctor said, "It hasn't killed him, and it won't if I can help it, but he won't be able to think about business for six or nine months. I ought to get hold of his second in command and warn him. Who'll be in charge while he's away?"

Oliver said slowly, "I suppose that'll be us."

(ix)

The paper was cream-colored and had "Marshall's Farm, Cullompton, Devon" put on, rather crooked, with a purple ink stamp at the top on one side and "Cullompton 27" on the other. It said:

This isn't really a farm, or not any more. It's a large cottage a little way outside the village. We've got what are lightly described as "mod cons," i.e. a telephone (but no gas for cooking, except in cylinders delivered irregularly) and a television set (but no main drainage). We're both in a honeymoon state about it still, seeing all the pros and none of the cons. Francis writes diligently all the morning while I do the housework, hindered rather than helped by a local girl of fifteen who, I'm sure, is going, any moment now, to tell me she is expecting a baby. Have you been reading Francis's reviews in the *Onlooker*? One author got so angry he rang him up and talked for hours at him. Incidentally, you were right about the books. We've got a bookseller in Exeter who buys them all back except one—a rather expensive one, unfortunately—which I spread marmalade over. Francis makes me wear gloves now when I read them. You've no idea how peaceful it is here.

Oliver turned the page. He was sitting in the office. Noise racketed round him. The steady rhythmic background of hammering, the occasional syncopation of the drill, sporadic outbursts in the bass key as the British workmen expressed their views on life, love, and holidays with pay. It had all been going on so long that he found he could ignore it now, as engineers in the bowels of a ship are said to ignore the hissing and thudding of the monsters that wall them round, being disturbed only should they fall silent.

The confusion in the office was, if anything, worse than it had been on that summer day—it hardly seemed two years ago—when he had first set eyes on it. Two years? Two years ago he had not met Philippa. Was it possible for someone like Serena to come into your life, and be so important to you, and then go out of it again so quickly and so completely?

He was under no illusions about that. That chapter was closed, completed, and done with. Helped by the perspective of distance, he could see that clearly enough. If Serena *had* double-timed on Francis, she would have insisted on going the whole distance. Confessions and lawyers and divorce and a Registry Office marriage, and a lifetime of loyally suppressed remorse.

Why were some women constitutionally incapable of separating the mental from the physical? And why were those women always the ones you really wanted?

"Come in."

Fred Fisher looked round the door.

"Hullo, Fred. What's broken down now?"

"Everything's going all right," said Fred. "I just wanted to tell you—I told Mr. Taylor—I'm handing my cards in at the end of the month."

"You can't do that," said Oliver. "You're a founder member of the firm. What's up? Aren't we paying you enough? Has someone been rude to you?"

"You're paying me all right," said Fred. "That holiday

bonus. Very handsome. Me and the wife appreciated it a lot."

"Well, then?"

"It's just that there isn't the scope, sir. And there'll be less to do when you get the new outfit going. They say we're going right over to chemicals. Is that right, sir?"

"Right enough," said Oliver, "but we shall still need a transport section, and you'll be running it."

"That's what I was thinking," said Fred. "It isn't really my line. I got this offer of a half share in a garage. It's down on the South Coast near Shoreham. The wife's very keen on the idea, she'd like the kids to grow up by the seaside, and there'll be plenty of money in it with all these new cars coming along and people who don't understand a thing about them driving down to the Coast in 'em and breaking down because they forgot to put any oil in the sump."

"All right," said Oliver. "I can't argue against your wife and the laws of economics. I shall be damned sorry, though. With Tom Everton going and opening his own shop it's the breaking up of a good team."

"Just before I go," said Fred, "I wanted to tell you something. I was talking to Palmer—he's a good bloke, he'll run your transport for you and do it well—he was saying that someone had told him that you thought old Snyder messed up your car that time you had the accident, remember?"

"I shan't forget it in a hurry," said Oliver, running the tip of his finger down the side of his face.

"Well, it wasn't."

Oliver stared at him. He said, "Explain that, Fred."

"To start with, Palmer said old Snyder didn't know a blind thing about motors. He got the business from his brother's widow. All he knew about was fiddling spares and making out bills. He couldn't have done a job like that. He wouldn't know how."

"Somebody did it."

"Ah," said Fisher, "and he reckons he knows who that would be. They took this chap on about a month before it happened. He was a clever enough mechanic. Then it transpired he hadn't got a work permit, so they had to get rid of him. He was under notice that week, and Palmer remembers seeing him one evening round the garage where your car was."

"Even if he was under notice," said Oliver slowly, "why would he want to take it out of *me?*"

"I wouldn't know about that," said Fred. "Perhaps he thought the car belonged to Snyder."

"And why did he need a work permit?"

"He was some sort of foreigner. A German, Palmer thought, though it seems a bit off, a German coming over here. You'd have thought they might have stuck to their own country for a bit after all the trouble they've caused."

"You can never tell what a German'll do," said Oliver.

When Fred had gone he picked up the letter again, but it was several minutes before he went on reading. His mind had flicked back two years into the past. A clearing in the forest, a ring of sentinel pines, a barbed-wire fence, four figures running across the swath of a spotlight, the juddering of the twin Vickers machine guns in the turret of the tank.

> We heard last week from Arthur [said the letter]. He's much better but it doesn't look as if he's ever going to get back to full-time working. His doctor's against it, and I think Arthur's beginning to see sense. He told me about your proposal to buy in his shares in installments with the money your Army pal (Blacker? Blackett?) is putting up. That seemed to me to be a sensible way of doing things. I don't believe two thundering individualists like you and Arthur ever would have got on well together. Hold on a moment, the boiler's making the *most* peculiar knocking.

There was a knocking on Oliver's door, too. One of the chemists, a flustered, elderly man called Toogood, put his head round the door and said, without opening it any wider, "There's a woman here. I told her you were busy."

He seemed to be holding the door against the determined efforts of someone outside to get in.

"Has she got a name?"

"It's Mrs. Williams. Mr. Taylor was away so she got hold of me. She insisted on coming along—"

Oliver said, "Then you'd better let her in."

"She's in rather a state."

"Let her in, man," said Oliver. "You can't have a fight in the passage."

"All right." Mr. Toogood opened the door reluctantly and Mrs. Williams came in. Oliver got up.

He had met Len Williams' wife only once, and he remembered her as a small, neat, compact woman with a worried expression and rather a nice smile. Now he hardly recognized her. Her face was white and there were livid patches under her eyes. It was as though some central cord which kept her parts taut had snapped suddenly, leaving a confusion of pieces where there had once been a woman. Her hands were jerking and her head scarcely seemed to belong to her body.

"Won't you please sit down?" he said. "What can I do for you?"

"You can't do any more," said Mrs. Williams. "You've done it all now, you filthy bugger." She took a pace nearer and spat at him. A wet blob of saliva actually hit his cheek as he turned his face away.

She was screaming. The dirty words, carefully manufactured and hoarded, were coming out like a jet from a poison sac, an eruption of pus, slowly gathered, now violently extruded.

The door burst open and Taylor strode in. He grabbed the woman by the arm, said "Out," and pulled her after him like a tractor towing a small car.

Oliver stood quite still, balanced on his feet as though he were in the ring, staring, staring ahead of him. He dipped his hand into his pocket without looking down, fumbled, pulled out a handkerchief, and wiped his face.

Taylor came back. He said, "I'm sorry about that. If I'd been here it wouldn't have happened."

"She must be mad," said Oliver.

"I expect it's shock."

"Shock?"

"You hadn't heard? Len killed himself last night. Put his head on the down line and the train went over it.

Messy way of doing it. I'll warn the people on the door she's not to be allowed in here again."

"Thank you," said Oliver.

He sat down, and picked up the letter. There was a postscript, scribbled on the back of the last page.

> The doctor tells me that I really may have started something at last. If it turns out to be a boy we're going to call him Rupert. Rather precious, but Francis seems keen on the name. Would you care to be a godfather? Or does that dislike of children which you once expressed to me extend to godchildren as well?

Oliver grinned as he read this. But he was really thinking of something quite different.

"A German," he said to himself. "It must be a coincidence."

FIRST INTERLUDE:

Oliver at Home (Radlett)

I DIDN'T hear all of this in the car on my way down to Radlett. I got the outline of it from Oliver then, and in the course of that evening, and I filled in the details from Dumbo and Taylor later on.

Oliver had rented a little house on the outskirts of Radlett, and had made himself comfortable enough in a bachelor sort of way. Mrs. Comrie had been Oliver's nurse, and his mother's nurse before that. She was one of those ageless Scotswomen who run their own lives with such economy that they have plenty to spare to look after two or three other people as well.

After dinner we settled down with a nearly full bottle of whiskey and Oliver brought me up to date.

"Partly it was luck. Partly it was hard work, but mostly it was a matter of swimming with the current. When things are going your way, all you've got to do is to avoid making a B.F. of yourself."

"What next?" I said. "No, no more for me at the moment."

I had learned by hard experience that it was no use trying to keep up with Oliver when he was drinking. If I refused two out of every three, I would have some chance of remaining sober.

"We've laid the foundations." Oliver poured himself a generous tot. "We've got decent premises far enough out of London not to cripple us with overheads but not so far out as to give us headaches about delivery. We've got enough capital for our immediate requirements—we shall need more if we're going to expand, though—and we've got a first-class transport section."

"Fine," I said. "You've got money to buy raw materials, you've got floor space to process them, and you've got a fleet of vans to deliver the finished product. The only point I'm not yet absolutely clear on is *what* product?"

"Proto-mycil," said Oliver.

"What the devil is proto-mycil?"

"It's an anaerobic spore."

"Come again."

"Basically it's a fungus. Botanically it's classed as a root because it grows underground."

I said, "I should think you'd have a terrific sale for it."

"We shall when we've done all that has to be done to it." I wondered if he was going to say any more. He never talked much about his own business, but he was in an expansive mood that evening. Or, since he wanted something from me, perhaps he was spreading a little ground bait.

(What he wanted became apparent later. He wanted me to come in as accountant and secretary to his group. I was very much inclined to say yes. Then a job I had been angling for with a firm of New York investment brokers came up, and I was out of England for the best part of eight years. During that time I occasionally read about Oliver and his doings. As he became well known, his photograph appeared from time to time in the financial press, and I used to stare at it with amazement and wonder how deeply the old Oliver was buried inside that increasingly impressive figure. It was a feeling schoolmasters must experience from time to time. One of the reasons I remember that night at Radlett so clearly is that it was the last time I caught a glimpse of the youthful Oliver before it finally became hidden under a carapace of thickening fat and dignity.)

"Did you hear about that spot of bother we had at Wolfsberg?" he was saying.

"I heard something about it. Prisoners trying to escape, wasn't it?"

"No one tried to escape. It was a rescue attempt. It damned nearly succeeded, too. We were running the Army cage at Wolfsberg. We weren't really equipped to do the job, though. You have to have trained men to guard a prison camp properly, and proper equipment—searchlights and miles of barbed wire and all that caper. Fortunately most of our prisoners had no real incentive to get out. Why should they bother? There was nowhere for them to go. They were going to get home just as quickly if they sat tight and let us feed them. All the same, there was a handful of hard cases—S.S. men mostly. You could tell them. They had their blood group tattooed under their armpits. One of them had tried to slice it off with a razor, I remember, and gave himself blood poisoning in the process and damned nearly died. But, as I say, they were a minority."

"How did you keep them in if you hadn't any barbed wire?"

"We had just enough to put two strands round the perimeter. I put a Sherman tank on each corner with a spotlight and a machine gun in the turrett."

It seemed simple but reasonably effective. I said, "Who tried to rescue whom?"

The man they tried to rescue was an Austrian called Kurt Engelbach. He was a doctor, an officer in the German equivalent of the R.A.M.C., a very decent citizen indeed. I was using him as an interpreter and got to know him quite well. He'd spent a year in London finishing off his medical training at St. Mary's. After he qualified he went to Switzerland, to the Rothenstein Clinic, and I gather he'd planned to settle there permanently with his wife when Hitler ordered him home. That was in 1938 when qualified men were being corralled from all over the place and drafted into the forces. Kurt had to go. His father and mother were still alive, and the authorities would have taken it out on them if he'd said no. But he left his wife behind in Zurich. He seems to have had a pretty interesting sort of war. To start with, he was attached to the Luftwaffe and did a lot of work on burned skin. Not skin-grafting. That's a surgical job. The treatment of skin that was badly burned but still rescuable. After that he went to Russia and had a lot of frostbite cases to deal with. Apparently the treatment is basically the same in both sorts of case. It involves renewing the dead tissue and softening the hardened layers of skin underneath it and encouraging it to grow again. He became rather an expert in this line and was given a good deal of latitude for research. That was when he discovered about proto-mycil. It's extracted from these fungi things—they're like little white mushrooms and there are only about two places in the world where they've turned up so far; one's in Russia and the other's in the Pont du Gard district in the South of France, and they're not at all easy to cultivate artificially, either. They need just the right soil and irrigation and atmosphere or they shrivel up and die."

Oliver helped himself to another drink. I said, "No," and, "What does proto-mycil do to the skin that makes it so special?"

"It doesn't do anything to the skin itself. It activates the capillary terminals just under the skin and brings the blood up from inside them. That encourages the skin to grow again. He told me that once, in the early days when they didn't know quite what quantities to use, they gave a sergeant in the Tank Corps a sort of permanent and rather attractive blush. His men nicknamed him Lili Marlene. He wasn't at all pleased about it. However, for a number of reasons which I couldn't entirely follow, it was decided that it had too many drawbacks to be used medically, so it was shelved. But Kurt was a forward-looking sort of chap. He thought of all the hardworking *Hausfraus* after the war who'd jump at the chance of rubbing a little into their work-worn hands and restoring their lovely pink-and-white texture, and he worked out a formula for a hand cream with a proto-mycil base. He got the formula out to his wife in Zurich and she patented it for him in Switzerland."

"And are you going to tell me that the men who tried to rescue Kurt were pharmaceutical magnates who hoped to nobble his process?"

"Certainly not. They were S.S. men. One of them, I've every reason to believe, was Kurt's younger brother, Steyr Engelbach. Kurt told me about Steyr. A rough type, an Austrian Nazi from way back. One of Schuschnigg's boys. He'd spent *his* war in various Special Service units and was planning, no doubt, to carry on the good work in the inner fortress, if that particular scheme of Hitler's had come to anything, which, of course, it didn't. He'd decided to rescue Kurt from the cage and take him with him, an idea which didn't really appeal to Kurt at all. Steyr had two friends with him, and they staged the operation one night when I happened to be Orderly Officer and Taylor was Orderly Sergeant. We were making a last tour of the camp before turning in, and we saw these four figures making for the wire and starting to climb through. Our sentries, in the tanks at either end of the line, seemed to have gone to sleep. They must have seen them and they weren't taking a blind bit of notice. I said to Taylor, 'Wake the bastards up.' I jumped up into the turret of the nearest tank, and Taylor sprinted for the other one. I had to tread on the sentry. He'd been garroted. I got the spotlight on. By this time they were all through the wire and running for the wood. I got off a couple of bursts. Taylor didn't have time to fire at all."

Oliver refilled his own glass and waved the bottle in my direction. This time I didn't say no.

"What was the score?" I said.

"Kurt and one of the men were dead. The third man was badly wounded. He died that night. He told us all about it before he died. The fourth man, Kurt's brother Steyr, was hit in the leg, I think, but he got off and got away."

"He must have had plenty of guts," I said.

"According to Kurt, who talked a lot about his younger brother, Steyr was a remarkable person altogether. A sort of superman. Very tough but very intelligent, too. If the truth be told, I think Kurt was afraid of him."

We sat in silence for a few minutes. As the night cooled off, a breeze had got up and was rustling the top of the poplar trees at the end of the garden. I was thinking how quickly we had all forgotten the war. Not the facts of the war, but the feeling. The idea that you could cut down three or four men with a squeeze on the trigger and the whole thing would affect you no more than bumping your neighbor's mudguard as you came out of your drive in the morning.

"There's one thing I don't quite understand," I said. "The proto-mycil ointment. The rights on it would go to

Kurt's widow on his death, presumably?"

"That's right," said Oliver. "And as soon as I was de-mobilized, I went straight to Zurich, and bought the rights off her. I'd got the bargain signed, sealed, delivered when Steyr turned up. I'd beaten him to it by less than a week. That gave him a second good reason for hating me."

PART II

Tendresse v. Lucille

IN THE spring of that year, the shipbuilding industry of the country was brought to a halt by a three-month dispute over the important question of whether the holes in a material containing alternate layers of wood and metal should be drilled by joiners or metalworkers; there were strikes of compositors in London, meat porters in Smithfield, and choirboys in Canterbury; the Guillebaud Committee reported and Archbishop Makarios was deported; consumption of wine went up and consumption of beer went down; whiskey and gin remained pretty steady; Mr. Harry Pollit unveiled a memorial in Highgate Cemetery to Karl Marx; and Mr. Malenkov, on a visit to this country, presented a stick of rock candy to a small boy in Blackpool. And Quinn & Nicholson, Ltd., held its first Annual General Meeting as a public company.

(ii)

"It is customary, I believe," said Oliver, "for the Chairman's speech, which has, of course, been circulated to all members, to be taken as read, and I expect that in future years we shall do that. I thought, however, that on the occasion of our first Annual General Meeting as a public company, it would be in order for me to say a few words."

He paused for a second to cast an eye over his audience. He was glad that he had chosen the smallest of the three available meeting places. An unexpectedly large number of people had turned up but they would have been lost in either of the big halls, whereas this one was comfortably crowded.

He recognized the representatives of the banks and the insurance companies who had come to see how the young Chairman would perform on his first public appearance. In future, and as long as all went well, they wouldn't bother. A number of private shareholders had turned up, too, including the inevitable old lady with a handbag big enough to hold three volumes of the *Encyclopaedia Britannica*. What on earth did she keep in it? Behind them were the reporters, mostly from the financial and City press, but at least one national daily he noticed, and the men in strategic positions near the door who intended to collar him as soon as the meeting was over and sell him everything from advertising space to typewriter ribbons. Dumbo should deal with them.

He said, "The year just passed has been a busy one for the company. The main event was, of course, the public issue of shares last summer. That was the moment when, if if I might employ a skiing metaphor, we left the nursery slopes and ventured out onto the hillside. I've no doubt that we shall find the going slippery, but I think we shall manage to keep our feet." (Laughter.)

The reporter from the City press made a shorthand note. He found Oliver a change from the normal run of chairmen.

"Our main selling line has, as in the past five years, been Handcharm. You will see the figures in the reports. It was widely predicted that sales would fall off, but in fact they have continued to expand. The export results have been particularly encouraging. We appear to have hit our European competitors so hard that they have been provoked, as you will have seen from my report, to counteraction. We have been notified of proceedings in the provincial court at Lyons, on the grounds that our formula and process is a breach of patent rights held by the Société Anonyme de Pharmaciens de Lyons. Fair enough! When a trader has to fly to the law to help him, it is usually a sign that he has been hit where it hurts—in his purse. I can assure you that these proceedings will be defended, and I am confident that they will be successfully defended."

Fergus Campbell stirred uneasily in his chair at the far end of the directors' table. As an experienced solicitor, he distrusted prophecies about the outcome of litigation, even in England, and litigation in France was going to be a great deal worse. Oliver noted the involuntary movement and shot him an amused glance.

"We do not, of course, rely entirely on one product. We are engaged in untiring research for new products in this fiercely competitive field. The sales of Quinn & Nicholson's Old-Fashioned Toilet Water and of our new Commando toothpaste are already extremely encouraging. While on the subject of trading, I will mention one point which does not, strictly speaking, concern the year under review. You may have seen in the papers that we have just concluded negotiations to purchase a controlling interest in Sandberg & Freyer. Sandberg's, as some of you will know, is a very old established firm of color printers with works at Hendon. Our stake in this company had a double object. First, we thought it was a sound way of investing some of the company's surplus assets. The other is that it gave us a reliable associate to attend to the packaging and advertising, which forms such an important part of our business. Finally, before I propose the approval of the accounts, I should like to mention that we have been glad to welcome a newcomer to our Board this year. Wilfred Harrap." He turned to the dark, impassive Ulsterman seated next to Dumbo. "Speaking as an ex-cavalryman, I felt the need of support from the sappers [Laughter] to clear away some of the mines which our evilly disposed competitors may have strewn in our path. [Renewed laughter.] Wilfred Harrap seemed to me to fill the bill admirably. Since the conclusion of hostilities, he has been working with his family firm in the City, and his experience is, I am sure, going to be of the greatest practical assistance to us in the financing of our various undertakings." [Scattered applause.]

Wilfred Harrap rose briefly to his feet, bowed, and sat down again.

"I now beg to move," said Oliver, "that the Directors' Report and Statement of Accounts for the year ended 31st March last be and they are hereby approved and adopted, and I will ask my colleague Mr. Nicholson to second the motion."

Brigadier Blackett and Wilfred Harrap shared a taxi on their way from the meeting to luncheon at the United Services Club. They were birds of a feather, soldiers of fortune, ready to carve out, with whatever weapon came most conveniently to hand, an agreeable niche for themselves in the world they lived in. Either of them might have stayed in the Army after a successful war, aiming at a lieutenant generalship, a knighthood, and a respectable pension, but the peacetime Army, as they had been quick to realize, offered no scope to their particular talents. It demanded people who were prepared to work as cogs in a complex machine, and a machine no longer operated from Whitehall, but with one of its poles in Versailles and the other in Washington. It needed political soldiers, men adept in the handling of committees, people who could talk to scientists and congressmen and trades-union leaders in their own language. The simple fighting soldier was now as much a myth as the Minotaur. A man who craved excitement, ambuscade and deceit, envelopment and attrition, the risks of defeat and the fruits of victory, could find them more easily in the square mile of the City than in the modern Army.

"Remarkable chap, our Chairman," said Harrap.

"He's come a long way in the last ten years," said Blackett.

"Did you know him in the war?"

"I knew him as a long-haired cavalryman who affected gabardine trousers and polka-dot scarf as a substitute for the battle dress provided for him by the nation."

"It was very curious how the old cavalry notions—shut your eyes, dig your spurs in, and charge—got transmogrified into tanks and came out exactly the same at the other end."

Blackett said, "He's got the right idea. Locate the enemy and hit him before he can hit you."

"Who's the enemy?"

Blackett considered this one as the taxi advanced down the Strand in a series of limited bounds.

"Our main competitor at the moment is the Mallinson Group. They've been a lot longer in the field than we have and they've got a sort of personal tie-up with Naumann."

"Jacob Naumann?"

"Yes. Do you know him?"

"Very well. Dodgy old devil. I knew he had interests in dyes and chemicals. I didn't know he went in for the toilet preparations."

"He's not a manufacturer, agreed. But he's on the board of two of the three biggest wholesale chemists in England. If he says, 'Buy from Mallinson,' they buy from Mallinson."

"Suppose he was to say, 'Buy from Mallinson *or* Quinn & Nicholson, whichever offers you the best product at the best price.' No favoritism?"

"If he only did that," said Blackett, "we should be very happy indeed." And to the driver, "You'd better turn into the Mall. We can walk up the steps."

The driver said, "O.K., guv, it's your legs."

"That lawsuit he was talking about," said Harrap. "Is it serious?"

"Oliver seems to think he can handle it."

"Our legal adviser didn't look too happy about it."

"Fergus Campbell's a cautious bird. Good thing, really. Oliver needs someone with a hand near the brake. This'll do!"

They got out of the taxi. Blackett paid the fare, adding a meticulously calculated tip, and the two middle-aged men then demonstrated their fitness to each other by walking, fast, up the twenty-nine steps beside the Duke of York's statue.

Other people were discussing Oliver Nugent that morning.

In his sixth-floor suite in the offices of Mallinson's Pharmaceutical Supplies, Ltd., in Clerkenwell, Victor Mallinson read the three typewritten sheets which his secretary had laid on his desk. He said, "Good work, Jennie. You managed to get it all down."

His secretary said, "Well, he talked a bit fast to start with, but I think it's all there."

"Did anyone think it was odd—your scribbling away in shorthand?"

"Not a bit. I sat just behind the press table, you see."

"Clever girl," said Mallinson. "Very good." He stroked his short, neat beard as he continued to read. His barber had been color-tinting his hair for some time now, but he had refused to let him dye out the gray streaks in his beard. He considered them distinguished. "I see you've even put in the laughter and applause," he said.

"Actually, it went down rather well."

"I'm sure it did, Jennie. The Chairman's speech always goes down well. When he has increased profits and a larger dividend to announce. It's what's known in sporting parlance as a walkover. Would you see if Mr. Crake is in his office? I'd like a word with him."

He had finished the report by the time Mr. Crake appeared, and was leaning back in his chair staring at the ceiling, his slim and beautifully tailored body forming a straight line from the top of his light-brown wavy hair to the polished tips of his shoes. He said, "Come in, Crake," but did not move his head. "I've got an advance copy of what our friend, Mr. Nugent, has been saying to his shareholders. I'd like your opinion on it."

Mr. Crake was squat, dark, and vulgar. His hair was so black and so strong that even had he shaved a great deal more carefully than he did, a large area of his face would have appeared to be permanently shadowed. His skin, where it could be seen, was pale, and this produced an illusion sometimes observable in people of this coloring that he was wearing white patches over his ears.

He read the typewritten sheets quickly and grunted. "Not a lot there," he said.

"Except an insufferable impression of self-satisfaction," agreed Mallinson.

"He's pleased with himself, and no error. There's only one thing I *don't* like about that setup. Them nobbling with Harrap."

"Is that something which ought to alarm us?"

"I dunno," said Mr. Crake. "It depends how easily you get alarmed. Harrap's still got one foot in his old man's setup, Latham's."

"Certainly. And Latham's, as we all know, is sound, old-fashioned merchant banking. Founded in the year of the Fire of London and hasn't changed much since. I understand their clerks still write in longhand with steel nibs."

"Latham's," said Mr. Crake, "is Feinberg's."

"How do you know that?" said Mallinson sharply.

"It's just one of those things I know. There's a tie-up behind the scenes. Cross guarantees at the bank. And Saul Feinberg is Jacob Naumann's cousin."

"I see." Victor Mallinson thought about this for a minute and then shook his neat head. "I don't think it'll make any difference," he said. "I don't think Naumann will upset a long-standing arrangement just because his cousin is interested in a firm that has a second-generation connection with one of our rivals. Do you?"

"You can never tell what's going to happen in the City," said Mr. Crake, "and that's for sure. I'd be a bloody sight happier if we had this long-standing arrangement you talk about in black and white and signed over a sixpenny stamp."

"It's rested for twenty years on a gentleman's agreement. They won't alter it now."

Mr. Crake expressed his opinion of gentlemen's agreements in language which made Victor Mallinson wrinkle up the corners of his mouth. Then he said, "One thing, as long as they've got this lawsuit hanging round their necks, they won't have too much time to bother us."

"Do you know who's running it?"

"That sounds a bit cynical to me," said Mr. Crake. "Are you suggesting it's a put-up job?"

"It occurred to me as a possibility. We'd all like to discover what the base of their Handcharm is. We can't get it by analysis, because it's vegetable not chemical. But if you forced their hand by alleging breach of an existing chemical patent, then they might be forced—in self-defense—to disclose what the base really is."

"Wouldn't work," said Mr. Crake. "Not in an English court. The plaintiff's got to prove his case. All the defendant's got to do is bloody well sit tight."

"In an English court, maybe not. What about a French court?"

"You never know what's going to happen in a Frog court," agreed Mr. Crake. "Case the other day. Divorce. The husband wasn't getting anywhere with his original case, so he switched ground and accused the barrister who was appearing for his wife of committing adultery with her. Tricky people."

Victor Mallinson said, "It would cost money to mount a case like that. I did hear a whisper the other day from

someone at my club that the money behind the case might
be coming from Germany."

Mr. Crake told Victor Mallinson what he thought about
Germany, too.

Other people were discussing Oliver Nugent that morning. Simon Bargulder, in his shirt sleeves, wandered out
of his office to look for Derek Wibberley. He could have
rung a bell and had him fetched, but he welcomed the opportunity to take a stroll through his kingdom. Sleeves
rolled to the elbow, displaying thick, hairy forearms, a
plaited leather belt encircling his equator, he rolled down
the passages of the advertising agency which he had
founded twenty-five years before with Harold French and
which was now competing on level terms with the big three
in the battlefield that is bounded by Kingsway, High Holborn, Farrington Street, and Fleet Street.

His course took him out of the executive suite, down a
flight of stairs, along the clean and sterile corridors where
the media analysts and data processors sat in their cells
and worshiped at the altars of Market Research; past the
room which housed their newest god, the computer, the first
to be installed in any advertising agency in England; down
a further flight of stairs and through double doors which
led into the television studio, silent for the moment with
the breathless silence of a soundproof room; and on into
the corridor which housed the copywriters.

Here he stopped a thin, untidy young man whose fair
hair came almost to his shoulders, and asked him if he had
seen Mr. Wibberley.

The young man started, threw his hair back from his
face, and muttered "I think he's in Art," then scampered
off down the passage.

Bargulder chuckled to himself. He had noticed that,
alone of all his staff, his copywriters resolutely refused to
call him "sir." This way they preserved their artistic inde-
pendence, he imagined.

He ran his man to earth in the color photography section of the art department. Wibberley was standing behind
a camera on a mobile crane, focusing it on a girl who was
dressed from the waist down in corduroy trousers and gum
boots, and for the remainder in a stretch nylon bathing

dress. Behind her was a boldly executed design of sand, cliffs, and sea. In front of her a cardboard sea gull rotated slowly on a wire.

"For God's sake," said Wibberley, "can't someone control that damned bird? Every time we get into position, the bloody thing twists round and blocks out Stella's right eye."

The girl said, "If you bring the camera any closer, they'll be able to look down my throat and see my tonsils sticking out."

"I'm sure they're as utterly beautiful as all your other projections," said Wibberley. "Oh, hullo, sir. I didn't see you."

"When you've finished," said Bargulder, "I'd like a word. There's no great hurry."

"I'll come now. Thomas can carry on. I'm only getting in his way, really."

Back in his office, which was furnished to look as much like a gentleman's study and as little like an office as possible, Bargulder pushed a box of cigarettes across the table to his subordinate and said, "I've been thinking. Might it be the right time to promote Quinn & Nicholson to three-star rating?"

Derek Wibberley flushed with pleasure. In a voice which he tried to keep carefully noncommittal, he said, "Well, sir. If you really think they're worth it."

"At the moment, to be honest, I doubt if they are. In a year they may be. This is a case when I should like to be ahead of public opinion, not behind it."

Firms who had accounts with Bargulder's were placed into three categories—one star, two star, and three star. These were as carefully considered and as hard to alter as the ratings of a *Michelin* restaurant. Not more than a dozen clients at any time would qualify for three-star status, and it was the first time that any of the accounts for which Derek Wibberley was responsible had been considered for for the accolade. It was more than an honor. It meant that a higher budget would automatically be allotted to his projects for them. It meant that he could get priority from any department in Bargulder's for their work. It meant an almost unlimited entertainment account for their senior executives—and for Derek Wibberley, too, come to that.

"I think they're the most enterprising firm in the toiletry market," he said. "It's extraordinary how they've come on in the last seven years. Mallinson's are the only people who are ahead of them, I should say."

"Who looks after Mallinson's?"

"Jacobsen."

"Ah, yes," said Bargulder. "Hendrik Jacobsen. A nice fellow. A very nice fellow." He sounded like a tiger saying, "A very nice goat."

"I'm talking to Oliver Nugent's partner, Nicholson, to-morrow about some plans they have for a new soap. We're having lunch together."

"Excellent. Where are you going?"

"I'd booked a table at the Columbine."

"The Columbine," said Bargulder, with a hint of re-proach in his voice. "For a three-star client? My dear boy! The Savoy."

Other people were discussing Oliver that morning. In small, untidy offices in Gresham Street and Old Jewry, where the real money in the City ebbed and flowed at the behest of a few inconspicuous but extremely shrewd men, his name was being mentioned, and the horoscope of Quinn & Nicholson was being studied and discussed by the sooth-sayers and astronomers of high finance.

(iii)

"It's not what goes into the bottle," said Derek Wibber-ley, "it's what you put on the label. Have some more sparrow grass. Waiter!"

"Not too much of the melted butter," said Dumbo. "Got my figure to think of. I've been getting very fat since I gave up squash last winter. Do you come here much?"

"It's handy for the office," said Wibberley. In fact, he had never been there before in his life, but a third glass of Corton had filled him with confidence and his youthful face was flushed.

"There's a lot to be said for working in London," said Dumbo enviously. He looked round the crowded grill-room, recognizing (at different tables) an actress, a pub-lisher, and a socially minded dean. "Normally I have a sandwich and a glass of beer at our local. Now that we've opened a London office, I may get up here a bit more often."

"I expect we shall be seeing a good deal of each other," said Wibberley. "You need us as much as we need you."

"That's right," said Dumbo. He thought Wibberley was a nice young man. Just the sort who would have made a good junior officer. An agreeable manner, but obviously a good brain, too. Much of what he had said about advertising seemed very good sense. Dumbo had never thought deeply about advertising before. It was money you paid out because it was the right thing to do, and in the hope of some vague future unspecified benefit. Like putting money in the plate at church. Now it appeared that there was more to it. Wheels within wheels.

"The trouble with toiletries," said Wibberley, "is that they're too easy to imitate. Take your Handcharm. Your rivals haven't discovered how you make it, and maybe they never will, but they've already started to market products of their own which are so like it, in make-up and general appearance, that the poor old muddleheaded public simply doesn't know which is which. Hand Lustre, Palm Balm, Finger Charm. All sold in packets and bottles which are just different enough not to infringe your trademark and registered design, but near enough to it to deceive anyone who's shopping in a hurry with a vague idea of what it was they heard last night on the telly."

Dumbo said, "It sounds—no more for me. Well, just half a glass, then. It sounds as though research is just a waste of time and money. I mean, why bother? All you have to do is wait around and see what your rivals are doing and copy it with a few subtle variations."

"You're forgetting one thing. The time element. It takes time to get your substitute out and advertise it. We reckon, at Bargulder's, that if you handle the original promotion properly you'll get an absolutely clear run for a year and a pretty favorable field for a year after that. At the end of the second year you might just as well stop pushing. There'll be so many people on the band wagon it'll come to a grinding halt."

"What exactly do you mean," said Dumbo, "by handling the promotion properly?" He had his eyes on the actress.

She had nearly finished and he reckoned she was going to have to squeeze past him to get off the banquette.

"The promotion itself has got to be based on a novel idea. It needn't be very profound, but it's got to be something no one's ever said before in exactly that way. The first man who was bold enough to tell girls that their armpits were smelly made a fortune. Most of the basic ideas have been thoroughly worked over by now, though, but you can get a new slant. Like that Commando toothpaste for men we did for you. BRUSH SEX INTO YOUR TEETH. You remember that?"

"I do indeed. I was so impressed by our advertising that I tried it myself for six months. It didn't seem to make much difference."

The actress was a disappointment. Seen from a range of one yard, the schoolgirl complexion had dissolved into a surface coating of matte color put on in apparently aimless blots and whirls. It was like looking too closely at an Impressionist painting.

"She models advertisements for the Mallinson group," said Wibberley. "You wouldn't think she was forty-five, would you? You'd like a glass of port? Or would you prefer brandy?"

"Neither," said Dumbo firmly. "A cup of black coffee."

"Just coffee then, waiter. And you might bring me some cigarettes. The other thing you've got to be terrifically careful about is security. If one of your rivals gets wind of what you're doing—the style of thing and the market it's being aimed at—there's nothing to prevent him preparing something on similar lines. Then you've lost the advantage of timing. In fact, you get the worst of both worlds, because if he times his exercise correctly and gets in just ahead of you, he gets an extra push from *your* advertising campaign."

When, at quarter to three, Wibberley finally called for and signed the bill, he added the name of the agency under his own and waited for a few minutes, finishing his cigarette before getting up. He knew perfectly well that the floor manager would be telephoning the agency to check his authority and he wanted to give them plenty of time to do it. In a month or so, when they knew his face, such precautions would be unnecessary.

As they were leaving, a pair at a corner table, deep in conversation, caught his eye. He said, "Isn't that your new director, Harrap?"

"That's right," said Dumbo. "Wilfred Harrap. I noticed him as we came in. Why?"

"That chap he's lunching with is Jacob Naumann's chief buyer, Horton. Mallinson won't like it when he hears about *that*."

"Will he hear about it?"

"Oh, certainly he will."

Mr. Crake said, "I told you not to bloody well write him down too soon. Nugent's crafty, and he doesn't box amateur three rounds of two minutes each and no holding in the clinches. He's a pro and the sooner we treat him as a pro the better."

Victor Mallinson thought that it was one of the rougher tricks of fate that he should have been given Mr. Crake for a partner, but he was sensible enough to realize that he needed him. They complemented each other. He thought of himself as an artist, a creator of beauty. He got an aesthetic pleasure out of an exquisitely conceived scent in a beautiful bottle, and he knew that the same bottle represented to Mr. Crake a sum of shillings and pence in raw materials and direct cost, plus overhead, plus advertising, plus retailers' return. It was a necessary discipline. Nevertheless, there were moments when he wondered whether it was worth it: a sordid grubbing after money, and anxiety about profit margins and dividends.

"I see he's advertising for a secretary," said Mr. Crake thoughtfully.

"Applicants for the post of Secretary to the Managing Director," said the neatly printed notice, "should obtain a card from the guichet on arrival. The number of the card will indicate the order in which you will be interviewed, and will avoid waste of your time and ours. Thank you."

The tall girl with the auburn hair read the notice and walked over to collect her card, which was handed out to her by a man with the look of a retired N.C.O. He seemed to have some difficulty in finding it, and she stood patiently in front of the window, the bright light showing up the tiny, almost invisible freckles behind her clear skin.

When she got her card, she saw that the number was fifteen. There were twelve girls in the room. That meant it was the second interview that was going on now. If they took five minutes each, she was in for an hour's wait at least. She took out a cigarette. No one else was smoking. So what? She lit it and cast an eye over the field. Half of them were upper-crust girls, debs or near it, probably quite inefficient, and out for the job on their looks. Two or three of the others were older women, probably highly efficient, but not the popular idea of a managing director's personal secretary. The most formidable was the neat girl nearest to the inner door. Good-looking enough to attract a wolf whistle and cool enough to freeze it, encased in a transparent outer skin of self-possession.

The inner door opened, a flustered-looking blonde came out, and the neat young lady went in. Five minutes passed. Then seven. This one must be making a hit. Ten. The auburn-haired girl was contemplating a second cigarette when the inner door opened again. This time it was the N.C.O. type who had given them their cards. He said, "I am sorry to inform you ladies that the post has been filled. If you will hand me back your cards, please, one at a time, I will refund you your expenses."

Auburn Hair thought that she wouldn't bother. She had come in her own car anyway.

(iv)

"I've got to go up to town for a meeting with our advertisers," said Oliver to Miss Doughty. "It'll go on late, and it'll mean staying up the night. You can deal with any routine stuff that crops up."

"I imagine so," said Miss Doughty coolly. She looked capable of running the firm singlehanded. "I think, before you go, you ought to deal with this letter from the bank about the fixed deposits."

"Mr. Nicholson can deal with that. He understands fixed deposits."

"Very well. Then there's a letter from the War Office asking if you can handle the Mepacrin contract for the Army in Malaya."

"That's Mr. Blackett's pigeon."

"If you say so. Only, seeing that their letter is a personal one from Major General Ferguson, I should have thought the answer ought to come from you, as Chairman, not from one of his own recent subordinates."

Oliver looked out of the corner of his eye at Miss Doughty, and said, "You might have something there. Incidentally, how did you know that Brigadier Blackett had been working under General Ferguson?"

"He mentioned it when he saw the letter."

"I see," said Oliver. "What other chores have you got for me?"

Miss Doughty consulted her book and said, "There's a staffing problem in the London office that wants your personal attention. The papers are in that docket in the 'in' tray. The auditors raised a number of queries which will need dealing with. I've got their letter here. You asked me to make some notes for you for your talk to the Pharmaceutical Trades Club. They're in that blue folder. And there's a long report from your new security man, Mr. Bolus. Suspected industrial espionage in the laboratory."

"Excellent."

"Which of them are you going to tackle first?"

"Actually," said Oliver, "I'm going to have a drink. If anyone rings up, you can tell them I'm in conference. With the president of the Pharmaceutical Trades Club."

Taylor said to Dumbo that afternoon, *"She* won't last long."

"Why not?"

"She's too efficient."

"It's time he had someone to keep him in order," said Dumbo. "He can't just play at it. We're a big outfit now."

When Quinn & Nicholson opened its London office in High Holborn, a flat had been found about a quarter of a mile away, in Lamb's Conduit Street. The flat was taken in the name of the company, and the rent featured in the accounts as a business expense (accommodation for directors and senior executives). In fact, it was Oliver's flat. It had been contract furnished and bore as much resemblance to a house as any suite in a hotel. The only unusual piece of furniture was a sizable safe, which had been hauled up to the flat with considerable difficulty and installed in the master bedroom. Oliver kept the whiskey in it.

He reached the flat at six o'clock that evening, had a word with the wife of the hall porter who looked after the flat for him and cooked his breakfast and whose name, by one of those coincidences which occur only in real life, was Mrs. Porter, and went up to bathe and change out of his office clothes and into a flannel suit. He was distressed to note that the trousers, which had been made for him less than a year before, were now uncomfortably tight round the waist. He slit the stitches at the back of the band with a razor blade, had a second drink, selected a shirt and tie with care, had a third drink, finished dressing, and went out.

A light drizzle was falling, almost a mist. Oliver spotted a taxi cruising down Theobald's Road from the direction of Gray's Inn and waved his umbrella imperiously. As the taxi swerved in toward the pavement, he heard footsteps running.

"Brett's Club," said Oliver.

"Excuse me!"

"Hold on a moment. This young man seems to want something."

"An awful liberty," said the young man, "but if you're going toward the West End could I share your cab? They're frightfully scarce in these parts."

"I can take you as far as St. Martin's Lane," said Oliver. "Get in."

"That's lovely. The Coliseum is what I want. *What* a bit of luck!"

Oliver was trying to place him. He was a good-looking boy, with fair hair and a very slightly effeminate face. The speech was pseudo upper class with its "frightfully" and its "lovely," but the accent (was it Cockney or was it a foreigner who had learned his English from a Cockney family?) peeped through like the lead in a snide half crown.

"Coliseum?" said Oliver. "Do I gather that you're late for the show? Or are you, perhaps, taking part in it?"

The boy flashed him a smile. " 'Perhaps' is right," he said. "I'm chorus. If they find they're short, they phone round the agencies to see who they can get to fill up with."

"And they got you?"

"That's right," said the boy. He had begun to search through the pockets of his jacket.

"Have you lost something?"

"I haven't actually lost anything, but I dressed in such a terrible hurry when I got the phone call from my agent I must have left my wallet in my other suit."

"Don't worry. I'm paying for the taxi."

"I was thinking about getting back. If I knew anyone in the show I could borrow from them, but I don't."

"You don't know *me*," said Oliver.

"That's perfectly true," said the boy, blushing prettily as he said it.

"All right," said Oliver. "I've bought it. I'll stake you a pound. That should buy your supper and get you home to bed."

"I hope you don't think I did this on purpose—just to borrow money, I mean."

"I think you've got a big future on the stage," said Oliver.

"No, really. I mean it. And I'll pay you back. Here's one of my cards. It's my stage name, but that's my address at the bottom. If you'll let me know where to send it."

He sounded so sincere that Oliver was almost convinced. He spelt out his name and address and the boy wrote it down on the back of an envelope.

"Here we are," said Oliver. "Cut down the back there and you'll find yourself in St. Martin's Lane. Good luck with the show."

"Good night, and thanks frightfully," said the boy. Oliver made his way up the seven worn semicircular steps which led to the swing doors of Brett's Club. To belong to Brett's Club was something. It was not the oldest club in London, and by no means the most expensive, but for reasons which were far from plain, it was very difficult to get into. It was not primarily political like the Carlton or bohemian like the Savage. It had been founded in the early nineteenth century in a fit of bad temper by a duke who had been refused permission to entertain a troupe of clowns at the Athenaeum, and it had retained a tenuous but persistent connection with the stage, although you were as likely to see a High Court judge as a theatrical knight at a long

center table. Oliver had been proposed for membership by
Jacob Naumann and seconded by a very ancient and very
notable military friend of his father's. He had had to wait
nearly a year for his turn to come up, and could still recall the thrill of pleasure he had felt when he learned of his
election.

As he walked upstairs to the bar, he was trying to answer
two questions. Why, if Maurice Merrivale, which was the
name printed in tasteful 24-point Palace Script in the center of the card, had really left his wallet in his other suit,
did he have his cards on him at all? That was a difficult
one, but the second was even more puzzling.

Mr. Merrivale's home address, printed in 8-point Gill
Sans in the bottom left-hand corner, was 72(a) Baxendale
Road, Fulham. But if he lived in Fulham and had just at
that moment rushed out in response to a telephone call
from his agent, how had he managed to be at the corner
of Lamb's Conduit Street in Holborn?

Oliver thought about this for a bit and decided that he
ought to make a telephone call. Then he went to the bar,
where he found Victor Mallinson. Mallinson had become a
member about a year after Oliver, who had been amused
to see that he described himself in the Candidates' Book
as "a collector."

Mallinson said, "If you haven't got to hurry home after
dinner, would you care for a game of bridge? I've got a
guest coming along. He's a Frenchman, actually."

"I'd like that," said Oliver. "We'll get Naumann to make
up a four."

Mallinson's friend had proved to be a small, quiet, gray-
haired man, with a name which sounded like Semolina.
There was no suggestion, Oliver noticed, that they should
cut for partners. Mallinson played with the Frenchman
against Naumann and himself. They had played five rubbers. One had ended more or less level. Oliver and Naumann had lost the other four, two of them quite heavily.
At the club stakes of ten shillings a hundred with one-
pound corners, this had not been disastrous, but when the
game finally broke up at one o'clock, Oliver found himself
paying out nearly thirty pounds for his evening's entertainment. The drizzle had cleared now and the stars were
showing. Oliver decided to walk home through Covent

Garden, already beginning to stir into life as the first lorries rumbled in from the country, up the deserted length of Kingsway and Southampton Row, and round a right turn into Theobald's Road. As he walked, he was trying to work out just how it had happened.

The cards had not run too badly. Old Jacob was a steady performer. Mallinson was one of the new school of educated bridge players who read every book and article that was written about the game, and had the latest conventions at his finger tips. Oliver himself played almost entirely by ear and would have backed himself against Mallinson six days out of seven. The Frenchman? Come to think of it, of course, it was the Frenchman who had made the difference. The turning point of the second rubber had been a small slam in hearts which Oliver had doubled and which had, against all the odds, been made. How? When he got home, he would write the cards down and work it out. Bridge problems were very like business problems. If you reduced them to simple terms and looked at them steadily, you could usually see a way through them or round them.

A black shape rocketed out of a shop basement and streaked across the road with a yowl, with a second black shape in pursuit. Oliver grinned to himself. If men and women were as open as cats about their lusts, what a lot of trouble everyone would be saved, and, incidentally, what a lot of damn silly books and plays wouldn't get themselves written.

A car was parked with side lights on against the curb opposite the entrance to his block of flats. He was fitting his key into the lock when he heard the car door open, and looked round. It was a big square man with a big square face.

"Mr. Nugent?"

"That's right," said Oliver. He shifted his weight on his feet, ready to fight or run. Running would be the safer option. The man was three classes above him in weight and looked as if he knew how to handle himself.

"Do you mind if we go up to your flat for a moment?" He put one hand inside his raincoat and pulled out a black leather case. Oliver studied the warrant card carefully. It was embossed with the Royal Arms and appeared to ident-

ify the stranger as Detective Sergeant (First Class) Warriner, G., attached to Q Division of the Metropolitan Police.

Oliver walked over to the car and said to the driver,
"Do you mind if I look at yours, too?"

"All right, Sergeant?"

"Certainly. Show him your driving license, and Bunny
Club card if he wants to see them."

"All right," said Oliver. "You can come along up."

Sergeant Warriner looked even larger indoors than he
had in the street. He removed his hat, revealing a guards-
man haircut, sat down on the hard chair beside the table,
and said no to a drink.

Oliver wandered across to the sideboard, decanted two
inches of brandy into a glass, and added some ginger ale
from an opened bottle. He thought, from the gleam in the
Sergeant's eye, that he might have joined him if pressed.

"Tell me all about it," he said.

"Well, sir, it's like this. One of our men from West End
Central picked up a nail—"

"A *what?*"

"A male prostitute, sir, outside Piccadilly Underground
this evening. He was soliciting for custom, and making a
nuisance of himself generally."

"Unpleasant," said Oliver.

"There's a lot of it about."

"Do you know, that's what my doctor always says. Last
time I went to see him, I told him I was pregnant, and he
said it quite automatically— But please go on."

Sergeant Warriner was staring at him with a baffled
expression. "Did you say you'd been pregnant?"

"I was pulling his leg," said Oliver. "Please go on with
your story. We'd just got to this young man soliciting in
Piccadilly. What happened next?"

"Well, sir, he was taken back to West End Central and
invited to turn out his pockets. In his wallet we discovered
a scrap of paper—"

"He'd found his wallet by then, had he?"

"What's that?" said the Sergeant. He sounded exactly
like a foxhound picking up the first real nip of scent on a
frosty morning.

"I'm assuming that the young man we're talking about

is called Maurice Merrivale. That's his *nom de guerre*—I don't think anyone could *really* be called that, do you?"

"Then you do know this man, sir?"

From a view to a chase.

"Oh, certainly."

From a chase to a kill.

"And have you known him for very long, sir?"

"I have known him," said Oliver, "approximately six hours longer than I have known you, Sergeant. He cadged a lift in my taxi this evening and conned a pound out of me. We exchanged addresses on the assumption, which I never had much faith in, that he might get round to repaying it."

"I see, sir."

"You don't sound happy."

"In a voluntary statement he made after his arrest, he asserted that he had known you for three or four months."

"When you say known me, you mean, I suppose, in the way of business?"

"Yes, sir. That was the implication. He mentioned visits to this flat."

"Over the last three or four months?"

"That's what he said, sir."

"I see," said Oliver. "Neat." He swirled the brandy round in his glass. "But not neat enough. Tell me, Sergeant, are charges like this usually investigated at Divisional level?"

"Sometimes."

"Because I understood that all charges of persistent soliciting by males were now referred to one department at Scotland Yard. Superintendent Glasgow, isn't it?"

"That is the arrangement, sir, but they can't always deal with all the cases that come along, so we sometimes have to investigate them, too."

"But you report them to the Yard, don't you?"

"We shall report this one, all right."

"I can save you the trouble. I've reported it to George Glasgow already."

"Do I gather you know Superintendent Glasgow, sir?"

"I met him when he came out to Austria on a war-crimes job," said Oliver. "I handed him over some choice S.S. specimens that I'd been put in charge of. I've kept up with him since, and I knew the job he was doing at the

Yard. So when this young hopeful tried to pick me up this evening, I gave him a ring."

Sergeant Warriner looked at him for a long moment; then he relaxed. His big body seemed to settle down in the chair. It was as though, without a word spoken, he had gone off duty. He said, "That was sensible of you, sir. Fortunate, too."

"There's one thing that puzzles me, though," said Oliver. "Why should he trouble to lie about me? I haven't done him any harm that I know of."

"Spitefulness. They're like that. If they can get anyone else into trouble, they'll tell any sort of lie to do it."

"Then he ought to have worked his lies out more carefully," said Oliver. "I've only had this flat for two weeks. Are you sure you wouldn't like a drink?"

"Not nearly as sure as I was," said Sergeant Warriner.

(v)

"Every effort will be made to comply with these specifications," said Oliver, "and the company are very grateful for your continued confidence in them."

"*Is* very grateful," said Miss Doughty. "Confidence in *it*."

"I beg your pardon."

"The word 'company' is neuter singular."

"It'll bloody well be feminine plural if I bloody well want it that way."

"Certainly. I was only pointing out the accepted usage."

"I don't give a damn for the accepted usage. It's my letter and it goes to Major General Miller, D.S.O., Contracts Department, War Office, Hobart House."

"You're quite sure?"

Oliver looked at his secretary suspiciously. "What do you mean?"

"I was asking whether you really wanted the letter addressed to Major General Miller. If you do, I'll send it that way. As you said a moment ago, it's your letter."

"Since this letter concerns an Army contract, and since Major General Miller happens to be in charge of Army contracts, and a personal friend into the bargain, can you think of any conceivable reason why it should *not* be addressed to him?"

"Only that he's been promoted to Lieutenant General. It's in the *Times* this morning."

Oliver said to Taylor as they were walking round the works, "Do you think there might possibly be such a thing as being *too* efficient?"

"Oh, I'm sure of it," said Taylor.

"You can pay too high a price—"

"I had an orderly room clerk once who was so efficient he could have run the whole regiment singlehanded. He could have done it in his spare time, actually. Every time I gave him something to type out, it came back different—you know what I mean?"

"I know exactly what you mean," said Oliver.

"Full of semicolons. He was nuts on semicolons."

"What did you do about him?"

"I had him posted as sanitary orderly."

Oliver said, "In the case I have in mind, although it would be an eminently satisfactory solution, I'm afraid it wouldn't be practicable."

They were walking round the factory. It was a very different place from the ramshackle outfit Oliver had found there twelve years before.

Built over the double site, backing on the canal, and fronting on the High Street, it was a roomy single-story building, constructed largely of steel and glass with a two-story brick annex at the east end sticking up like the bridge and upper works of an aircraft carrier. This annex, housing all the office and executive staff, had a private entrance into the side road and a car park behind it, filling the space between it and the canal.

The main entrance, a wide bay with a one-way traffic circuit, opened directly onto the High Street. Following the logical progression of incoming materials, Oliver and Taylor had gone through the left-hand entrance into a reception section where goods were checked, sorted, stored, and issued. ("Quartermasters' Stores," said Taylor.) Behind this, and running almost the full length at the rear of the building, were the make-up departments. This was where the various processes of grinding, pulping, slicing, mixing, distilling, boiling, cooling off, and molding went on. Old hands still referred to it as the kitchen.

A short corridor then took them across to the packing department, but before reaching it they had to pass on their left the heavy teak door which led down a couple of steps to the experimental laboratory. Here Bernard Lewin, the company's head chemist, worked at his brews.

"Eye of newt," said Oliver, "and toe of frog, wool of bat, and tongue of dog."

"It's an odd sort of outfit," agreed Taylor, "and he's an odd sort of bloke. Tell you the truth, I don't understand one word in ten he says, but he's clever. You can tell that."

"He's not clever," said Oliver. "He's a genius."

Bernard was not everyone's cup of tea, but Oliver had been taught by no less an authority than Field Marshal Montgomery that idiosyncrasies of dress and manner might be overlooked if, and so far as, they were compensated for by brain power.

"How's he getting on? He looked a bit off-color last time I saw him."

Taylor paused to consider this. It was a serious question and one which it was his job to deal with seriously.

He said, "I thought he was settling down all right. It was a bit difficult to start with. Those shirts. And that hairdo. The men used to whistle at him, and, of course, that made the girls laugh, but it was all quite friendly, if you follow me. But just lately there's been something on his mind. No doubt about that."

"I can't have him worried. The job he's doing is the most important thing in the company at this moment. You could almost say it's going to make the difference between success and failure. For the next few years, anyway."

"I'll do what I can," said Taylor. It occurred to him that there was very little difference between a works manager and a sergeant major.

They strolled on into Packing, which occupied the whole of the northeast corner of the building. Through this department flowed the unending stream of three-color wrappers, pictorial labels, special displays, instruction leaflets, and advertising material, designed by the artists at Bargulder's and specially printed for them by Sandberg & Freyer. Here were machines which would turn a roll of cardboard into five hundred cartons in the twinkling of an eye, machines that would fill bottles with three different liquids in the right proportions without spilling a drop in the process, machines which would count out tablets and dispense them into a container, seal the container, and label it.

"If I had to look after one of those machines," said Oliver, "it'd drive me mad in a day."

"They get used to it," said Taylor. "What they like is not having to think."

"By the way, how's your daughter getting along?"

"She's getting above herself," said Taylor. "When she was just a typist, it wasn't so bad. Now that she's a secretary, she'll hardly talk to her own family."

They moved out through the invoicing room and by a communicating door into the office annex.

Oliver said, "I've got a Board meeting in five minutes' time which will drag on most of the morning. Could you see Jim Bolus and ask him to have a word with me before lunch?"

There were five small square bottles on the Board Room table, each labeled and numbered, and five glass dishes, each no larger than a half crown.

"Take your choice, gentlemen," said Oliver. "They're all subtly distinct, or so Mr. Lewin tells me, but it needs a more educated nose than mine to be certain of the differences."

Brigadier Blackett unscrewed the cap of one of the bottles. There was a glass dipper inside the cap which he inserted, drawing out a drop of the liquid and spreading it on the glass saucer. Then he lifted the saucer to his long brown nose and sniffed.

"Can't smell a damned thing," he said.

"If you actually sniff at it, you won't. Hold it in front of your nose and let it assail your nostrils."

The Brigadier allowed it to assail his nostrils, and said, "Ah. I got it then. Rather nice. Reminds me of something, too. Can't think what." He screwed up his eyes in an effort of memory. The others watched him anxiously. "Reminds me of my wife," he said at last.

Dumbo tried them next. He said, "If you want a personal

opinion, I should say the order was Number Five first, Number Two second, the rest also ran."

"Fine," said Oliver. He turned each of the little dishes over, told Dumbo to turn his back, and put a drop of scent on each of them.

"Now try again," he said.

Dumbo tried again. He said, "The one at the end's Number Five. The one in the middle is Number Two—I think. I'm not sure about the rest. And I still prefer Number Five. What's the joke?"

"Those were all out of bottle Number Three," said Oliver, "and I didn't do it just to pull your leg, Dumbo. I wanted to demonstrate what I've always thought—that there isn't one man in a hundred who can really tell two scents apart."

"When I was in South America," said Harrap, "I proved conclusively that I hadn't any sense of smell at all. It was an advantage there in some ways."

"Let me try," said Wibberley.

He held each bottle briefly up to his nose, then said, "Cover up the labels and change the order round." He then tried them again, more slowly this time, and said, "This one's Number Four—it's definitely sweeter than the others, more ambergris, I should say. This one's either Number One or Number Three and this is the twin. They're not very easy to distinguish but I think I've got Number One in my right hand and Number Three in my left. This is definitely Number Two. It's got that smell of wet fern which is very popular nowadays. And this is certainly Number Five. I agree with Mr. Nicholson, it's the best of the bunch."

There was a round of applause from the Board.

"How do you do it?" said Harrap. Technique of any sort interested him.

"It's practice," said Wibberley. "You have to associate something physical with each smell. It isn't always a flower or a tree. There's one skin lotion that smells of hospitals and another one of scrambled egg."

"Fascinating," said Harrap. "What does our Number Five remind you of?"

"It's got a strong, distinctive smell," said Wibberley. "I was trying to locate it."

They tried in turn.

"An old-fashioned conservatory," said Dumbo. "Lilies, musk roses, and passionflowers."

"Call it Maud," said the Brigadier. His fellow-directors looked blankly at him. He said, "I can see you weren't brought up on Tennyson, as I was. 'Come into the garden, Maud, for the black bat, night, has flown.' There's a bit there about something which still gives you a kick even if you've been dead for a hundred years. Come to think of it, Wibbers, it might make a good advertising line."

Wibberley promised to look it up.

Harrap said, "Christmas morning, around twelve o'clock, with a nice pine log fire crackling in the grate and the first pre-lunch gins being poured out."

"A brand-new pack of cards," said Oliver. "It's that very faint pear-drop smell you get when the cellophane's taken off."

"Girls," said the Brigadier. "Young, and slightly silly girls who are just beginning to realize what it's all about."

"A psychologist would have a field day with our reactions," said Oliver. "What about you, Wibbers?"

Derek Wibberley recognized the compliment. It wasn't every day that he was called in at Board level, particularly at such a climactic moment in the history of a company.

He said, "It's feminine, and that's something to be thankful for. A lot of perfumes which are being turned out nowadays are about as feminine as the elephant house at the zoo. It's young and tender, like a flower that hasn't quite reached maturity. Yet it's got quite a distinctive smell. Most of the stuff the French are exporting is labeled 'Subtle' or 'Elusive.' It's so damned elusive it's got no smell left."

"Young and tender," said Harrap. "Feminine, distinctive, and Tennysonian. What price Princess?"

"On the right lines," said Oliver.

"Junior Miss?"

"Much too hearty."

"Jeunesse?"

Wiberley said, "I think that's been used. Wait a moment. What about Tendresse?"

A pause, as they turned it over.

"By God," said Oliver, "that's it. Tendresse."

After the meeting he had a word with ex-Squadron Leader Bolus. Bolus had one eye, one and a half ears, and only two fingers on his right hand. The remainder had been lost in an encounter with a Messerschmitt over the Western Desert in 1943. He was Security Officer to the group and was disliked by almost everyone in it except Oliver.

Oliver said, "I've got a bit of a problem on my hands. The way I look at it there are two ends to it, and the thing is to find out where they meet in the middle. One end is a temporary motor mechanic, thought to be of German extraction, employed by Snyder's garage about seven years ago."

"That's the outfit that went bust, isn't it? We use it as a transport section now."

"Correct. We took some of their people over, too. Palmer was one of them. He'll remember this chap. It was the time when I had my smash."

"And you think this Kraut mechanic was responsible for it?"

"I thought so at the time and I still think so now. The other end of the trail's a bit fresher." He handed Bolus Maurice Merrivale's card.

"You think this is the same chap?"

"No. I don't think that," said Oliver, "but I think they might have the same employer."

"One club," said Oliver.

Victor Mallinson was sorting his cards out. He continued to do so, deliberately prolonging the process, as if he enjoyed the feel of the slippery pieces of pasteboard. It was one o'clock in the morning and they were alone in the cardroom at Brett's. Finally he said, "One no trump."

Jacob Naumann stared glumly at his hand. It contained nothing to encourage him. Five small spades, four hearts headed by the knave—the only honor in the whole deplorable collection—a singleton diamond, and three of his partner's declared suit of clubs.

It looked like the end of the evening. A pity. Until that moment they had not been doing too badly. They had been a few hundred points up at the end of the last rubber, and he would very much have liked to have called it a day and gone to bed, but the others had been keen to go on.

He recognized that the game had developed into a private duel—a trial of strength between Nugent and Mallinson —and he regretted it. He liked to keep his private feelings out of games, in the same way that he kept them out of business. Now the opposition was a game up, and it looked very much as though they had the rubber in their pockets. Unless, of course, Nugent was going out on a limb to sacrifice, which would be expensive.

He said, in what he hoped was a strictly expressionless tone, "No bid."

Victor Mallinson's partner thought hard before saying anything. M. Sermoulin was not in the least tired. In Egypt, where he had learned his bridge, and later in small private parties in France and Italy where it had earned him a steady income, he had often played right through the night. What made him hesitate was the current of private hostility which he, too, had sensed between Mallinson and Nugent. Once two players at the bridge table really started gunning for each other, it was apt to color every bid that they made. (He recollected a night's play near Annecy which had proceeded on the same lines. It had ended at six o'clock in the morning on the dew-soaked lawn behind the Château with the sun peeping over the Dents de Lanfon. Fortunately both men had been rotten shots.)

Also, there was something wrong with the bidding.

Nugent had opened one club. Since he wasn't playing any artificial system, this surely meant that he had at least five clubs, maybe more. His own partner had then bid a confident no trump. This surely meant at least a guard in clubs. Three or four of them at least. And there was he, *staring at five clubs in his own hand, headed by the king and ten.* He also, incidentally, held the ace, knave of spades and the king of hearts. Quite enough, opposite his partner's strong no trump, for a raise to three no trumps and game, which would conclude a comfortably lucrative rubber.

Nevertheless, he hesitated.

Instinct told him that Oliver Nugent was going to bid again, and to keep on bidding. He had the look of a man who did not give up lightly. Very well. If they pushed him high enough, a double could be lucrative.

So he, too, said, "No bid."

Before the words were spoken, Oliver had snapped out, "Two clubs."

Victor Mallinson, without looking at his cards again, said, "Two no trumps." Naumann passed quickly and M. Sermoulin, feeling that the time had come to conclude the farce, said, "Three no trumps."

Now, if Oliver dared to mention his paltry club suit once more, he was booked for the most expensive double of the year.

Oliver said, "And I double that."

Victor Mallinson said, "Redouble."

Naumann was in agony. He thought for a wild moment of staging a rescue operation with his five small spades, but abandoned the notion. Such attempts were nearly always futile. He said, "No bid."

His next headache was finding a card to lead.

In normal circumstances this would have been no problem at all. When your partner has bid a suit twice, and doubled a subsequent no-trump contract by his opponents, he is announcing that his own suit is long, solid, and unbreakable. He is not advising you to lead it. He is ordering you to do so.

And yet—and yet—unless both his opponents were raving mad, they *must* have guards in the suit. Mallinson particularly. And since he was sitting over Oliver, a club lead might be quite fatal. It might present the opposition with four or five tricks in the suit. And each redoubled, vulnerable overtrick was going to cost them four hundred points, or two solid pounds in cash.

But if this was the true picture, then Oliver was mad. It really boiled down to a question of which of the two men he trusted.

A spade if he trusted Mallinson; a club if he trusted Oliver. Coming out of an agonizing trance, he laid down a small club.

M. Sermoulin exposed his hand. Mallinson said, "Thank you very much indeed, partner," and selected the king of clubs. Oliver topped it with the ace. He had no option. It was the only club in his hand. He then proceeded to play out the ace, king, queen, and four other small diamonds.

"Eight tricks to us," said Oliver. "That makes you four down, vulnerable, doubled, and redoubled. Twenty-two hundred."

"Never try it again," said Naumann. "My nerves won't stand it."

M. Sermoulin said, "Nicely done. I saw exactly the same coup executed by an Italian at Venice three years ago, but on that occasion it was even more gratifying, for I was playing with him."

Mallinson said nothing. He had lost his temper. He lost the next two games as well.

Oliver was reflecting, with pleasure, on all these things as he walked back to Lamb's Conduit Street, and the seventeen pound notes which he had extracted from Victor Mallinson was the smallest part of the sum total of his satisfaction.

It had been, as the Frenchman had suggested, a whiskery old coup: the concealing of one suit by bidding another, the luring of one's opponents into a no-trump contract, the provocative double. But it needed correct timing, and, above all, it needed exactly the right sort of opponent. An egotist. A man cunning enough to set traps for you but too self-satisfied to perceive that you might be setting the same traps for him. "In short," said Oliver aloud, "a clever player who is not quite as clever as he thinks he is."

This observation was answered by the flinging open of the door of a car standing at the curb just ahead of him, and a girl's voice which said, "You're wrong about that."

"Come back and don't be a fool," said a man's voice thickly.

"I'm not going to be mauled about by you," said the girl, "and what's more, I'm not going to let you drive the car any further. You're drunk."

"If you don't want to drive, you can bloody well walk."

"I'd rather walk than finish up dead."

"Stupid bitch."

"That's no way," said Oliver, "to talk to a lady."

"What the bloody hell's it got to do with you?"

"Nothing at all," said Oliver. "That's what makes it such fun." He opened the car door, twisted his hands into the driver's collar, braced one foot against the car, and pulled.

The driver was half out of the car before he realized what was happening; then he grabbed the steering wheel and started to bellow.

Oliver half turned, still holding his collar, and yanked him over his shoulder in a fireman's lift, straightening up as he did so. The extra leverage was effective. The man came out and, as Oliver loosed his hold, slithered over his shoulder and onto the pavement. On the way down his head bounced off the lamppost.

"I say," said Oliver. "I do hope I haven't killed him."

"I don't care if you have," said the girl.

They examined the man. Blood was trickling from a deep black cut over his right eye.

"That's all right," said Oliver. "If he's bleeding he *can't* be dead. Let's make him comfortable, shall we?" He dragged the man across the pavement and propped him up in a sitting position against the low wall. As an afterthought, he got a rug from the back of the car and tucked it round the man, who was starting to mutter.

"He'll have a hell of a head in the morning," said Oliver. "Now, where can I drive you to?"

"It's his car," said the girl doubtfully. "I live in Kensington."

"Fine," said Oliver. "I'll drive you home and bring the car back. He may be stirring by then. Unless, of course, a policeman comes by, in which case he won't be stirring, he'll be in stir. Joke."

He had had time to look at the girl by now. She was worth looking at. Taller than average, she had the current model-girl look which had been invented by David Bailey, and had swept the country along with the clothes his girls modeled: the elongated thoroughbred, compounded of good bones, large eyes, and a lower lip turned down like a sheet on a well-made bed. Her hair formed a thick, square helmet round her face. The street lamps made it impossible to be precise about the color but he thought it was reddish.

"Well—all right," she said. "If you think you can drive it. It's a sports car of sorts."

"I know this model well," said Oliver. "I drove my first one when I was thirteen."

By the time they got to Hyde Park Corner, he had found out that the girl's name was Philippa, that after leaving school she had taken a shorthand and typing course, had got a job in a lawyer's office, which she loathed, and had been angling for a post as secretary to a television executive.

"That lout you left on the pavement pretended he could fix it for me. He said he had pull."

"He looked as if he had just enough pull to get a cork out of a bottle," said Oliver. The girl laughed for the first time that night. She had nice teeth.

By the time they were turning into Kensington Church Street, Oliver had returned the compliment and told her something about himself. She was an easy girl to talk to.

She lived in a cul-de-sac off Camden Hill, in a house which had been converted into five maisonettes. There were five names beside the bells on the door.

"Just for the record," said Oliver, "which are you?"

"I'm the one at the top," said the girl.

"It must be a lovely view," said Oliver. "Good night, and sleep well."

He climbed back into the car, turned it neatly, and drove off. The girl stood on the doorstep looking after him. As the car reached the corner, a hand came out and waved. She waved back.

"We-e-ll," she said to herself. "Lovely view. That's quite a new gambit. We thought, just for a moment, he was going to suggest we might go up together and admire it. From my bedroom window, perhaps."

(vi)

"The way I see it," said Wibberley, "we need a series of twelve half-pages in color in the better-class monthly glossies—with perhaps an option, subject to penalty, to break at six. The first one to appear in the month before D Day, step up the campaign in the last fortnight with a regular spot in the weeklies, and turn on the heat in the last week with the dailies. After D Day we cut right back on the newspapers and start in with a weekly television quickie and then just keep things simmering with placard advertising, bus and underground, free displays and hand-outs in the shops, and maybe a short film for the local advertising circuits."

"I like that," said Bargulder. "I tell my clients always,

'Don't run before you can walk. Do your promotion in the good, old-fashioned way in the papers and magazines. Once your product is really selling, you can puff it along with television and films.' What's the budget?"

"For the initial campaign, twenty thousand."

"That's good," said Bargulder. "Very good. I like the name, too. Tendresse." He scribbled on the pad in front of him. "We'll get our clever little Hungarian to do some sketches for us. I see it with the tails of the 'S's coming right back under the word, almost to the beginning."

"Something like this?" Wibberley laid a slip of paper on the desk. "I got Dino to rough it out for me."

"Yes. Yes. I like that very much. You can tell Dino from me. Now—who are we picking for the lead?"

He meant, as Wibberley well understood, which of the many models who were prepared to sell their faces, or celebrities who were prepared to sell their names, was going to be the subliminal image of the new product, the Tendresse type.

"We had a difference of opinion over that," said Wibberley. "I thought we'd be aiming to make most of our sales in the lower middle-class bracket and we ought to ask the agencies for a sweet little face—not fluffy. You know, a touch of character—slightly retroussé nose, big mouth, perhaps a couple of freckles."

"What you were looking for," said Bargulder, "is the girl that every middle-class mother would hope her own daughter would turn out to be, and that the mother would give anything to be herself once again."

"Exactly," said Wibberley, "but I couldn't get it across to Nugent. He says that when it comes to scent, all women are snobs. He's after something right out of the top drawer. Black velvet, diamonds, false eyelashes, and a title."

"We'd better see if we can get him his Lady."

"You don't think perhaps that we ought to try to persuade him to see it our way? I'm not at all sure he's not making a mistake about this."

"My dear Derek," said Bargulder, and it was a sign of the highest favor that he should even remember, let alone use, an employee's Christian name. "Never try to change a client's mind. We are here to interpret his wishes. That is our sole function."

"All the same," said Wibberley, "I think he's wrong. He's twenty years out of date. People don't imitate duchesses now. They laugh at them."

"You mustn't allow yourself to get personally involved in this, Derek."

"But I *am* involved, sir. It's my biggest assignment to date. Easily my biggest. If it goes wrong, I'm the one who's going to carry the can."

"No such thing. The agency stands behind every member of its staff. Bear that in mind." He got up and laid a fatherly hand on the young man's shoulder. It was a benediction and a dismissal.

Victor Mallinson said to his secretary, "What would *you* say was the nicest smell in the world, Jennie?"

"Fish and chips."

"An agreeable taste, if you like that sort of thing. Not really a nice smell. Burned fat."

It was one of the reasons she liked working for Mr. Mallinson. He always talked about interesting things in a sensible way. Yesterday it had been an argument about modern art in which he had got the better of that odious Mr. Crake. The day before it had been preference shares, when Mr. Crake had come out top.

Jennie had been brought up in a rough home, where you got belted if you stepped out of line, where culture had been the television set and conversation a shouting match. She hadn't been unhappy, but it had been a revelation to her that another sort of world existed. Another sort of man, too. All her early friends had been girls. If any male person outside the family showed an interest in you, they had one reason, and differed only in the seriousness of their intentions and the skill of their technique. Mr. Mallinson wasn't like that at all. She thought he was probably a bit of a pansy, really, but not an obvious one. He didn't talk in an affected voice or wear peculiar clothes. Most of the time he behaved in a sensible, grown-up way, but there were moments, when he was being opposed or obstructed, when he could be childish. She found then that she could laugh at him and like him at the same time.

Since he was being serious about this, she had better be

serious, too. She said, "I've always sort of liked the smell of burning leaves."

"I don't think we could call a new scent burning leaves. Or could we?"

"What about Bonfire, then?"

"That's not bad. In fact, it's nearly right. It would do for a man's product. You can call them things like Commando and Ringcraft and Tang. It won't quite do for girls."

"Wood smoke?"

"No. That's not as good as Bonfire. You need a joined spondee."

"Come again?"

"One word, of two syllables. And it's got to suggest— oh, a nice, simple, feminine girl without too many airs and graces."

"But a bit of a chick," said Mr. Crake, who had joined the discussion.

"The nicest girl I know," said Jennie, "is the girl who lives in the flat below mine. She's simple, and feminine."

"What's her name?"

"Lucy."

Mallinson considered it. Mr. Crake murmured, "I love Lucy," to himself.

"Nearly," said Mallinson, "but not quite. Simple and girlish, yes."

"But not enough chick."

"Lucy, Lucinda, Lucilla. What about Lucille?"

"I like that," said Jennie.

"Not bad," said Mr. Crake. "Probably been used before. Most of the best names have."

"Check it," said Mallinson. "If it's available, I think it's what we want. We'll have to see what Hendrik Jacobsen thinks of it."

"If you're selling something," said Oliver, "it seems to me that the main thing you've got to decide is who you're selling it to. In other words, which class you're aiming at. Upper, middle, or lower. Right?"

"It's simpler than that," said Wibberley. "For a start, you can cut out the lower classes. They've got more spending money than they used to have, agreed, but still not enough to push a luxury product. And as for the upper class, they're a dead loss. They don't read advertisements."

"My grandmother," said Dumbo, "who is definitely upper class, spends most mornings reading advertisements and most afternoons buying the goods which have caught her eye. She's got the largest known collection of unread encyclopedias, unused trusses, and uneaten breakfast foods."

"Don't take any notice of him, Wibbers," said Oliver. "Go on with what you were saying. What classes *does* a professional huckster like you recognize?"

"For advertisers there are two, and two only. The upper middle class and the lower middle class. You must make your mind up quite clearly from the start which you're aiming at."

"Why not sell to both?" said Harrap.

"If you aimed at both you'd hit neither, because the approach is completely different. The U.M.C. likes solid worth. Nothing flashy, nothing risky. Twenty shillings' worth for a pound. It's been brought up to believe the old fallacy that you get what you pay for. That an article which costs two pounds will be twice as valuable as one which only costs one pound. If you're aiming to sell to them, you confine yourself to plain statements about how reliable and durable the thing is, and it's a top selling point if can add that it's been sold, unchanged, for a hundred and twenty years."

"It doesn't sound a very hopeful line for scent," said Oliver. "What about the L.M.C.?"

"The thing to remember is that they're much more adventurous. You give them color, superlatives, free gift coupons, and severely reduced prices."

"I don't think we can compete in that field, either," said Oliver.

"It's where most of the money is."

"Maybe," said Oliver. His mouth was settling into a line of obstinacy which Dumbo recognized. "But I don't think we want to go for them straight away. What I think we ought to do—following your own line of reasoning, Wibbers—is to start by selling Tendresse to your upper middles. Get it established, get the name known. Then reverse the process. Step up the advertising, reduce the prices, and go after the lower middles. The one thing we've got to avoid is any suggestion that it's a cheap scent. What do you think, Wilfred?"

"Sounds sensible to me," said Harrap.

"I agree," said Dumbo.

"All right," said Oliver. "We're all agreed."

Wibberley looked, for a moment, as if he wanted to say something, but before he could get round to it Oliver had swept on. "The next point, I take it, is *how* are we going to sell? What line are we going to take? The high road or the low road?"

"I'm not sure that I follow you," said Dumbo.

"This is something I've quarreled with Wibbers a good deal about." Oliver accompanied this with a friendly grin which robbed the words of their sting. "There are two quite different approaches. Either you can try to persuade your purchaser that Tendresse is what the girl next door is using. That it's what makes Jean so popular at the tennis club dance."

"A blooming English rose," said Harrap, "as a substitute for a decadent French lily."

"That's the idea. Or else you can shoot high and tell them that this is what the film star smothers herself in before appearing at the Grand Charity première, and the duke smells behind the duchess's ear when he dances the cotillion with her at the Hunt Ball."

"Which line do you fancy?" said Dumbo cautiously.

"Me? I'd go for snobbery every time."

"It's a nice point," said Harrap. He considered it carefully as if it were a question of dismantling a particularly tricky fuse. "Is the strongest urge in human nature to be like the crowd and do what everyone else is doing, or is it to better oneself and ape the class above?"

"I'll back snobbery," said Dumbo.

"Maybe," said Harrap. "I gather our adviser doesn't agree with us."

Wibberley looked embarrassed. In fact, he was as sure as he could be that Oliver was backing the wrong horse. Instinct and experience told him so. What Oliver had said might have been true twenty years ago, but people nowadays didn't think like that. The war had shaken them up and thrown them together. They were more independent and, unconsciously, a lot more Americanized. You didn't sell them anything now by throwing duchesses at them; you antagonized them. He thought of all this and then he thought of Simon Bargulder's injunction.

He said rather weakly, "I'm not here to persuade you, you know. Just to interpret your wishes."

"Fine," said Oliver. "Now, let's get down to details."

Victor Mallinson spent the morning with his own advertising agent, Hendrik Jacobsen. Mr. Jacobsen was small, round, and resilient, his elasticity permitting him to absorb shocks which would have shattered a more rigid person. Even now he was not worried. If he had allowed the ideas of his clients to worry him, he would have collapsed long ago. But an instinct, bred by long experience in his difficult, fascinating, and much-maligned profession, was warning him that there might be trouble ahead.

He said, "To sum it up, Mr. Mallinson, you want a double-barreled campaign. A normal advertising effort, to launch your own new perfume, Lucille. Quite a good name, that. Easy to remember, and not too difficult to pronounce." He repeated it softly to himself, rolling it round his tongue, as if he were savoring the bouquet of a fine wine. "But you also want a destructive effort—aimed at killing your rival's product."

"Correct," said Mallinson. "Might I—"

"Of course. Of course." Mr. Jacobsen pushed the huge silver cigarette box across the desk. It was a sign of his preoccupation that he had not noticed that his client had finished his own cigarette at least two minutes before. "You have good reason to think that Quinn & Nicholson are about to market a similar product?"

"I know they are. I can even tell you its name. Tendresse. What I want to do is, really, two different things. I want to get on the market a clear week before they do. No sooner, no later."

"That will involve a certain amount of guesswork."

"There'll be no guesswork. I shall be able to give you a firm date very shortly."

"I won't ask you how you propose to obtain it," said Mr. Jacobsen with a tight smile. "And the second thing?"

"The second thing is that I want our campaign to be as

near in type and style and approach to theirs as is possible—only more so, if you follow me."

"Your idea being that if you get out ahead of them, their show will seem to be an imitation of yours."

"Not only an imitation," said Mallinson. "A rather cheap and feeble imitation."

Jacobsen noticed the vindictiveness in his voice and was somewhat disturbed by it.

"Good God," said Oliver, "it's five to eight. We better call it a day." He looked at the pile of papers on his desk. "And a very good day's work, too, if I may say so."

Wibberley was able to agree with that. Once the main lines had been decided, he had found Oliver remarkably quick and willing to learn. In the last four hours, they had covered ground which would have taken two or three days with less intelligent clients.

The three of them—Oliver, Wibberley, and Philippa—were alone. Dumbo and Harrap had stuck it until seven o'clock and had then made their excuses and taken themselves off.

"I'll tell you what. I'll stand you both dinner. The best the local pub can provide."

"Very kind of you," said Wibberley.

"I could eat a horse," said his secretary.

"Don't jest about sacred subjects," said Oliver. "The last steak I had there never came off an Aberdeen Angus. We've been so busy that I've not had time to introduce you to each other. Derek Wibberley, the pride of the advertising profession, my newest secretary, Philippa Pearce."

Wibberley had noticed the girl as soon as he came in. She had a mass of auburn hair cut severely *en casque* and the white skin and green-golden eyes which often go with such hair.

"She's been with me a week," said Oliver. "We're still in the honeymoon stage. We haven't had time to quarrel yet."

"That happens about the end of the first month," said Philippa. Wibberley noticed that she had a pleasant voice, not aggressively educated, certainly not common. U.M.C.?

"We'll get cleared up in here. I expect Bolus is still about somewhere." He pressed a bell under the ledge of the desk.

"We're all getting very security-minded these days." As he spoke, he was gathering up all the papers on his desk into a fat pile. "Nobody takes anything in writing out of this room. I don't mean you, Wibbers. You'll have to take your stuff, but don't leave it about in taxis like the Air Vice-Marshals. Oh, Bolus, we're ready to knock off, I expect you'll be glad to hear."

Squadron Leader Bolus inspected Oliver's desk and his secretary's table, opening the drawers and peeping into them. Then he carried all the papers over to the wall safe, put them inside, and locked the safe with his own key. He tore the top two sheets from Oliver's blotting pad, screwed them up, and threw them into the wastepaper basket, and as an afterthought took the cover off the typewriter on Philippa's desk. In preparation for the morning she had rolled in two blank sheets of foolscap with a carbon between them.

Bolus extracted the paper, examined the carbon, screwed that up, and tossed it into the wastepaper basket, too.

"Bad habit, that," he said. "Keeping old carbon papers."

"Sorry," said Philippa meekly.

Bolus picked up the wastepaper basket in his sound left hand and made for the door. He said, "I'll let you out by the front entrance and lock up after you."

"Fine," said Oliver. "Good night."

The three of them walked out across the deserted packing department. Oliver stopped for a moment, put a hand on Wibberley's arm, and said, "Look. I meant what I said. About your being an up-and-coming advertising man. This is a pretty big account you're handling now. Oughtn't Bargulder to recognize it?"

"In what way?" said Wibberley cautiously.

"I don't know a lot about your organization, but I should have thought that the least a person handling an account like that ought to have would be a place on the Board."

"If I asked for it, would I have your backing?"

"To the hilt," said Oliver. "Come on. Bolus is wanting to get rid of us."

They went out through the small door cut in the great iron shutter which masked the entrance to the loading bay and round the corner of the administration block to the car park.

Apart from Oliver's, there was only one other car in the

park. He recognized it as Bernard Lewin's battered Ford Consul. Looking back, he could see a fan of light from the window of the experimental laboratory. The chief chemist was working late.

When he came up to the car, he saw something else. Someone had written in yellow chalk across the door panel, "Filthy Jewish Nit."

(vii)

"We were two of the last away," said Dumbo. "My car was parked alongside Lewin's, and Wilfred's was next to mine. We'd certainly have seen it if it'd been there then."

"No doubt about it," said Harrap.

"Luckily we managed to get it cleaned off before he came out," said Oliver. "Has this sort of thing happened before?"

Bolus, to whom this remark was addressed, said, "It's difficult to say. I've been making a few inquiries this morning. I don't think there's any general feeling against Lewin. They thought he was a pansy and laughed at him a bit, but he took it very well and it died down—or I thought so. I've never heard any of this anti-Semitic stuff."

"It was a careful job," said Oliver. "Done in big, thick letters. It must have taken five or ten minutes, and it was done between seven o'clock when Mr. Nicholson moved his car and eight fifteen when we came out. If any member of the staff was seen hanging round the car park between those times, I want to hear about it."

"I'll do what I can," said Bolus.

"You'd better," said Oliver, and he said it so savagely that everyone in the Board Room was startled. "Because at this moment in time Lewin happens to be about the most important person in this outfit."

Simon Bargulder rotated in his chair and stared out of his pale-blue eyes at Derek Wibberley. It was impossible to tell whether he was surprised or annoyed. His massive and battered face efficiently concealed his feelings.

He said at last, in tones of surprising mildness, "It's a tall order."

Wibberley, who had expected an explosion, felt relieved.

"It was the client's own suggestion," he said. "He felt

that as it was such a big account, his representative ought to have Board status."

"We've got half a dozen as big or bigger," said Bargulder, and named them.

"Quite so," said Wibberley. "The first four are looked after by Mr. Raven and the other two by Mr. Moore. And they're both on the Board already."

"It's not as easy as that. Directors can only be appointed by a general meeting of the company. That's not for another six months."

"When Mr. Brooksbank left, you made Moore a director, didn't you? And the meeting confirmed it later. Couldn't you do that again?"

"Moore had been with us nearly ten years and was handling a number of large accounts. Suppose we did what you suggest and they *didn't* confirm the appointment?"

"Six months from now, if certain moves that are planned come off, the Quinn & Nicholson account will be the biggest we've got. I don't think your shareholders are going to risk losing it."

Bargulder opened his eyes a trifle.

"Are you suggesting," he said, "that if you were to leave us, the Quinn & Nicholson account would go with you?"

Wibberley said, with a smile, "I'm certainly *not* suggesting it. But, as you said yourself, clients get attached to the people who look after their affairs. They also have to let them into a good many trade secrets. So they tend to stick to them."

"Humph," said Bargulder. "This isn't something I can decide myself, you know. I'll have to consult the other directors."

When Wibberley had gone, he sat for a long minute, almost unmoving. Then he hitched himself up to his feet and lumbered out of the room. Curiously enough, he did not turn to the left toward the rooms of his fellow-directors, which formed an executive suite at the end of the passage, but to the right and down a short flight of stairs toward the copywriters' department. He went into one which had "Llewellyn-Davis" on the door, and spent the next half hour in it.

"He's weakening," said Wibberley. After missing him at the works and the London office, he had caught Oliver at his flat. "To tell you the truth, I felt a bit of a louse putting it to him quite so bluntly."

"In business," said Oliver, "as in war, you'll never win if you don't exploit a favorable situation to the full. You'll never be in a better position to get what you want."

"If it came to the point—I mean if I had to make good what I said—you'd back me up, wouldn't you?"

"Every inch of the way. And I'm not being altruistic. I think you have the right touch for us. If you go, the account goes with you. It's as simple as that."

"Thank you," said Wibberley.

The call had caught Oliver as he was changing. He put back the receiver and went on with the job of tying his tie. He must have been preoccupied, since it took him three shots to get it right. When he had finished, he remained for a further ten seconds peering at the face above the tie. He wasn't very happy about his face, either, but there was nothing he could do about that.

When Victor Mallinson arrived at Brett's, he went into the reading room to look for an evening paper and found a lanky figure stretched in one of the leather armchairs in front of the fire.

"This is an unexpected visitation," he said. "Come upstairs and have a drink."

"It's kind of you," said Horton, "but I think I'd better not. My host will be here any minute now."

As chief buyer to the largest chain of retail chemist shops in London, he received, in the course of duty, a great many pressing invitations to eat and drink, most of which he refused very willingly, since he suffered from chronic dyspepsia.

"You're sure you won't?"

"Quite sure, really. And I think that's them."

Oliver Nugent came in, followed by Wilfred Harrap and Saul Feinberg.

"Ah, there you are," said Oliver. "I hope we haven't kept you waiting. You know Wilfred Harrap, don't you? And Victor Mallinson, too?"

Mallinson said coldly, "Horton and I have known each other for something like twenty years."

"Amazing," said Oliver. "Let's all go up and have a drink."

It was far from clear whether the invitation was intended to include Mallinson. He evidently considered that it did not, since he remained standing rigidly in front of the fire.

Crake said, "I told you to watch it."

"*If* you said that," said Mallinson, "and I don't remember your doing so, it was just about the stupidest remark you could have made."

"Temper, temper."

"What was the point of it? Watch it! Watch what? Do you think I could have prevented Naumann and Feinberg getting together?"

"I don't say you could have prevented it."

"Then what could I have done?"

"We might have tied 'em up legally, like I said. I never gave a sausage for gentlemen's agreements. What we wanted was something in black and white."

"And how do you suggest we make them sign an agreement if they didn't want to? Deep hypnosis?"

"Well," said Crake, "it's no use crying over spilt milk. The fact is we're wide open. And it won't only be Feinberg's lot. The others'll follow suit, you'll see. We haven't got a tame market any more. It's a straight fight. We've got to outproduce them, outadvertise them, and outsell them. And if we don't we'll be up shit creek without a paddle."

It was one of Crake's less pleasant characteristics that he always stated unpleasant facts in the most unpleasant manner possible. Mallinson accepted this. He knew that when it came to a fight, Crake was worth every hair on his ugly face.

He said, "Instead of blowing off a lot of hot air, suppose you make a few positive suggestions for dealing with the situation."

"There's only two things we can do. Produce better stuff or sell it cheaper."

"That means a price war."

"We could stand it longer than they could. We've got more reserves."

"They've got Latham's behind them. And Feinberg."

"They're behind them as long as they're making money. They're coldhearted bastards. If Quinn & Nicholson strike a rocky patch, their new chums in the City will drop them as quick as they've taken them up."

"Then it's up to us to see they *do* strike a rocky patch."

"We're not the only people gunning for them."

"Oh?"

"I was talking to Malim and he told me that Jack Tovey —he's the currency market man on the *Financial News*— had heard in a roundabout way from their man in Germany that the Westfälischer Gesellschaft für Pharmazeutische Artikel were the people who were putting up the money to bring this case against Quinn's in the French courts."

"It sounds a bit farfetched to me. They've got a fair-to-middling import trade into this country. It's mostly Galenicals, though. I shouldn't have thought they had enough at stake to make it worth their while fighting a toiletry firm like Quinn's."

" 'Tisn't entirely business. There's a personal angle to it, Malim thought."

"Personal?"

"Something to do with Nugent."

"Interesting."

"I thought so," said Crake, "because, speaking for myself, if anyone wants to stick needles into that cocky young bastard, I'm prepared to lend 'em a couple of dozen."

"I entirely agree," said Mallinson. "Jennie, see if you can find out the name of the English Managing Director of the Westfälischer people. It's Hartmann or Hartfeldt, or something like that. I met him at a Guildhall lunch last year."

Oliver looked at his watch and said, "Time for one more letter."

Philippa said nothing. In the three weeks she had been at Quinn & Nicholson, she had found that a private secretary had no set working hours. Some days she had nothing to do but tidy the pencils and paper clips in her desk and file her nails; other days she worked sixteen hours with a twenty-minute break for lunch if she was lucky.

All the same, there was something different about tonight. Previously, when she had stayed late, it had been because of some palpable crisis in the affairs of the firm. On this occasion Oliver was dragging it out deliberately. The last two letters had been unnecessary. Both of them could have waited until the morning, and one, she was pretty certain, would never be sent.

She toyed with the idea that this might be a prelude to a seduction and dismissed it. The furniture of the office was plainly unsuitable; anyway it would have been out of character. When Oliver wanted to seduce a girl, he would be more direct, or a great deal more subtle.

Bolus put his head round the door and said, "All clear now. You can make your exit. You'd better come out of the side door and I'll lock it after us."

The three of them went out the side door. Bolus slammed it. They stood for a moment under the light of the street lamp.

"What about Bernard?" said Oliver. "We haven't locked him in for the night, I hope."

"He's got his own key," said Bolus. "He can let himself out."

"Fine," said Oliver. "Good night," and to Philippa, "I'll give you a lift to the station."

They walked toward the car park. A light mist was coming up off the canal, putting muslin round the street lamps and tickling noses and throats.

Oliver backed his car out and turned into the High Street.

"What was all that in aid of?" asked Philippa.

"What do you mean?"

"It went like badly rehearsed amateur theatricals."

"Was it as obvious as that?"

"You are up to something, aren't you? You and holus Bolus?"

"As a matter of fact, yes. We are."

"You might let your secretary in on it."

Oliver swung the car into the layby in front of a row of shops and stopped. "You can watch the fun if you like. One of two things is going to happen. Either we're going to have a long, cold, and pointless wait or we're going to see some brisk and healthy action."

"It sounds like a second-feature film," said Philippa.

Oliver locked the car and they started to walk back the way they had come. A hundred yards short of the factory, they turned left down a side road and right again when they reached the canal. They were now on the track which led behind a row of shops and houses, finishing up at their own car park.

Oliver slowed his pace and motioned Philippa into the shadow of the wall. They were moving now along the narrow strip between the factory itself and the canal. Above her head she could see a fan of light, milky in the mist, and located it as the window of the experimental laboratory. Beyond the row of windows in the north wall of the packing department there was a small iron gate, a back entrance to the car park. It was usually kept locked. Oliver put his hand on it and pushed. The hinges must have been oiled because it swung open without a sound.

Oliver put his mouth close to Philippa's ear and said, "Now we wait."

For the next thirty interminable minutes which dragged past—every separate minute ten minutes long—nothing happened at all. Philippa was a long way past simply being cold. She had lost all feeling in her feet. The mist made her want to sneeze, and in an effort to stop it she bit her lip until the tears ran down her frozen cheeks. Then the muscles in her right leg started to twitch with cramp, and when she put a hand on the gatepost to steady herself, she found that all feeling had gone from her hands as well.

Oliver saw her moving and put out his hand to steady her. Then she saw that he was pointing.

A figure had materialized in the car park behind Bernard Lewin's car. He was carrying something in his right hand which made a metallic "chink" when he put it down.

Philippa suddenly forgot the cold and discomfort. After the long wait in the dark her night sight was now excellent, and although the only light was a street lamp outside the far gate, she could make out well enough what was happening.

The newcomer was carrying a heavy Army knapsack. That was what had made the "chink" when he put it down. Now he was unstrapping it and taking out a tin. It looked as if it might be paint. It must be paint because he was now taking out a brush as well.

There were other people there, too. Two or three of

them closing in on the car. Then all the car-park lights came on.

Philippa started forward, but Oliver's hand closed on her arm.

"We'll keep out of this," he said.

The man with the paintbrush she recognized. He had a mop of graying hair, an old-young face, and he dragged one leg when he walked. She had seen him in the dispatch department. Bolus was behind him and with Bolus were three of the lorry drivers. Palmer was one of them. She didn't know the other two.

"Doing a little overtime, Jarvis?" said Bolus. "Touching up Mr. Lewin's car for him? I don't know that I'd have chosen just that color myself."

He took the brush from Jarvis's hand, dipped it in the open paint pot, and drew it out, thickly covered in red paint.

"I wasn't doing anything wrong," said Jarvis. The panic in his voice made it run up into a squeak.

"You didn't do anything wrong because we happened to be here in time to stop you," said Bolus. "Pity to waste good paint, though. Grab his arm, you two."

Jarvis saw what was coming, twisted round, and tried to run. It was a futile gesture. Two of the drivers had him by the arms. Palmer had one hand on his collar and the other in his hair.

"Let's try our hand at a spot of home decorating," said Bolus. So saying, he drew the full brush of thick red paint over Jarvis's face and down the front of his coat. Jarvis said feebly, "Lay off, will you? A joke's a joke."

"You're talking too much," said Bolus. He had another brushful now and a lot of this went into Jarvis's mouth.

"Never leave a job half done," said Bolus. He dipped the brush into the pot once more and slapped it vigorously over his squirming captive.

Jarvis started to scream. It was a horrible blubbering noise, thick with pain and outrage.

"He looks a right mess," said Palmer. "What do you say we give him a wash down?"

"Good idea," said Bolus.

"Suppose he can't swim?"

"Everyone ought to be able to swim. Up he goes. One, two, and away."

A flailing of arms, a splash, and Jarvis disappeared under the murky waters of the canal. When he reappeared, the men started to laugh. The canal was so shallow at that point that the water came only up to Jarvis's waist. He plodded across, feet squelching in the mud, and dragged himself slowly up the bank.

"Don't bother to come back for your cards," said Bolus. Philippa was shaking.

"Come on," said Oliver. "Run. It'll warm you up." He led the way back to the car. "What you want's a stiff drink. I know just the place."

The saloon bar of the Connemara Arms out on the Watford bypass had a roaring fire in the grate. Oliver bought two large whiskies and carried them over to a table by the fire. Philippa's teeth had stopped chattering, but she still looked a bit white round the lips.

"Put that down the hatch," said Oliver. "You asked to come, you know."

"It was horrible," she said. "Four of them and that silly little man."

"That's the sort of thing that happens to spies when they're caught."

"Spies?"

"Jarvis was carrying out orders. He'll get adequate compensation from his employers, I don't doubt."

"What are you talking about? What orders?"

"We happen to have the best analytical chemist in the market, and Bernard Lewin's a genius. Absolutely the strongest card in our pack. If our rivals can trump him, it's an important trick to them. Bernard's a bit eccentric, like most geniuses. And he's a Jew. So they put someone in to pester him. It's been going on for some time now. Someone sewed a yellow patch on the back of his overcoat in the cloakroom. Not very pretty. One of the men spotted it and reported it to Bolus, who had it off before Lewin saw it. There was that scribbling on his car. We got that off, too. Tonight's little effort was intended to be something permanent. Something that *couldn't* be rubbed off."

"But why?"

"Don't be a cuckoo," said Oliver. "It's perfectly obvious.

If he's unhappy here, he puts himself back on the market.
And guess who'd give him his next job?"

"Mallinson's, I suppose."

"It's a fair bet."

"I think it's horrible," said Philippa. "Do you think I
could have another drink?"

"That's the girl," said Oliver.

By the time he brought the second one back, Philippa
was looking more her normal self again. She said, "Do you
think you'll be able to prove it was Mallinson?"

"We shan't even try. There'll be no direct link. There's
a firm in the West End of London. It operates as a genuine
employment agency, but if you've got the proper introduc-
tions and see the right partner, you can hire industrial spies
and saboteurs as easily as you can get—"

"Secretaries?"

"If any secretary of mine tried to double-cross me,"
said Oliver, "I'd give her such a beating she wouldn't be
able to sit down for a week."

"I believe you would, too," said Philippa.

They drove back in the car toward Elsfield Wood in a
warm and companionable silence. Philippa was thinking,
"When we get to the station, I know exactly what's going
to happen. It's sort of inevitable. The whole evening has
been leading up to it. He'll park his car at the far end,
away from the lights, he'll switch off the engine, he'll say
'We've got ten minutes before the train comes. Why waste
it,' and he'll put his left arm under the middle of my back,
which I'll lift up just slightly from the seat to show him I'm
not fighting, and he'll put his right arm on my left shoulder and pull me toward him, and he'll kiss me very thoroughly. I don't think he'll start undressing me because he
isn't the sort of man who undresses a girl in the front seat
of a motorcar in a station yard. If he wanted to do that,
there'd be another time and another place altogether."

Oliver swung the car into the station yard, drove it up
to the far end away from the lights, switched the engine
off, and said, "By the way. I'm going to France on Monday. It's about this lawsuit. I thought I'd take the car and
we'd take it easy."

"We?"

"I'll need my secretary, naturally. I thought I'd warn

you so that you could get any clothes you needed for the trip. As it's business, the firm will pay, of course. And here's your train."

(viii)

The Silver City biplane tilted its wings, circled round the salt marsh and sand dunes which border Le Touquet's golf course, skimmed the roofs of Etaples, and touched down on the runway.

"I've never done that before," said Philippa. "It was fun."

"Best way of crossing the Channel," said Oliver.

"Until they build that tunnel," said the girl in the seat behind them.

There were seven of them in the tiny cabin and they had talked to each other in the offhand, friendly way that English people sometimes do when they are thrown together. Philippa had gathered that the middle-aged couple were coming over to pick up a daughter who had been staying with a French family in Rouen, and the young man and girl were starting their first-ever touring holiday in France. The older man with the gray mustache and briefcase, who looked like a retired Army officer, had said good morning pleasantly enough, but had not told them anything about himself.

When Oliver had told the young couple that he and Philippa were also motoring in France ("business and pleasure, fifty-fifty"), the girl had glanced at Philippa's ringless left hand and then looked quickly away. Oliver had noticed it and decided that it was something he had better attend to.

They had lunch on the terrace of the Escale restaurant and sat over their coffee watching the shuttle service of little silver planes drop out of the sky, taxi round, deposit their cargo of two or three motorcars apiece, pick up a new load, and take off again. The two couples had driven on.

The military gentleman was sitting by himself in the far corner drinking beer. He waved genially to them as they left. After he had watched them drive away through the pine trees toward Etaples, he strolled down to the telephone booth in the reception hall and dialed a number at Montreuil, which is oddly called "sur-Mer" although it stands ten miles from the sea. All southbound traffic from Le Touquet passes through Montreuil.

Oliver never found it possible to dawdle when he was driving a car, but on that afternoon he was in no hurry. They dipped down the long, winding hill into Rouen as the clocks sounded four, crossed the river, and ambled through the area of docks, factories, and oil refineries on the south of the river. As the road swung up, past the castle of Robert the Devil, they were suddenly in deep countryside, running between woods of oak and chestnut and lime.

It was after seven and the kilometer stones to Alençon were running out of numbers when they turned off the main road, twisted through a tangle of byroads, and came suddenly on the village of St.-Pierre-sur-Orcq and the Hotel Grâce Dieu.

"But it isn't a hotel at all," said Philippa. "It's a château."

"And so it was not so very long ago," said Oliver. "It's a hotel now, and unless it's changed hands since I was here last, it's a good one. For some reason or other it's not in the *Michelin Guide,* so it doesn't get overrun with tourists."

As they drove into the paved yard, Oliver ran an eye over the cars already parked there. Five with French number plates, one from Germany, one from the Netherlands.

He parked alongside, jumped out, lifted his own suitcase and Philippa's quickly from the trunk, and handed them to the man who had appeared. The man said something in French. Oliver nodded and gave him a five-franc piece. The man stumped off.

"Come and have an *apértif.* You can wash afterward."

"They know you here?"

"I've been here once or twice before. I telephoned for the rooms from the airport. I usually do that for the first night in France. When you're within driving distance of the Channel, the hotels tend to get booked up. Later on I take a chance on it. Dubonnet, Byrrh, Campari-soda, or something with gin in it?"

By the time they had finished their second drink, it was

eight o'clock and the waiter was hovering over them with a menu. Oliver chose the meal for both of them with loving care.

"Your first meal in France," he said, "is more than a feast. It's a festival. Do you know why the French are so good at food? It's because they hold to the tradition of eating out on Sunday. While the English family huddles round its unchanging weekend joint, the French family departs, en bloc, to its favorite restaurant. That means that every restaurant, however small, however casual its weekday trade, must cook and serve at least one large, first-class meal a week. This keeps the chef on his toes and makes the whole thing an economic possibility."

They were in the dining room by now. Philippa noticed that the idea of going up to their rooms for a wash and brush-up seemed to have been dropped.

"It would be a mistake to rush things," said Oliver. Philippa looked up sharply. She thought she detected a gleam of amusement in his dark-brown eyes. "I was talking about food," he said. "In a day or two your stomach will have acquired a French appetite."

He ordered quenelles de brochet, deciding regretfully against the lobster sauce as being too rich, and guinea fowl à la belle maman, with a salad of watercress. "After that we shall pause for breath," he said, "and see if we can manage something ambitious to finish up with, or perhaps just a sorbet."

"You're in love with food," said Philippa.

"It's a mutual affection," said Oliver. "Food and I love and respect each other. Perish the man who eats only enough to replace the energy he expends. Is food petrol? I eat much more than I need, and year by year I acquire additional layers of fat, each a memento of some enjoyable engorgement."

"Like an oak tree. One more ring each year."

"An apt and charming simile. Sommelier!"

He chose a Sancerre to go with the quenelles and a Chambertin for the guinea fowl. Philippa did some mathematics.

"You've ordered two bottles of wine just for us?"

"Correct."

"But that'll mean we've got to drink a bottle each."

"It's a mistake to make actuarial calculations about wine. We shall drink exactly as much of each bottle as we feel we need."

The dining room was filling up and most of the tables were now occupied. One car at least had arrived after them. Its driver, obviously an Englishman and less obviously a commercial traveler, was demanding "saumon fumé" in the loud clear tones which English people use when dealing with foreigners who don't understand their own language.

As the waiters bustled from table to table, as the spirit lamps flickered under the chafing dishes, as the brandy flared, as the wine sank in the bottles and the blessed smell of good coffee permeated the room, the atmosphere seemed to warm and thicken. Philippa leaned back in her chair. She was as happy as any cat given a cushion in front of the fire and a dish of cream.

She turned her head to look at Oliver. He seemed relaxed and contented, but there was a hint of wariness in his eyes. In just such a way, thought Philippa, and at just such a moment, having dined and wined a business acquaintance, would he introduce casually, lightly, almost as an afterthought, the proposition which had been the *raison d'être* of the whole meal.

She said, "When you spoke of one's first meal in France, you meant your first meal on each visit, I take it. Or did you mean your first meal ever?"

"I wasn't sure," said Oliver. "You haven't told me a lot about yourself yet. Have you been to France before?"

"I lived here from the age of four to the age of fourteen. I had holidays in England with my father but I went to French schools—a kindergarten in Paris and then the lycée at Fontainebleau."

"I see," said Oliver. The wary look was back in his eyes again. "Then I imagine you speak French pretty well."

"Of course. I understand it, too. When that man took our bags, he said, 'Room twenty, as on the previous occasions.' "

"Naturally," said Oliver. "I booked us in as Mr. and Mrs. Nugent. I thought it would save a lot of explanations and embarrassment."

"D'accord," said Philippa demurely.

Never was fortress more charmingly surrendered.

The next three days were spent in demonstrating how long you can take, if you give your mind to it, to get from Alençon to Lyons. On the first day they got no farther than the Loire and spent a long, hot afternoon bathing in it. On the second day they followed the Loire almost to its source and spent the night in a tiny chaletlike hotel at Le Monastier. On the third day, for no better reason than that Oliver knew of an excellent restaurant at Talloires which served fish called "ombles," they made a long diversion to the Lake of Annecy.

It was while they were sitting over lunch here that Oliver said, "As you will have guessed, this legal business at Lyons is partly an excuse. I have to go there, it's true. Twenty-four hours would have covered the trip. But I came to the conclusion that I had earned a holiday."

"I'm not complaining," said Philippa. She was watching the sails of the little boats tacking up the lake into a fresh breeze off the foothills of the Alps.

"I worked the whole thing out with my usual skill. We get to Lyons tomorrow—that's Thursday. I shall have settled my business with the lawyers by Thursday evening. We motor back on Friday and Saturday, fly across on Sunday, and are back at our desks by Monday morning. That gives us exactly eight working weeks before D Day."

"D Day?"

"When we loose Tendresse on an appreciative upper middle class."

"Is it as soon as that," said Philippa. A cloud had crossed the sun, sending a blue-black shadow across the lake, and the little boats were driving into it.

On Thursday morning at Lyons, Oliver said to Philippa, "I shall be spending the whole morning with our lawyer, Maître Philippon. He is very distinguished and has a gray beard exactly like the late Sir Henry Wood. But he would consider it frivolous if I took you to his office, which is staffed, incidentally, entirely with male clerks. In the afternoon I shall want you because I shall want to dictate my affidavit. It's called a declaration of exceptional solemnity here, but it's the same thing as our affidavit. Then it'll have to be typed out. The hotel is providing a machine. Then we have a date with the Vice-Consul, who will authenticate my signature and stand us a drink. And don't forget that we have two children back in England."

"It's sweet of you to tell me," said Phillipa. "Have they got names?"

"The boy is called Philip, after you."

"And the girl? I suppose Olivia, after you."

"The darlings," said Oliver. "How *could* we have deserted them, even for a week? Here is Maître Philippon."

The French lawyer, who did, indeed, look startlingly like the late Sir Henry Wood, bowed to Oliver and kissed Philippa's hand. A young man with sandy hair was hovering in the background. He was not introduced, and Philippa imagined that he was one of the lawyer's male assistants.

She had the morning to fill. Lyons is not the most picturesque of French cities, but it has the brash attraction of a place which is full of people getting on with the business of making money. Philippa did some shopping and one or two other chores and then sat at a table under a striped umbrella in the Place Victor Hugo, sipping at a citronade and watching the traffic tying itself up in a free-for-all round the statue of the novelist. At one point she thought she spotted someone she recognized. He was strolling down the pavement opposite, but he was swallowed up in the exodus of homegoing lunchers as the clocks struck twelve.

At quarter to one she walked to the restaurant where she had arranged to meet Oliver. Missing it the first time, she swung back and came face to face with the man. This time there was no possibility of mistake. It was the sandy-haired lawyer. He stepped politely to one side and she went into the restaurant. Oliver, who was already installed at a table in the corner, rose to meet her.

She said, "I'm being followed by one of Philippon's assistants. Why?"

"Do you like to face your fellow-lunchers or sit with your back to them? Facing's better, I think." He signaled to the waiter, who pulled the table out from the wall and adjusted her chair for her. When he had taken their order and gone, Oliver said, "I'd hoped you wouldn't notice. He must have done it very badly."

"But why?"

"Lyons is a lot nearer Germany than London or Elsfield Wood."

"I don't understand."

"There's someone in Germany," said Oliver, "who hates my guts. He's had one shot at killing me and one shot at framing me, and it's his money that's behind this lawsuit."

"A trade rival?"

"He's the head of our biggest German competitors, but that's by the way. He's gone up as quickly on his side of the fence as I have on mine, because he happens to be a ruthless sort of sod with an above-average outfit of guts and a knack for picking other people's brains."

"Him and you," said Philippa. "Did you really think he was going to abduct me?"

"It'd be corny, I know, but supposing he had whisked you away in a taxi to some back-street den and held lighted matches against the soles of your feet. Wouldn't you have told him all my secrets?"

"Before he struck the first match," said Philippa. "I'm a frightful coward."

"According to Philippon, this lawsuit is a big bluff. He hasn't got a chance of succeeding. The most he could have hoped for was what we should call an interim injunction to hold up our exports of the raw material for Handcharm—which is a fungus and grows in only two known places, one of which is the wrong side of the Iron Curtain."

"Please don't," said Philippa.

"Don't what?"

"I thought you were going to tell me *where* the stuff grew. I could feel the soles of my feet tingling."

"He wouldn't bother to torture you to discover our source of supply," said Oliver cheerfully. "He knows that. It's the process he wants."

"Why does he hate you? You personally, I mean."

"Here comes the pâté," said Oliver. "It's made of goose and truffles. Very rich." When he had finished the last crumb of the pâté and four slices of buttered toast with it, he said, "He's got pretty good reasons for hating me. I killed his brother and had a shot at killing him. And I bought the Handcharm process off his brother's widow for a hundredth of what it turned out to be worth. I'm not sure that in his eyes that's not the greatest offense of the lot."

Wibberley said, "But I *must* speak to him."

"I'm terribly sorry," said Dumbo. "I could have given you the number of the hotel in Lyons, but he was due to leave there this morning."

"When'll he be back?"

"He'll be in the office on Monday morning."

"Back in England, I mean."

"On Sunday night."

"Today's only Thursday. It can't take him four days to get back from Lyons."

"I don't think he's hurrying. It's business, but it's a sort of holiday, too," said Dumbo, and heard Wibberley at the other end of the telephone line draw in his breath with a hiss as if he had been hit in the stomach. He said, "This can't wait. I've got to talk to someone."

"Why not come down here and talk to Harrap and me?"

After a short pause Wibberley said, "All right. I'll do that."

"He sounded a bit narked," said Harrap, who'd been listening in on the office extension. "If this is going to be a council of war, we'd better get hold of Bill Blackett, too. Did Oliver say anything to you before he left?"

"About what?"

"About Wibbers—and his advertising campaign."

"He said we were to support him to the hilt, but he wasn't to be given the signal for the kickoff until he got back from France."

"I see," said Harrap. "That was all he told you, was it?"

An angry Wibberley came straight to the point. "I was as good as ordered by Nugent to stick my toes in with Bargulder and ask for a seat on the Board. He said the Quinn & Nicholson account was important enough to justify it and ought to be represented by a director."

"Fair enough," said Dumbo. "What happened?"

"I saw Bargulder this morning. He told me"—Wibberley's voice still shook with outrage at the recollection—"that I was getting too big for my boots and that if I didn't like it I could hand over the account."

Harrap said, "A bit tough that, certainly. What happened?"

"I was so flabbergasted," said Wibberley, "that I didn't know what to say. But I can tell you this. If he persists in his attitude, I'm not stopping with him. There are plenty of other firms who'd be glad of my services, I can tell you."

Harrap and Blackett looked at each other. Dumbo said, "Look here, aren't you being a bit hasty about this? Suppose *I* had a word with Bargulder."

"Someone had better," said Wibberley, "and quick, or there's going to be real trouble. I assure you."

When he had gone, Dumbo said, "What the hell's Bargulder playing at? If he rocks the boat now, we really shall be for it. Suppose Wibbers trots across the road and joins up with Mallinson's agent—what's his name—Jacobsen?"

Harrap looked at Blackett and said, "I suggest we let it run until Oliver comes back. He'll sort it out."

For most of the journey back they talked about things that didn't matter. On the Saturday, south of Orléans, Philippa said, "What shall I do with this when we get home? Wear it on a ribbon and hang it round my neck?"

She indicated the plain gold circlet which Oliver had bought for her on the second day of the journey.

"Don't waste sentiment on it. Sell it. You'll get a good price."

"Is that what the others did?"

"The others?" said Oliver innocently.

"When we got to the hotel on the first night. The man who took our bags. You remember. He said, 'The same as on previous occasions.' "

"That was my third visit. On the other occasions, believe it or not, I was alone."

"I'll believe you. Thousands wouldn't."

"And the fourth time will be tonight. I booked the same room, too. For our last night in France."

"It was a sweet thought," said Philippa.

Next morning after breakfast, Oliver went down to find a conference going on in the yard. The place stank of petrol.

"Someone's been throwing the stuff about," he said.

The Dutchman whose car was parked next to his had opened the bonnet of his Mercedes and was examining the petrol tank anxiously. Oliver did the same. The truth was apparent at once. There was a jagged hole an inch across in the bottom of Oliver's tank.

The proprietor, who had joined them, exclaimed aloud at the sight. "Who can have done such a thing?" he said. "It is clearly deliberate."

"It wasn't done by a woodpecker," agreed Oliver. He was thinking furiously. There could be no important reason that he knew of for stopping him from reaching London that night, and yet someone had taken a lot of trouble about this little bit of sabotage. The bonnet was self-locking with a release inside the car itself, which was also locked. He took a quick look at the windows and found, as he had suspected, that one of the side vents had been forced. A wire loop, dropped through the opening, would have lifted the inside locking catch. Quite an expert job.

He said, "Where's the nearest garage? And, more to the point, will it be open?"

"There's a garage in Alençon, and it will certainly be open for sales of petrol and oil, you understand, but not necessarily the workshop."

One of the men said something, and the proprietor's face lightened.

"I had forgotten. A fortunate chance. There is a man who might repair it for you. He is an itinerant mechanic. He works at the Rocambeau farm."

"Let him be sent for."

The mechanic arrived driving a tractor. He examined the damage in silence, watched by the large crowd which gathers round any comfortable contretemps. Then he straightened up and said something to Philippa, who had assumed the position of interpreter.

"He says the hole's too large to plug with cement or anything like that. It would need a patch and the patch would need welding."

"Has he the kit to do it?"

The mechanic's response to this was a lengthy monologue ending with an expressive gesture in which he blew out his cheeks, said "boom," and threw both hands in the air. It earned a murmur of applause from the audience.

"He says that he could very easily solder on a patch, but if you use a red-hot soldering iron on a tank which has recently held petrol, it will ignite the fumes and—"

"All right," said Oliver. "I understand the last act. Has he got any other suggestions?"

The man considered the matter. There was, he said, one chance. In the tractor shed at the farm there was a derelict motorcar. He had the impression, but could by no means be held to guarantee it, that the tanks in the two cars were roughly of the same size and shape. If that was so, it would not be impossible to effect a substitution. It would be easiest to do the job at the farm, where he had his equipment. If Monsieur concurred with the suggestion, the tractor could tow it there.

"Fine," said Oliver. "How long?"

Much depended, said the man, on whether it was necessary to fit a sleeve over the petrol union. If they were fortunate, two hours.

It took just under two hours and cost the surprising sum of fifty francs. "And where in England would you get a job like that done on a Sunday for under four quid?" said Oliver as they drove along the *route nationale,* going fast to make up for lost time. "Or where would you find a mechanic like that?"

"You had a real stroke of luck there," said Philippa. "I gather he'd only installed himself at the farm two or three days ago. He's a traveling mechanic. He does odd jobs for farmers. They said he was an absolute wizard—anything from motor mowers to ten-ton tractors."

"He's certainly fixed this one," said Oliver.

The hotel had got them up a picnic lunch, and they ate it in a field south of Rouen.

As they were packing up to go, Philippa said, "How much petrol did we have?"

"I'm not sure. I told them to fill it up. Why?"

"When we stopped, I noticed the gauge was registering empty."

"I don't suppose that means a lot," said Oliver. "The gauge wouldn't register on the substitute tank. All the same, we don't want to run out. Better dip her and see."

He broke off a thin branch from the hedge, unscrewed the petrol cap, and pushed it in.

"What's up?" said Philippa.

"There's something damned odd about this tank," said Oliver.

"What do you mean?"

"Come and feel."

Philippa took the stick and prodded cautiously.

"Now take it out and look at it."

"It's as dry as a bone. No petrol there at all."

"No, but there *is* something there. Something soft and rather bulky. You can feel it with the stick."

Philippa said, "Do you think it's a bomb?" She meant it as a joke but it suddenly struck her that it might quite easily be true, and the words came out with a dry croak.

"I don't *think* so," said Oliver. He had got out a torch and was trying, without much success, to shine it through the opening of the tank. "It's a damned odd bomb if the heat and vibration haven't set it off by now."

"And if there isn't any petrol, what's the car going on?"

"There's petrol, all right, and I think I can see how it works. This is one of the old-fashioned tanks with a smaller spare tank inside it. It's a sort of baffle-plate arrangement. The first lot of petrol that you put in fills up the rear compartment. As soon as that's full, it flows over into the main part of the tank. When you've finished the main, you switch over and use the gallon or so in the first section. You can see the joins on the outside of the tank."

"I expect you're right," said Philippa. "But *what is it?*"

"Whatever it is, we're not going to get it out through the petrol cap. We'll have to cut one end of the tank open, and I've got nothing to do it with. Let's try the next garage."

The proprietor of the next garage opened up the shed at the back, which served him as a workshop, and showed Oliver a useful assortment of tools.

"I find myself unable to comprehend," he said, "why Monsieur should wish to cut a piece out of his petrol tank, but if such is his wish he should find here suitable tools to do it with."

"Thank him a thousand times," said Oliver, "and tell him not to bother. I'll do the work."

He selected a small drill and bored three touching holes with it to form an entrance for the point of the metal saw. The rest of the operation was laborious but straightforward. Three cuts defined three sides of an oblong flap. Oliver took a pair of pliers, gripped the top of the flap, and bent it outward. The proprietor and Philippa craned forward. Oliver put in a gloved hand and eased something out from the bottom of the tank.

"Well," said Philippa, "it doesn't look very exciting."

"Is that what Monsieur was looking for?"

"What we need now," said Oliver, "is a sharp knife."

It was a flat package, some six inches square, enclosed in a thick plastic covering taped and glued at the edges.

"Do be careful," said Philippa. "This may be where the trick comes. Suppose it's full of acid and spurts up at you when you cut it?' '

"I don't think it's acid," said Oliver. He was slicing carefully round the edge.

It was a package of photographs. There were forty of them, beautifully printed, absolutely clear, and cold-bloodedly filthy.

Oliver fed them, one at a time, into the workshop stove.

"I would have asked for one as a souvenir," said the proprietor wistfully. "It would have attracted custom. On the other hand, I fear my wife would not have been amused."

"The next thing," said Oliver, "is to repair the tank. Our pal this morning told us that you couldn't use a soldering iron on a petrol tank. I thought he was talking balls at the time. Anyway, I'm going to have a shot at it. You two can get outside if you like, but honestly I don't think there's any danger."

At Lydd Airport a customs officer called them out of the passport-control room. Oliver noticed that his car had been parked to one side to let the others through. There was a second and senior officer by the car and a mechanic with him.

"We were looking at this tank of yours," said the first officer. "Was it on your car when you took it abroad?"

"For God's sake! You don't image I normally drive round with a prehistoric arrangement like that, do you?"

"When was it fitted?"

"At eleven o'clock this morning at a small village outside Alençon called St.-Pierre-sur-Orcq."

"Were you aware, sir, that under Rule 17(c) of the Customs and Excise Rules governing the temporary export and reimportation of mechanically propelled vehicles *any* fitment made abroad had to be reported at the port of re-entry?"

"I will confess," said Oliver, "that I had no idea that Rule 17(c) existed."

"I see, sir."

The two customs officers looked at each other. The senior one said, "In that case I'm afraid we shall have to examine the tank, sir."

"Rule 17(d)?"

"I beg your pardon."

"I was just wondering what your authority was."

"The rules give us authority to examine *any* vehicle entering or leaving."

"All right," said Oliver. "I'm not arguing. How long do you think it'll take? Half an hour? You'll find us in the bar when you've finished."

"He doesn't *look* as if he's got a guilty conscience," said the first officer.

"Hardened criminal," said the second. "It's the one we're looking for, all right. You can see the place where the tank's been cut open and sealed up again."

(ix)

"Of course it was a put-up job," said Oliver. "And, of course, the customs at Lydd had been tipped off about it. We could hear them licking their lips half a mile before we came in to land."

"If you *hadn't* spotted them," said Dumbo, "what would have happened? They'd have confiscated the photographs, I suppose, and you'd have been fined."

"I should have been bust," said Oliver. "Bust, flattened, and finished. Can't you see the headlines? 'COMPANY DIRECTOR HELD AT AIRPORT. SMUGGLING FILTHY PICTURES.'"

"It wouldn't have been very happy," said Blackett.

"It was worse than a bomb," said Oliver. "If I'd been blown up, at least I'd have got some sympathy. This I should never have lived down."

"How did they organize it?" said Harrap. He sounded more interested than shocked. "They were taking a pretty long chance, weren't they?"

"I asked for it," said Oliver. "I walked into it like an innocent child. I forgot my Kipling. Do you remember the girl who tells a soldier, 'My mother always warned us when we went out on a trek not to come back the same way'? We not only came back to the hotel I stayed at on the way out, but I actually signaled my intentions. I booked the room for the last night in a loud clear voice in the foyer of the hotel after breakfast that first day. Anyone could have picked it up. There was one chap who looked a bit too like an English commercial traveler to be true. He arrived after us and could easily have been tailing us."

"One thing I can't see," said Dumbo. "Suppose you had been caught, couldn't you have explained what happened? There were plenty of witnesses."

"Certainly I could have explained," said Oliver. "And I might even have brought over witnesses. The only person I shouldn't have been able to get hold of would be the mechanic. He's back in Germany by now."

"Then wouldn't it have proved—"

"All that it would have proved was that I was a damned clever smuggler. So clever that they would probably have assumed that I'd been working the racket for years. I arrange to meet my confederate with a petrol tank full of filthy pictures, or cocaine, or the plans of the latest French atom bomber. I make a hole in my own petrol tank. He appears like a good fairy and installs a substitute tank in the presence of lots of impeccable witnesses. If I get past, fine. If I get caught, I blame him. Too easy."

"All the same," said Harrap, "it was a long shot. You might have changed your mind. You might have insisted on sending your car to a garage. You might have jibbed at having the tank changed."

"What if I did? What had they got to lose?"

"The money and effort they'd put into it."

"The man who is now head of the Westfälischer Gesellschaft is prepared, I would guess, to expend a great deal more effort than that, and a lot more money for the pleasure of putting me down."

"Look here," said Blackett. "Who *is* this chap? Don't

you think you ought to tell us? I mean—suppose someone
pushed you under a bus. It's been done before."

"It wouldn't make any difference. Bolus has got all the
facts. He'd take the file to the police. It probably wouldn't
do much good, because if there's one thing this crowd is
absolutely expert at it's covering their tracks."

"All the same," said Harrap, "I think you ought to put
us in the picture."

Oliver thought about it. Then he said, "All right. It's
not a story I'm a hundred per cent proud of, but perhaps
you ought to know about it. Dumbo here and Taylor were
in at the start in the S.S. camp near Klagenfurt."

He told them about the night on which he had shot Kurt
Engelbach and two of his companions, and wounded Steyr.

"In retrospect I could wish it had been the other way
round," he said. "Kurt was a genius. If he was alive now,
he'd probably be a Nobel Prize winner with three rows of
letters after his name. Steyr, on the other hand, is a prime
bastard."

"Fascinating," said Harrap. "I wish you'd told us this
before."

"Why?" said Oliver.

"It's such a damned fascinating story," said Harrap,
with a faraway smile. He was thinking of all the oppor-
tunities which must have passed *him* by in six years of
war. There was an old woman in the Apennines who had
shown him a way of making a drink like Chartreuse out
of alcohol, sugar, and herbal drops.

"That Steyr sounds like a vindictive sort of swine," said
Blackett.

"I think he might have forgiven me for killing his
brother," said Oliver. "What he couldn't overlook was my
pinching the patent rights in proto-mycil."

"It's a good many years ago," said Dumbo. "He's worked
himself up into a top position in German industry. I should
have thought he might have forgotten about it by now."

"He may have cooled down a bit. I hoped he had. This
last effort doesn't look like it, though. I did wonder if I
might buy him off."

His fellow-directors stared at him.

"You know what they say. If he's American, offer him
money. If he's English, offer him a title. If he's French,

offer him a woman. If he's German, offer him a formula."

"What formula?"

"We could always start by offering him Handcharm. If Tendresse goes big, we shall be concentrating on that anyway."

After a moment's silence Dumbo said, "I take it you're joking."

"That's right," said Oliver. "I'm joking."

(x)

"When Lady Fortune Smiles," said Mr. Jacobsen—long association with the world of advertising had conditioned him to thinking in headlines—"Why Reject Her Advances?"

"It seems almost too good to be true," said Mallinson. "I can't think what Bargulder's playing at. Would *you* risk losing the copy head who was handling an important campaign on the eve of that campaign's being launched?"

"*I* shouldn't," said Mr. Jacobsen, "but I'm not Bargulder. He's God Almighty, and he's as obstinate as the Rock of Gibraltar. If he'd make a single move toward Wibberley, Wibberley would go trotting back to him, good as gold."

"Quinn & Nicholson can't be very happy about it."

"I don't suppose they are. The point is how far can we go ethically?"

"I didn't know that there were any ethics in advertising."

"Men in Glass Houses," said Mr. Jacobsen. "Advertising's such a vulnerable job that if we started cutting each other's throats we'd all be in a mess. We've got an unofficial ethical code which is a lot stricter than anything the Medes and Persians ever thought up. All the same—"

"It isn't as if *you'd* seduced Wibberley away from his present employers. His employers threw him out."

"True."

"He came to you. You thought well of him as a copywriter. Is there any reason you shouldn't have offered him a job?"

"Caesar's wife. We've got to be above suspicion. For instance, if he'd offered to bring proofs of all the proposed

Tendresse advertisements with him, we'd have had to say
no. That wouldn't have been playing the game."

"I suppose not."

"On the other hand, once he is in our outfit—if he
should happen to talk about them—in a general way—give
us an idea of the sort of line they've been going on—"

"You can't stop someone talking," agreed Mallinson
happily.

"It's Derek Wibberley," said Philippa, "and it's the third
time he's telephoned this morning."

"How many times did he ring up yesterday?" said Oliver.

"Seven times."

"If he keeps it up, he'll establish some sort of record."

"Don't you think you ought to talk to the boy?" said
Dumbo.

"What good would it do? I know what he wants and he's
not going to get it."

"It would be civil," said Dumbo.

"It would be a waste of time."

"The point is," said Dumbo, "that he thinks you encouraged him to present some sort of ultimatum to Bargulder. He duly presents it and gets kicked in the teeth.
You might at least say you're sorry."

"Give me one really good reason."

"Well," said Dumbo. "Put it at its lowest, if he feels sore
with you he's going to be very tempted to run off to Jacobsen's—who'd welcome him with open arms—I can't help
thinking."

"He's gone there already," said Oliver. "He starts working there on Monday."

"How do you know?"

"We've had a man in Jacobsen's for a long time. He's the
chap who carries the tea round and he hears all the gossip."

Harrap said, "It reminds me very strongly of the three
months I spent on Monty's staff under Bill Williams, working out the deception plans before Alam Halfa and Ala-
mein. There's the same sort of atmosphere of 'If we do A
he'll think we're bluffing, but if we do B he'll think we
want him to think we're doing A and he'll assume we're
doing B.' "

"Then we do C," said Blackett. "Time for one more before dinner."

They were in the small bar of the United Services Club.
In the months they had worked together on the board of
Quinn & Nicholson, they had grown to appreciate each
other's qualities. Both knew that if anything happened to
Oliver they would have to carry the firm.

"The person I'm sorriest for," said Blackett, "is Dumbo.
He's a decent, straightforward soul. He'd be perfectly
happy running a small family business. He's out of his
depth in this sort of league."

"I still think he ought to have been told what we're up
to. The same again please, Bob, but don't be shy with the
pink. I'm an eight-drop man."

"If he'd been told, he'd have jibbed."

"It was the lesser risk. You can't fight a battle with half
the staff thinking you're going in one direction and half
thinking you're going in quite a different one. That's much
better, Bob. I like to taste the stuff."

"Do you think Mallinson will accept the gambit?" said
Blackett.

"It's such an attractive one. Nothing to lose as far as he
can see and everything to gain."

"The point about gambits," said Blackett, "is that you've
got to weigh up the person who offers them. You remember
what the great Botvinnik said: 'If Tal offers you a pawn,
take it. If Petrosian offers you a pawn, decline it. If I offer
you a pawn, think it over.' "

Victor Mallinson drew a thick ring round the date Monday, May 31st. He then counted forward five weeks and
drew a second ring round July 5th and a third round July
12th.

"That's the timetable," he said. "Lucille explodes like a
ten-ton bomb on July 5th. Tendresse goes off like a damp
squib on July 12th."

"You're sure about these dates?" said Jacobsen.

Mallinson looked across at Crake, who nodded.

"I think," he said, "we can assume that our information
on that point is accurate."

"Because you realize that they could play the same trick

on you. If they moved back their start date *two* weeks, they'd be a week ahead of you."

"*Could* they do it?" said Crake.

Jacobsen considered the question. "They could do it but it'd be very difficult to do it without our finding out about it. A big advertising campaign isn't like an earthquake. It doesn't just happen. It's more like a hurricane. It gives plenty of warning; that is, if you happen to be tuned in to listen for it. Extra space has to be booked well ahead in newspapers. Retailers have to be warned about special displays and about clearing out old stock, and a lot of printing has to be done."

"Quinn's have got their own printing subsidiary," said Crake. "We shouldn't get much warning there, and they might decide to launch it without warning the shops."

"They'd still have to book newspaper space," said Mallinson. "I take it you've checked on that."

"I've checked," said Jacobsen, "and the picture is reasonably plain. You've both got advance space in the glossies. That's the normal outrider stuff. Introducing the name, tickling people's curiosity. Standard curtain raisers. There's nothing big breaking in the first four weeks. There's quite a heavy booking for Nortex, the shirt and underwear people, midweek on July 1st and 2nd. That's the Thursday and Friday before *yours* comes out. I don't see that they should conflict with you. It's clothes, not toiletry. And it's men, not women. The Quinn & Nicholson bookings start on July 12th. They were made in another name, incidentally, and by a small agency in the City, but we've traced them back to Bargulder's."

Mallinson said, "Suppose they *did* jump the gun somehow and got ahead of us. It wouldn't do us much harm. As we've planned it, our line is both to advertise our product *and* to take the steam out of their advertising." He was looking at three pairs of advertising rough-ups which had been placed side by side on the table beside his desk.

Jennie, who was sitting quietly in her chair, couldn't help reflecting that Jacobsen had swallowed his scruples pretty quickly. She seemed to remember his saying that he couldn't ask Wibberley to bring across proofs of the Tendresse advertising when he joined Jacobsen's, but it was apparent that this was precisely what he had done.

On the left were three rough drafts for Tendresse advertisements. Each showed an exquisitely gowned and heavily bejeweled lady smiling at a man in full evening dress with decorations. Underneath, a peeress, an Olympic swimmer, and a well-known film heroine were presenting a plug for Tendresse, "the upper-class perfume on sale at last at a price within *your* reach."

"To be fair to him," said Jacobsen, "Wibberley disclaimed any responsibility for them. They were Nugent's brain children, and no amount of talking would shift him. Twenty years ago they might have been quite effective."

"People haven't stopped being snobs in twenty years," said Crake. "It's the sales line that's all wrong. What they're really saying is 'An upper-class perfume at a lower-class price.' People stop believing that when they stop believing in fairies."

"I agree," said Jacobsen. "What you've got to say to them nowadays is 'All right, it *is* expensive, but it's well worth the extra money.' "

"I think we've struck the right note throughout," said Mallinson. He was looking at the three Lucille advertisements.

THE BOY NEXT DOOR

Don't bother what the Duchess thinks. It's when *he* turns his nose up that you want to watch it because, let's face it, *he's* the one whose opinion really matters. May we suggest a simple method of making sure that he looks at you twice. . . .

The second one said:

ARE YOU A NAME DROPPER?

People who talk about the great only succeed in making themselves small. Why not be yourself! *You're* the most important person in *your* life. And when you want to be yourself, plus something, might we make a suggestion. . . .

The third one simply said:

FIRST IMPRESSIONS COUNT

What did *he* think when he met you for the first

time last night? If it didn't go off quite as well as you'd
hoped, here's a hint. . .

"It's the right line," agreed Jacobsen.

Crake was examining the advertisements side by side. "I
should call it anti-advertising," he said. "Are you sure we
can get away with it?"

"Get away with what?"

"It's quite obvious we're taking the piss out of 'em, isn't
it? They come out with a line of duchesses and film stars
and such, and a week later we come along—using the
same size and type of print in our headlines, incidentally—
and say, 'Don't take any notice of duchesses and celebrities—' "

"Our legal department examined that aspect of it," said
Jacobsen. "They don't *think* that any action could lie.
Quinn's would only make fools of themselves if they tried
it."

"There's nothing to prevent us getting out headlines in
the same print, surely," said Mallinson. "That type face
has been used for years."

"They'll be bloody angry, all the same," said Crake.

Back in his own room he rang for Mr. Rowland. Mr.
Rowland suffered from a permanent head cold, but was a
careful and experienced operator. Mr. Crake referred to
him, in moments of affection, as his truffle hound. He
said, "Hop down to the companies' registry and see if you
can get a line on Nortex, the shirt people. It's at the back
of my mind that they had some trouble about five years
ago and had to go to the City in a hurry. They weren't
actually taken over, but someone's got a big hook in them."

Mr. Rowland snuffled and said he would see what he
could root out.

The City Carlton Club, despite its three-hundred-guinea
entrance fee and fifty-guinea annual subscription, has a
five-year waiting list. Saul Feinberg and Jacob Naumann
often shared a table there at lunchtime.

Feinberg said, "I met Wilfred Harrap at Latham's the
other day."

"I thought he'd left them."

"He doesn't work there now. I had the impression that

he was there to pass the hat round for Quinn & Nicholson."

Naumann stared suspiciously at the smoked trout on his plate and said, "I thought Quinn's had been doing all right. Their last account looked as healthy as— Waiter!"

"Sir."

"This isn't a smoked trout at all. It's a buckling."

"I'm afraid you're right, sir."

"Take it away. It looked pretty healthy to me."

"That was six months ago. They've been spending an awful lot of money lately. Developing this new line of theirs. It's all under security hatches at the moment, but Wilfred says it's good."

"It had better be," said Naumann. "The amount of money they're paying out on advertising it. I was given the figure in confidence. It seemed incredibly high to me."

Feinberg said, "The mistake a lot of people make—the Americans in particular, if I may say so—is in thinking of advertising as a science. Market research and computers and all that taradiddle. It isn't a science and it never will be. It's an art."

"The chef apologizes, sir. He made a mistake over your order."

"He'd better not try it on again."

"When Jacobsen mentioned Nortex," said Crake, "it rang a bell and I got Rowland to dig round. It took some doing because the sort of information we wanted isn't on the public files, but I knew Nortex went off the rails five years ago and had to get in outside money. There's a first debenture on their property. The bank holds that but it's limited to twenty thousand pounds. The real money's on second debenture. That's held by a nominee company."

"Let me guess," said Mallinson. "The real holders are Latham's."

"Bang on the arse."

"And you think they've induced Nortex to lend their name to Quinn's and that the real booker of the advertising space on July 1st and 2nd is our old friend Oliver Nugent, who plans to spring a big surprise on us by launching Tendresse three days *before* we launch Lucille?"

Since this was exactly what Crake had thought, he contented himself with looking sour and saying, "It's just the sort of bloody trick he would pull, isn't it?"

"Right up his street," agreed Mallinson. "Only in this case it's going to hurt him more than it hurts us. If he does come out next Thursday and Friday with a lot of corny advertisement chock full of duchesses and such, it's exactly the curtain raiser we want for our campaign telling girls not to be so damned silly. That's the beauty of it. *It doesn't matter if he comes out before us or after*. If we come out first, we scoop the pool. If he comes out first, he looks silly."

"You could be right," said Crake. "There isn't a lot we can do about it anyway. We can't bring our stuff forward, because we couldn't get the space now, and we can't put it off without losing a hell of a lot of money. I wonder—"

"What's up now?"

"You don't suppose it's a double bluff? Do you think Nugent guessed we'd find out about Nortex and be so scared of his coming out first that we'd try to bring ours forward at the last moment and get into a hell of a mess doing it?"

Mallinson thought about it. He said, "I don't say he *couldn't* have worked it out that way. It's the way he plays bridge, but it'd mean that he knew an awful lot about our plans. Not just generally, but in detail. By the way, you warned Jacobsen about that tea man of his, didn't you?"

"He sacked him on the spot. The chap was very upset. He's suing him for wrongful dismissal."

"The best of British luck to him. But my point is Nugent would have to know a lot more than a casual spy like that could possibly tell him. He'd have to be right in the middle of our plans."

"We're probably getting jumpy for nothing," agreed Crake. "The only thing is we've got more money sunk in it now than I'd care to see go down the plughole."

When Crake had gone, Mallinson said, "You're very quiet, Jennie. Don't tell me you're getting worried, too. That really would upset me."

"I've got a feeling," said Jennie.

Mallinson came over and perched on the corner of her desk. He said, "When my secretary has a feeling, I insist on sharing it."

"I've got a feeling you're underrating this man Nugent altogether."

"He's demoralized Crake. For heaven's sake, don't let him start demoralizing *you*. Do you realize, Jennie, that you're the girl Lucille is aimed at? Not the Rolls-Royce-Berkeley Buttery set with long white fingers and pointed fingernails who've never done an honest day's work in their lives, but girls like you." He picked up her left hand and laid it in his. "With stubby fingers and short nails and an honest, down-to-earth approach to life." He closed his fingers lightly over hers and said, "If we've got you, we've got the lot."

"Hares," said Oliver from the depths of his armchair by the fire.

"Wassat?" said Philippa sleepily. She was coiled up on the sofa, her head on the crutch between the arm and the back.

Oliver waited until the clock on the mantelshelf had tinkled out midnight; then he said, "Rabbits," and, "Didn't you know it was lucky to say 'Hares' the very last thing in one month and 'Rabbits' the first thing in the next one? And, by God, we're going to need all the luck we can get this July."

Philippa said, "I hate all this waiting. I haven't got the temperament for it."

"Waiting's finished."

"Not quite," said Philippa. "Nearly a fortnight to go. *We* don't come out till the twelfth."

"We're coming out tomorrow."

Philippa slowly uncoiled and looked at him.

"Are you serious?"

"As a judge. Odd, when you come to think of it. You say 'Sober as a Judge' and 'Drunk as a Lord,' so how would you describe a Law Lord?"

"Stop fluffing," said Philippa. *"What* advertisements have we got coming out tomorrow?"

"National coverage. Booked for us by the kindness of Nortex and Latham's. Good, rousing stuff."

"Then what about all our space on the twelfth? Has that been canceled?"

"Certainly not. We're using that for Tendresse as planned, only we've got a new line of approach. We've changed the emphasis a bit. We're abandoning duchesses and going for the girl next door."

Philippa was bolt upright by now staring at him. Oliver had not stirred. He was lying back in his chair, hands folded on his lap, legs spread, as relaxed as a discarded puppet. If she had known him longer, she would have recognized the ringside pose. He was at battle stations.

"Do you mean you're using *both* slots for Tendresse?"

"That would be excessive," said Oliver. "And in advertising, as in bombing, you must avoid saturation. A little in the right place is the ticket. The advertising splurge which comes out tomorrow and Friday could most fittingly be described as counterbattery work. We're firing a few rounds to knock out their guns before they can shoot back at us."

A thought struck her.

"Who arranged it? I can't remember any letters about it."

"There weren't any. It was all done on the telephone."

The blood mounted slowly in Philippa's face, then ebbed, leaving her white with a burning patch in the middle of each cheek.

She said, at last, in a voice which she scarcely recognized as her own, "Why did you do that?"

"It seemed a sensible precaution, since I knew you were working for Mallinson's."

"How long have you known?"

Oliver got up and came across. Philippa wondered if he was going to hit her. She would have been happier if he had. Instead he by-passed her, went to the desk, and took out an envelope. From it he extracted a handful of photographs, selected one, and gave it to her.

She examined it curiously. It was certainly she. She was leaning forward looking almost straight into the camera with a polite half smile on her face.

"What is it? When was it taken?"

"Some months ago. I advertised for a secretary. Remember? We reckoned the opposition wouldn't pass up a chance like that. I had a candid camera behind the reception desk and we photographed *all* the applicants. I gave the post to the first girl who looked possible. My God, I got more than I bargained for there." He laughed.

Philippa said, "I see. And then you just waited for one

of the others to turn up somewhere in your life."

"It was nicely done. That drunk car scene. If I hadn't known it was you, I'd have fallen for it every time."

She said, "What are you going to do? Have *me* covered with paint and thrown in the canal?"

"I wouldn't dream of it," said Oliver. "You have been a comfort to me"—he eyed her speculatively—"in so many ways that I really feel that I am in your debt."

Philippa said nothing. She had got over the first shock and didn't know whether she was going to laugh or cry. The uncertainty made speech risky.

"As long as they had you planted in my office," said Oliver, "I felt comfortably certain that they wouldn't try anything else. It was useful, too. If I had any particular little tidbit of false information to pass back, such as the start day for our advertising campaign, I could do it through you. I take it, by the way, that you *did* telephone Mallinson from Lyons. Maître Philippon's young man says you made a long-distance call that morning. He was able to find out that it was a London call, but not the number."

"Then all that talk about the German who hated you was makeup?"

"I only wish it was. That branch of the opposition is real enough. *They're* the ones who fixed my car."

Philippa said quickly, "I had nothing to do with that."

"Of course you didn't. You didn't know we were going back to that hotel until I told you. And it was you who pointed out to me that there was something screwy about the petrol tank when we stopped for lunch. It crossed my mind for a moment that that might be some sort of elaborate double bluff, but I dismissed the idea. I knew you well enough by then to realize that you're a simple girl at heart."

"Gloat away," said Philippa. "I can't stop you."

Oliver sat down on the arm of the sofa. "I'm not gloating," he said. "There are no morals in business and damned few rules, either. It's not a game. It's a way of life. The stronger go up, the weaker go down. You did what you had to do and you did it very nicely. The only reason I'm telling you all this is because there's going to be a hell of a row, starting tomorrow. There's going to be a lot of dirty infighting and people are going to get hurt. There's no real reason you should be one of them."

He got up and went back to the desk.

"That's why I'd like you to have this." He dropped a long envelope onto the sofa beside her. "It's got enough in it for you to stand yourself a month in France. You've got friends there. I should lie low till the dust settles."

Philippa said, "You—you're quite impossible."

She made the mistake of trying to laugh, and the tears came coursing down her cheeks in a steady stream.

Mr. and Mrs. Jacobsen lived at Epsom, five minutes' walk from the station and the shops, and the first caller at their house every morning was the paper boy who delivered one copy of each of the nine ranking national dailies. Mr. Jacobsen liked to skim through the advertisement sections over breakfast and peruse them more thoroughly during the train journey to town.

That Thursday morning he had finished a slice of toast, had drunk a first cup of coffee, and was starting a second as he turned his attention to the pile of newspapers.

Normally this process was accompanied by a cheerful commentary, touching on the successes of his own firm, the inadequacy of his rivals, and the scandalous advertising rates charged by newspapers which artfully inflated their net circulation figures in order to raise those rates even further.

It suddenly occurred to Mrs. Jacobsen, who was attending to the wants of their daughter Violet in her high chair in the corner, that something out of the ordinary was happening.

Her husband was racing through paper after paper, tearing them open, glancing at them, and throwing them aside. His face was white.

She said, "What is it? What's up?"

Mr. Jacobsen said nothing. He had finished with the last of the papers and was glaring at it as if it had insulted him personally.

Then he jumped to his feet and bolted for the door.

Mrs. Jacobsen said, "Your coffee—"

She heard the front door slam.

Mr. Jacobsen ran down the front path. Halfway down it he tripped over Violet's doll pram and relieved his feelings by kicking it into the rockery.

Back in the breakfast room, Mrs. Jacobsen was looking through the pile of crumpled papers. She knew enough about her husband's business to confine her search to the areas in which the advertisements of Jacobsen's more important clients appeared. If there had been the most terrible mix-up, these important and expensive places might be filled with "stand-in" advertising, repeats of old advertisements kept ready for such a contingency. Everything seemed to be in order. The new Glubbo cartoon series was running nicely. Brekklbrix was offering children numbered components to build their own motorcycles. Mastodon underwear had launched their new ("natural-scented") mini-briefs. All seemed well.

The only new advertisements occupying the spread position in six of the papers were not, so far as Mrs. Jacobsen could see, anything to do with her husband's firm at all. They were drawing the attention of housewives to the merits of a new lavatory cleaner named Loo-Seal.

"FIRST IMPRESSIONS COUNT," said the headline.

What did *they* think when they came to your house and had occasion to visit the smallest room? Loo-Seal, the miracle cleanser . . .

The second said: "THE FAMILY NEXT DOOR," and inquired:

Are you in good odor with your neighbors?

And the third asked: "ARE YOU A GERM DROPPER?"

We tend to think of germs as unpleasant things which other people pass on to us. Might the boot be on the other foot? If you feel any doubts about it, have your lavatory pan regularly sealed with Loo-Seal, the miracle cleanser.

Mrs. Jacobsen thought the advertisements rather effective. She particularly admired the way in which the headlines were set out. It was a bold and distinctive type, much used by her husband's firm. She made a note to order a large economy size tin of Loo-Seal herself.

"It's an outrage," said Jacobsen.

"Is there no way we can stop it?" said Mallinson.

"I've already spoken to our lawyer. He doesn't think so. To get an injunction, we should have to show some cause of action. Breach of copyright or plagiarism or something like that."

"Well?"

"The trouble is," said Jacobsen unhappily, "that they can hardly be accused of plagiarizing our advertisements when theirs came out first."

"Do you think the Advertising Council might be asked to intervene?"

"Stop blatting," said Mr. Crake. In a crisis his language, never delicate, deteriorated alarmingly. "You're pissing against the wind. You haven't got a chance in hell of getting an injunction, and *if* the Advertising Council did do anything, which I doubt, it'd be five years too late. Face facts."

"We've got till Monday," said Mallinson. "It'd be a rush job but if you put every man onto it do you think we could get out an entirely new line in advertisements?"

"I expect they could," said Mr. Crake, "and it'd be as much use as a bull's udder. You haven't grasped the problem. *What you've got to change is the name,* and that's already printed on fifty thousand labels, on fifty thousand bottles, sitting in five hundred chemists' shops waiting to go on the shelves on Monday morning. How long do you think it's going to take to get *them* back, steam off the labels, and get new labels and new containers and new handouts printed? Monday morning? Don't make me laugh, it's bad for my ulcers."

"A month to do the job at all," said Jacobsen, "but that would bring us out at just the *wrong* time—a fortnight after Quinn's and looking like a carbon copy of them. If we've got to postpone, better make it six months until the steam has gone out of their effort, and do the job properly."

"I suppose we've *got* to change the name?"

"For Christ's sake," said Crake. "Unless you want every-one to think that Lucille, which we've put more money into promoting than I care to think about right now, is the name of something you use to clean the lavatory pan. If you bring the stuff out now, you'll have stockbrokers' clerks cutting out the adverts and sticking them up side by side in the House."

"We've *got* to change the name," agreed Jacobsen.

He, like Mr. Crake, was watching Mallinson. The de-cision had to come from him. His face was white and he was biting at his top lip and he seemed to be having trouble with his breathing.

"If he had a gun in his hand and Nugent came through that door," thought Jacobsen, "he'd shoot him and glad to do it. It's not just the money. It's pride. He's raw."

Mallinson sat down in his chair, stretched his legs in front of him, and went through the motions of relaxing. He even managed to laugh.

Jacobsen thought he had never heard a sound with less mirth in it.

"It's a game," said Mallinson. "We've got to remember that. Just a game. That's right, isn't it?"

"That's one way of looking at it," said Jacobsen.

"It's the only way. The first thing I want to find out is which member of our team has been letting us down. Be-cause until we attend to that little matter, we're not going to make much progress in any other direction."

"That girl we planted on him," said Crake.

"Impossible. She knew nothing about our advertising. And the one date she gave us, in fact, was right."

Jacobsen said slowly, "I'm afraid there's really not much doubt about it, is there? We've been sold a pup. To use a gambling expression, we've had a card forced on us."

"Wibberley?"

"I underrated that young man. He had me fooled all along the line. I thought he really was angry with Bar-gulder. Of course, the whole thing was a put-up job. Bar-gulder pretended to sack him knowing we'd snap him up. He comes along with a lot of so-called Tendresse advertise-ments—we shall never see *them* in print—and gets all our stuff from us, and hands it to Quinn's on a plate. That's the only possible way they could have done it. Whoever pulled this job didn't only know dates and timings, they knew *the actual wording and layout of our advertisements.*"

"I think you've put your finger on it," said Crake.

"I only hope he's been well paid for this little job. He'll have to live on it for a long time, because, as far as advertising's concerned, he's had it. In this country *or* in America. We've got associates there and I'll make it my business to have him black-listed wherever he goes."

"You're locking the stable door after the horse has gone," said Mr. Crake. "Not that I'm opposed to it. That young man's earned a kick on the cruppers and we'd better see he gets it. Now, let's get down to cases."

"The first thing," said Mallinson, "will be to draft a circular to all our retailers. 'Owing to last-minute difficulties over international patent rights'—I think that'll do as well as anything—'we regret that we have to ask you to postpone.' Take this down, will you, Jennie?"

When the others had gone he said, "There's so much to do. I hardly know where to start."

"The best thing," said Jennie, "when you feel like that, is to have a cup of coffee. I'll go and make it."

Mallinson laughed for the second time that morning. This time there was some genuine amusement in it.

(xi)

"We've got to do something about Derek Wibberley," said Dumbo.

"He's old enough to look after himself," said Oliver.

"I mean it," said Dumbo; his normally good-natured face was pink with embarrassment and determination.

"But why?"

"Because we've dropped him into the mud for our own ends, and I don't see why he should be the one to carry the can when we've scooped the pool."

"That's one of the finest mixed metaphors I've ever heard," said Oliver, "but I still don't quite see what you're getting at."

There was an undertone of caution in his voice. He knew Dumbo well enough to realize that a crisis of some sort was impending.

"What I'm getting at," said Dumbo, "is this. First you persuaded Derek that he ought to be given a seat on the Board at Bargulder's. Then you got together with Bargulder and arranged that *when* he asked for it he was to be kicked downstairs with a flea in his ear. And you knew that when this happened he'd resign and that the opposition would snap him up and that, as likely as not, he'd tell them all he knew about our Tendresse campaign—might even take copies of the stuff with him."

"Quite right," said Oliver. "Exactly what he did."

"And because the stuff he gave them wasn't the stuff you were going to use, his new employers have jumped to the conclusion that he's double-crossed them, and have sacked him *and* black-listed him so that he can't get another job."

"Incidentally, how do you know all this?"

"Derek came to see me."

"And cried on your shoulder?"

"All he wanted us to do was to tell Jacobsen the truth."

"It'd be an interesting exercise," said Oliver. "What do you suggest we actually say? Wibbers is quite a decent chap, really. A double-crosser maybe, but not a treble-crosser?"

"If you won't discuss this seriously," said Dumbo, getting up, "I'm sorry I'm wasting your time."

"I am discussing it seriously. I'm asking you what you suggest we do for Wibbers. Jacobsen won't take him back. If we told him the truth he wouldn't believe it, and if he did believe it he'd still be furious with Wibbers. You don't love a Trojan horse even when you realize it wasn't all the poor animal's fault."

"All right. But we ought to do *something* for him."

"Pension him?"

Dumbo was still standing, and his face had gone white. He said, quite quietly, "Is this firm Quinn & Nicholson or is it Quinn & Nugent?"

"What on earth do you mean?"

"I've been wondering. If you had an elaborate plan like this hatched up, why didn't you let your fellow-directors in on it? Why did you have to play the whole hand alone?"

"Wilfred and Bill Blackett knew about it."

"Then why was I left out?"

"Because," said Oliver, "I was perfectly certain that you wouldn't have agreed to it."

There was a moment of silence; then Dumbo said, "I don't believe in outstaying my welcome. You can have my resignation in writing." He went out.

Oliver sat looking after him in silence. Then he started to swear very softly.

"It's a great pity," said Blackett, "but I suppose it had to happen sooner or later."

Harrap said, "It was a bloody awkward decision to have to make. Dumbo's a good chap. He's the ideal person to run a small family firm. Everyone would like him and respect him and know that they'd get a square deal from him. It's just unfortunate that he's got out of his depth. There's no room for sentiment in a public company. It's eat or be eaten. Two more like the last please, Bob."

Blackett waited until the barman had brought the drinks and retired out of earshot before he said, "You often got the same choice during the war, didn't you? Whether you'd prefer to serve under a complete shit who knew his job or a nice chap who might wobble at the critical moment."

"And you always opted for the shit."

"Mind you, I'm not saying that Oliver—"

"No, of course not," said Harrap. "He's got a lot of good points. You realize that he could quite easily have ridden Dumbo off?"

"How?"

"For a start, he could have given him the real reason for not telling the opposition the truth about Wibbers. If they'd once grasped the fact that he was a fool and not a knave, they might have started looking round for the person who really *was* giving away their secrets."

"True," said Blackett. He sipped at his whiskey. It was the second of the two drinks which he allowed himself before dinner and he liked to take it slowly. "Why didn't he?"

"There's a streak of ruthlessness in him. Ruthlessness for its own sake. He enjoys making his own plans, setting his own objectives, and going straight for them, no matter whose toes he treads on."

"He's a bit like Monty in some ways," said Blackett. He

thought about Oliver for a moment and added, "Only in *some* ways, of course."

As Oliver approached the steps leading to Brett's Club, a figure detached itself from the darkness and lurched forward. Oliver stood still.

"Wanna word with you."

"Oh, it's you, is it? If you want to see me, come to my office in business hours."

"Don't give me that stuff," said Wibberley. He was swaying on his feet under the joint influences of anger and alcohol. "You know bloody well if I come to your office I'll be given the about turn. I wanna talk to you now, and you're bloody well going to hear what I've got to say to you. You're a twister. Do you hear me? A bloody twister. And I'm going to follow you into that bloody club of yours and say it to all the stuck-up sods inside there, too. I'm going to tell them you're a twister. How are you going to like that?"

"We shan't like it at all," said Oliver gently. He was balanced on his feet, peering forward in the dim light from the lamp above the steps at the figure swaying in front of him.

"I thought you wouldn't. But that's what I'm going to do." Wibberley put out a hand and caught Oliver by the lapel of his coat, as much to steady himself as to detain his victim. "I'm going to follow you round and tell everyone what you are. You're a bloody crook."

Oliver said, "What you want to do, old son, is go to bed and get a long night's rest. Come and see me in the morning."

He disengaged the clutching fingers, side-stepped past him, walked quickly up the steps, and disappeared through the swing doors of the club. Wibberley followed more slowly.

In the lobby a large man in porter's uniform barred his way. He said, "Excuse me, sir, but are you a member of this club?"

"If you imagine for a bloody moment that I'd be a bloody member of this bloody club, you can think again."

"In that case, sir, I'm afraid you'll have to leave."

Five seconds later Wibberley was picking himself up from the pavement.

Oliver, watching from the window of the club, saw him get up, make an attempt to get back up the steps, think better of it, and start away down the pavement, walking as if he had unequal weights attached to his feet. Oliver went to the telephone and dialed a number.

"Wimbledon Police Station? My name's Nugent and I'm speaking from Brett's Club. There's a man outside who's been annoying several of the members. His name's Wibberley. I'll spell it for you. That's right. I think he has a house on Lodge Road. You might watch out for him. He's much too tight to be in charge of a motorcar. I thought you ought to know. I only hope he doesn't kill someone on the way home."

The voice at the other end thanked Mr. Nugent for his public-spirited behavior and said that the matter would be attended to.

Sylvia Nicholson said, "Can't you *see*, Oliver? Dumbo was simply bluffing. He lost his temper, that's all. If you would take a single step in his direction, he'd come back at once."

Oliver said, "It's a month since he left the Board and I haven't heard a word from him. Not a letter or even a telephone call. I've had to assume—we've all had to assume—that his decision was final."

"He hasn't said anything because he's too proud to do it. If he knew I'd come round here this evening, he'd slay me."

"I'm sure he wouldn't do anything so silly. And please won't you sit down and take your coat off and have a drink, so that we can talk this over?"

Sylvia shook her head. She was a nice dumpy person, half girl, half woman, and, Oliver suspected, a stronger character than Dumbo in almost every way.

She said, "There isn't a lot to talk over, really. If you invite him back he'll come. If you don't he'll stay out. And don't misunderstand me. We're not starving. He's still got his shares in the company and I've got money of my own. It's just that he's miserable. He's too young to retire. If he's got nothing to do he'll go mad. Or do something silly like putting all our money into a chain of bingo parlors."

"I sympathize with that," said Oliver. "If I had nothing to do I'd go mad myself. Or start some really serious drinking. Look, Sylvia, why can't you leave this alone for a bit? Give it time. We'll think something out for him."

"A branch managership? He's not a boy, you know. His grandfather founded this firm, and his father put it on its feet. It's been the family's business now for nearly a hundred years. I'm not asking for much. A word from you and he'll come back."

"It'd be very easy to say yes."

"Then why not say it?"

"All right," said Oliver. "I'll tell you why, but only if you're sure you want me to. You probably won't like it."

"I'll risk that."

"If I'd had to explain everything I was going to do to Dumbo and get his approval, we couldn't have gone through with the last fight. I told Blackett and Harrap because they're natural bastards and they understand that sort of thing. And that was really why Dumbo flew off the handle. He was huffed because I'd taken them into my confidence and left him out. That's the truth. And if I go to him now and beg him to come back, the assumption would be that I'd have to take him into my confidence in future. That's why I said wait. In a year or two, when we've finished with Mallinson's and we're in smoother waters, we could afford to have someone as nice as Dumbo on the Board. But we haven't got there yet. We've won a battle. We haven't won the war. And I can't fight in the way I have to fight if I've got to carry Dumbo's conscience. I should be weighted out of the race before I started. You asked for it and there it is."

Sylvia listened in complete silence and then said, "I think that's the most absurd explanation I've ever heard."

"All right. It's absurd. The truth's often absurd."

"Why not be honest? Why not say that the only thing you're interested in is being boss? Harrap and Blackett are your creatures, but Dumbo isn't. He might stand up to you occasionally. That's why you want him out. That's the real truth, isn't it?"

"If it's a comfort to you to think of it that way," said Oliver politely, "by all means do."

"You know," said Sylvia, her lips trembling, "you ought to stop sometime and take a look at yourself. At what you've done, and the way you've done it. Then you mightn't be so damned happy about yourself."

"Please, Sylvia."

"No, I'm going to say this now because I probably shan't see you again. You really ought to carry a notice round your neck. 'Keep off. Danger.' You use people. And when you've used them up, you hurt them or kill them. I heard all about Derek Wibberley. Drunk in charge and assaulting the police. Thirty days. That was a laugh, wasn't it? Well, at least he didn't end up with his head on a railway line like poor Len Williams."

For a long time after she had gone, Oliver sat perfectly still. Only his eyes were alive and dark and angry.

The flat was very quiet.

Without moving his head he could see the exact spot on the sofa where Philippa had sat curled up, her head resting on the join between the arm and the back. The room was clean, orderly, and airless. Like a very expensive room in an exclusive nursing home. He wished now that he hadn't stayed up in London. He wished he had gone home. He wished he had refused to see Sylvia.

Vivi was a girl of originality and enterprise. Driven off the pavements of Soho by the Street Offenses Act, she had not, like many of her sisters, retreated into the doorway of the closest near-beer hall but had moved east into the quiet streets which lie between Southampton Row and Gray's Inn Road. She had argued that police surveillance would be a lot less strict in these respectable quarters, and she knew that quite a few business and professional men had flats in this area.

She spotted Oliver as a possible customer as soon as he turned the corner. It was something to do with the way he was walking. A man by himself either walked fast, as if he had somewhere to go and intended to get there, or he strolled. Oliver was strolling.

Vivi moved out under the street lamp. She had a small,

not unattractive face and was wearing a chinchilla coat with a big turned-up collar, fur-lined suède boots, and nothing else at all.

Oliver stopped in front of her and said, "Well?"

Vivi thought, "Damn. He's sozzled to the eyebrows. Pity. Promising customer." She said, "It's a cold night, duckie. Oughtn't you to be in bed?"

As she said it, she swung the front of her coat wide open.

Oliver was swaying slightly on his feet. He examined her with as much interest as a housewife pricing fish on a slab. Then he said, "How much?"

"I'm expensive, dearie. Probably more than you've got."

"How much?"

Vivi was puzzled. From the way he was walking and standing he was tight. On the other hand, his voice was clear and unslurred. Maybe he wasn't as drunk as she'd thought.

"For a nice boy like you," she said, "twenty pounds."

Oliver felt in his pocket. Very deliberately he extracted an envelope, opened the top, and shook out a dozen photographs onto the pavement.

"Take your pick," he said. "They're all whores." Then he turned on his heel and wandered back down the street.

SECOND INTERLUDE:

Oliver at Home (Sevenoaks)

DURING the years I had spent in America with Manson, Fulweider, Glanz, Cotton & Hicks I got generous vacations which I often spent skiing in the Adirondacks. And I thought I knew something about the game, but I had found the snow at Gstaad faster and the runs more tricky than anything I had met there, and I limped into my flat that February afternoon with a twisted knee and the aftereffects of concussion.

There was a pile of letters inside the door, mostly unwanted circulars and unpaid bills, but one of them caught my eye. It had a well-bred look about it, a good quality envelope, the name and address put on with an electric typewriter, common enough in America but not so common in England at that time. Also it spelled my name right, which a lot of people don't do. It was from Oliver. It said that he had heard from friends that I was back in England and planning to stay put, and would I drop in and have a word with him before committing myself in any other direction?

I guessed, of course, that he meant to offer me a job, and that was something that needed thinking about. I was tired of working for other people and had come back to England to find a partnership I could buy into with the capital I'd saved in the States. I wanted to be my own boss. However, that was no reason not to go and see him.

The London office of Quinn & Nicholson (Holdings), Ltd., as they now called themselves, was in the big new block with that odd statue in the forecourt opposite the Pearl in High Holborn. I saw from the plates in the lobby that this was also the registered office of Quinn & Nicholson, Ltd., Sandberg & Freyer, Ltd., Quinn & Nicholson (Sales), Ltd., Quinn & Nicholson (Properties), Ltd., and Bassett & Munk, Ltd.

I went up to the fourth floor, was taken in hand by a commissionaire, shown into the Managing Director's outer office, and handed over to a brunette whose horn-rimmed glasses seemed to be a form of protective camouflage. (The female bark beetle of Colorado has similar circular markings on the face, but in her case they are thought to attract rather than repel the male.)

She smiled sweetly at me, relieved me of my coat and hat, straightened my tie for me (or perhaps that was my imagination), and allowed me in.

Oliver jumped up from behind his desk, came across and grabbed my hand. "The return of the native," he said. "Sit down. What have you done to your leg?"

I told him, and he said, "Lucky devil. I haven't had a real holiday for three years."

I was trying to get used to the changes in him. Cumulatively they were startling, but it wasn't so easy to itemize them. He was a lot fatter, but a first-class tailor can hide that; his face was settling into the heavy mask which I had noticed on so many American businessmen, the product of soft living and hard decisions. He looked as if he had used up about twenty years of life in the eight years since I had seen him, but there was still a look of the old Oliver in his eyes.

He sat me down in the chair of honor and asked me a lot of questions about my doings in America. I realized that he had kept fairly close tabs on my movements, and was flattered by the thought that he should have bothered. Soon, but not too soon, he eased round to what was in his mind.

"We've changed a good deal in the last few years," he said. "I expect you've noticed."

I said I had. I'd also followed *his* fortunes in the financial press, since it had been in my mind that our paths might cross.

He said, "Bill Blackett and George Taylor look after

the production side at Elsfield Wood. We put Taylor on the Board when Dumbo pulled out."

I knew enough about that not to pursue it.

"Wilf Harrap and I look after the marketing and finance side. We've got a separate sales company that does that."

"You've got a hatful of companies," I said. "I saw their names on the door."

"That's mostly the property side. We've been buying up chemists shops. Basset & Munk is a North Country chain. We've got our eyes on a much bigger one in Scotland—Macfarlane & Rae."

"What on earth do you want with shops?"

"Tied house principle, old boy. We run 'em for profit but they have to take our special lines."

I was impressed in spite of myself. Macfarlane's was a big outfit, a household name north of the Tweed. I said, "What would it cost you to take them over?"

"We'd have to offer cash and shares. The cash handout would be about half a million."

"Have you got half a million?"

Oliver laughed. When he laughed, he sounded a lot more like the old Oliver. "No one in business ever has half a million. It'd mean a loan transaction. That's what I want you for. You've been doing that sort of work in New York. You know all the tricks of the trade. You'd start as Secretary to the group and there'd be a reversion to a seat on the Board in about three years' time when you got into your stride."

We talked about it. The terms were generous. If I'd been looking for a paid job, I'd have jumped at it, and I said as much. After half an hour Oliver said, "Don't say yes or no today. Can you come down for the weekend? Mrs. Comrie would like to see you. She was talking about you the other day. She says you're the only accountant she knows who has an honest face."

The house was on the Wilderness side of Sevenoaks where all the nobs live, and was a very different proposition to that unpainted box of bricks at Radlett. A whole-time gardener, I guessed, to look after three-quarters of an acre of garden and a local girl to help Mrs. Comrie run a house which had so many labor-saving gadgets it was practically self-propelled anyway.

We settled down after dinner, in front of a log fire, with a man-sized whiskey each.

"You're pretty comfortable here," I said.

"Too comfortable," said Oliver. "If I wasn't so comfortable, I shouldn't be so bloody fat and unfit. That was the real cause of the trouble last winter."

"I didn't hear about that."

"It was pleurisy. I was in bed for a month and away from work for another month."

"It must have been bad, to keep you away from your office for two months."

"It was my heart." Most people, when they say things like that, say them with transparent bravado. Oliver really sounded indifferent. He'd taken no care of himself when young, and wasn't going to start worrying about the afflictions of middle age.

"Of course, I drink too much, too. The doctor told me I ought to lay off altogether. I did for a bit, too. But I was so bloody miserable that I soon gave up trying."

He poured himself out a second whiskey, and topped my glass up. Then we got on to Quinn & Nicholson, and the change he had in mind. The future, as he saw it, lay in the American aerosol can.

"It started with fly sprays and things like that," he said, "but it's catching on fast. People are so damned lazy. If they can get something by pressing a button instead of unscrewing a cap or taking out a cork, they'll go for it every time. We shall be cleaning our teeth with pressurized toothpaste before long. The machinery's damned expensive. A lot of it's under license from abroad. And the stuff's potentially explosive, which means elaborate safety precautions, and that costs money, too."

Later on I mentioned a lawsuit and saw his face darken.

"It's Mallinson," he said. "He couldn't take what we did to him lying down. So he started this action. I think he sometimes wishes he hadn't. I certainly do. It's not just the money. You've no idea the amount of sheer bloody *time* a lawsuit takes up. It's been going on for eighteen months and we haven't got anywhere near the actual hearing yet."

"If it's wasting so much time and money, why doesn't he stop it?"

"It's pride," said Oliver. "Real deep, basic, old-fashioned pride. The sort of thing that used to make gentlemen meet at first light on Wimbledon Common and take pot shots at each other from twelve paces. It wasn't only the cash, although it must have cost him a packet. The real trouble was that the story got about and people laughed at him. He couldn't take that."

After that, we talked about me for a bit. I said rather feebly, "There are lots of good company accountants."

"It isn't only an accountant I need," said Oliver. "I want someone I can talk things over with from time to time. Someone from the old times, in the war. George Taylor is the only one left now."

If I really had meant to keep out of Quinn & Nicholson, it was a fatal mistake to let Oliver talk to me. He was a wonderful negotiator, with a flair for saying exactly the right thing at the right moment. He'd have made a successful politician. Lloyd George had the same touch.

Around midnight I capitulated and agreed to give it a try.

PART III

Mallinson's v. Quinn's

NATIONAL HEALTH SERVICE charges were doubled, Mr. Benn failed to remain in the House of Commons, and Bradshaw ceased publication. The *Daily Mirror* extended its empire by outbidding Lord Thomson for the *Daily Herald*, and Mr. Cecil King said that he saw nothing wrong with power so long as the power belonged to him. For the first time in nearly fifty years, two British girls were seen in the Women's Single Finals at Wembley and a bluethroat was seen at Cley, in Norfolk. June 1st was the coldest June day for eighty-one years. A group of British models visited Moscow to display Western fashions and the bank rate went up to 7 per cent. The Conservatives proposed a pay freeze and the Labour Party proposed a vote of censure on it, on the grounds that it undermined the well-established machinery for freely negotiating wage settlements. And the case of Mallinson's Pharmaceutical Supplies, Ltd., v. Quinn & Nicholson, Ltd., was finally set down for hearing.

(ii)

As soon as he had had a chance of assessing him, Oliver realized how lucky he was in his solicitor. Fergus Campbell was nondescript in appearance. He was not clever. He would have considered the adjective "clever," if applied to a solicitor, an actionable insult. He knew as much about the details of the law as most practicing solicitors, which was precious little, but he had an infinite capacity for taking

in the details of other people's problems, and he had a
nature which acted as a flywheel or governor to his clients'
mental mechanisms. If they were rash, he was cautious. If
they were sticky, he would add the requisite dash of im-
petuosity.

"I thought a good deal about counsel," he said. "It was
quite clear that we wanted a strong leader. That's why I
briefed Kendrick Starkey."

"What exactly do you mean by strong?" asked Oliver.
He was stretched out in the very comfortable chair, almost a psychiatrist's couch, which Campbell supplied for
his clients.

"In this context I mean one who is capable of being
rude."

"I thought rudeness went out with F. E. Smith."

"In criminal cases, yes. In civil cases even now it is
sometimes necessary. I think this is one of them. The whole
case is a try-on. A monstrous piece of impertinence."

"Then you don't think they've a chance?"

"I didn't mean that. Impertinence sometimes comes off
in the Law Courts, as in other walks of life. No. We've
got to fight this every inch of the way. That's why I was
particularly glad to rope in Lewis Moffat as a junior. He's
a good lawyer. He'll supply the ammunition. Starkey will
shout it."

"We're really coming under starter's orders at last?"

"We're in the 'warned' list. It'll be the end of this week
or the beginning of next. I'd prefer to start on a Monday
if possible. High Court judges are human, and they're
mostly old men. They get tired by Friday. And when they're
tired they don't want to listen to you. It'd be a pity to get
brushed off after all the work we've put into the preliminaries."

"How long *has* the thing been going on?"

Campbell turned back the pages of a bulging folder and
said, "I see that the writ was issued almost two years and
three months ago."

"As long as that," said Oliver. "It's been quite an experience. Like having your large intestine wound off on a
roller."

"Grab your hat," said Campbell. "We mustn't keep
Starkey waiting."

Mr. Starkey greeted them cordially. Lewis Moffat, pale and serious, was already installed at the conference table in the first-floor room overlooking the Temple Church.

The Q.C. was a surprisingly ugly man: small, squat, and heavy, with a face like a dyspeptic bulldog. His voice, in ordinary conversation, was soft and agreeable. He said, "It was clever of them to mount this case as slander of title. It enabled them to ask for a jury. Defamation and breach of promise are almost the only civil cases you can get 'em for now—thank goodness."

"You don't approve of juries?"

"Only when I've got a very weak case. There may be something to be said for 'em in the criminal courts."

"A relic, don't you think, of the time when judges were in the king's pocket?"

"Maybe." Starkey was weighing Oliver up carefully as he talked to him. He was visualizing him in the witness box under examination, and then under cross-examination. The impression he made on the jury was going to be a vital factor. "But in civil cases juries are an anomaly. After all, if you had something wrong with you and got a competent surgeon to cut you open, you wouldn't ask twelve good men and true to peer inside you and assess the result."

"If they're as bad as that, why on earth do we put up with them?"

"It takes a long time to change anything in this country," said Lewis Moffat sadly.

"Particularly a public image," said Starkey. "And you have to realize that the public image of businessmen is one of the things *we're* up against. A jury automatically assumes that any undergraduate who is driving a car is speeding, that any actor who is friendly with a woman is sleeping with her, and that *all* businessmen are scoundrels. That's what they'll start from."

"I'm afraid it's going to be a witch hunt," agreed Moffat.

"No doubt," said Oliver, "but which witch?"

"Quite apt," said Starkey. "Might use it in my closing speech. Which witch? That's the case in a nutshell. If the jury comes to the conclusion that you were behaving unscrupulously, while your opponents were conducting themselves in a perfectly honest and aboveboard way, they'll lean over backward to award them substantial damages, whatever the lawyers say."

"And if that's their line," said Moffat, "they've picked the right counsel for it. There's no one at the bar who can drape a white sheet more effectively round a grubby client than James Snow."

"It was after one of his most effective perorations," said Starkey, "in defense of a fraudulent stockjobber, if I remember rightly, that he earned the nickname of Driven Snow."

Oliver said, "If Mr. Snow thinks he can transform Mallinson and Crake into a pair of lily-white innocents, he isn't a barrister—he's an alchemist."

"We haven't necessarily got to attack *their* characters," said Moffat, in his soft Lowland voice. "After all, they're the plaintiffs. It's up to them to prove their case."

"As my learned junior reminds us," said Starkey dryly, "it's up to them to prove their case. He also implies, I fancy, that I am straying from the point. So let's get down to business. We'll take the proofs of evidence first. You realize that one of the most important witnesses is going to be this advertising man—what's his name? Wibberley."

"It's a difficult business," said Simon Bargulder. "Very difficult. What I'd like to do most is to have nothing to do with it at all."

"That's what we'd all like," said Oliver, "but we've got no choice. We didn't start this action. We're the ones who are being attacked. You don't suggest we lie down and let them walk over us?"

"That I don't suggest, but it is a private fight between Mallinson and you. Must the agency be involved?"

"You're involved already."

"Shall I have to give evidence?"

It was perfectly astonishing, Oliver thought, how big, tough businessmen wilted at the thought of having to stand up in court and answer a few questions. He said, "It all depends on Wibberley. Whether he decides to tell the truth and, if so, how much of it."

"What *can* he say?"

"If he wanted to be devastatingly truthful, he'd say that

he was made a fool of from beginning to end. That he was deliberately encouraged by us to ask for a seat on the Board, knowing that you'd smack his bottom for him and guessing that he'd walk out in a huff and go across to Jacobsen's with a load of carefully planted false information which would lead them up the garden path."

"*If* he is truthful," agreed Bargulder, "that is what he would say, but do you think he will say it?"

"I'm damned sure he won't. No one's going to stand up in court and admit that he's been both a fool and a rogue. He'll put across some carefully slanted version of the truth. The question is, which way is he going to slant it—and how far?"

"Do you think that if we made some approach?"

"What sort of approach?"

"Suggested perhaps that we found him a suitable post in the advertising industry. He would like to return."

"It might work. On the other hand it might backfire badly. We wouldn't want him to get up in court and say we'd tried to bribe him to change his story."

"It's very difficult."

"Don't misunderstand me," said Oliver. "I'm not averse to a little judicious bribery. What I draw the line at is unsuccessful bribery. I'd like to keep Wibberley out of this as much as possible. He's an unnecessary complication, and, God knows, we've got enough complications without him."

Bargulder looked at him curiously. Oliver was pale, and for the first time in their acquaintance he thought he detected a note of weariness, almost of despondency, in his voice. "It must be very trying for you, all this," he said. "I have something which will do you good, I think."

He waddled across to the corner cupboard and got out a squat brown bottle.

"They are our clients. When we launched their last campaign, the Managing Director gave me this." He measured out two generous shots. Oliver said, "This is damned good whiskey."

"You will not buy it in the shops. To get hold of it, you have to be a distiller yourself."

"Maybe I'm in the wrong line," said Oliver. "None of the stuff that Quinn & Nicholson brew does you half as much good as this." He accepted a refill and stood with it in his hand for a moment. The color had come back to his face. He added, "I don't mind a fight in the ordinary way, but this is different. When the lawyers get in on the act, they seem to turn it all sour."

"I want all your opinions on this," said Oliver, "and I'm not just asking for them in order to disregard them—"

"Makes a nice change," said Harrap.

"—as I've sometimes been accused of doing. This is really important. What it boils down to, as I see it, is a straight choice of tactics. Defense or attack? Do we sit tight and hope Mallinson's will make fools of themselves, or do we counterattack and try to blast them out of their positions?"

"Which do the lawyers advise?" asked Blackett.

"All they can really say is that it's up to the plaintiff to prove his case, which sounds fine but doesn't get you anywhere."

"It seems to me," said Harrap, "that a lot depends on *how* they put their case. Are they simply going to prove a string of facts—one lot of advertisements appeared on July 2nd and a second lot was due to come out on July 5th only it couldn't because the second lot happened, by coincidence, to look so like the first that the second lot had to be scrapped. If that's their case, I'd say let 'em get on with it and try and prove it, and the best of British luck to them."

"Quite so," said Blackett. "But are they going to stop there? Aren't they going to try and ferret out what went on behind the scenes?"

"Which scenes?" said Oliver. "Ours or theirs, or both?"

"You have a point," said Blackett. "We know, of course, that they were planning to do the dirty on us. We just happened to outsmart them."

"We *know* it," said Harrap, "but can we afford to prove it?"

Both of them were looking at the fourth member of the Board.

George Taylor had developed surprisingly with promotion. A little awkward at first with a brigadier, a colonel, and a major, he had soon found his feet and now dealt with the others on a basis of perfect equality. With his hair graying at the temples and a pair of reading glasses straddling his thick nose, you might have taken him, at first glance, for any business executive, a bit healthier perhaps than the run of men on the eight-thirty. It was only when you looked closely at him, noticing the barrel chest which threatened to burst out of his well-cut waistcoat, the square shoulders, and the thick neck, that you might realize that you were looking at an ex-sergeant major who had also been a cruiser-weight boxing champion and was now director of a public company.

He said, "Under all the circumstances, I'd say let them make the running."

"I agree," said Oliver. "If you think your opponent's got a bad hand, there's no point in playing his cards for him."

Blackett nodded, and Wilfred Harrap said, "Well, that seems to make it unanimous, doesn't it?"

(iii)

"I suppose your head office knows that you were going to see me this morning," said Mallinson, "and present me with this—this ultimatum."

"It's not an ultimatum," said Mr. Partridge patiently. "It's just a word in season. And I certainly wouldn't have done it without a direct instruction from our Board."

As Manager of the City branch of the London & Home Counties Bank, he had often to deal with petulant industrialists and had developed a certain technique. It made it more difficult in this case that he knew and liked Victor Mallinson personally.

"You can wrap it up much as you like. It's an ultimatum. Unless we peg our overdraft at its present figure, you're going to ring down the curtain."

"You're greatly overstating what I said. Head office would like you to keep your overdraft where it is—or even to lower it. They would have to consider very carefully any request for an increase."

"Which means they would refuse it."

"Not necessarily."

"Mallinson's has banked here for thirty years. We've often exceeded our present figure. Why are you suddenly getting cold feet about us?"

"It's a matter of trends and tendencies," said Mr. Partridge. He looked out of the window at the rain which was belting down and wondered whether any explanation was going to do any good. He knew exactly how Mallinson felt. He had been hit in his most vulnerable place. The financial integrity of his business had been questioned. His pride had been hurt and he was shocked and furious and needed someone to kick. Mr. Partridge had often served as whipping boy in such circumstances. It was one of the ways he earned his very large salary. He said, "In the old days, when you were building up the business and we could see a valid and productive use for our money, it is true that your overdraft rose above its present figure. And our confidence was fully justified. The money went into machinery and stocks and building, and produced an excellent return."

"What do you think it's going into now?" snarled Mallinson. "Strong drink and dancing girls?"

"We don't think that, but an examination of the figures over the last two or three years has been—well—disturbing. It seems that you have been attempting to undercut other firms—at least, that is the only explanation I can see for a cumulative drop in profits."

"We're fighting a trade war. You can't fight without reserves. We've used some of our reserves. It's what reserves are for."

"That's perfectly true. I pointed it out myself to head office. They then queried this figure of twenty-five thousand pounds written off for abortive advertising. That would be a nonrecurrent item, I assume."

"You assume correctly."

"And the further provision this year for legal expenses?"

"Both these last two items are recoverable, and will shortly be recovered."

"If that were to transpire, of course, it would make a considerable difference. You're referring, I take it, to this litigation with Quinn & Nicholson?"

"I'm not fighting Quinn & Nicholson," said Mallinson. "We had a perfectly good relationship with them in the past and we will again in the future. I'm fighting that crook Nugent, who's taken them over. This time he's bitten off more than he can chew, and it's going to choke him."

"You sound confident about that."

"If I sound confident," said Mallinson, smiling for the

first time that morning, "it's because I am confident. I've been advised that we have a very strong case. But I am taking no chances. As a matter of fact, I've arranged to take certain steps this morning which should place the issue beyond any doubt."

"I'm most relieved to hear it," said Mr. Partridge.

When his visitor had gone, he rang for his secretary and dictated a short letter.

> On your instructions I said nothing about calling in our debenture, since I agree this might be premature. We should await the outcome of the present litigation, but meanwhile I am quite clear in my own mind that no increase in overdraft should be allowed. If you will authorize me to do so, I will confirm this in writing forthwith.

The rain had stopped and a pale sun was shining. Mallinson walked back down Moorgate without seeing or hearing anything that was going on round him. Crossing Finsbury Square, he nearly walked in front of a taxi. The driver jammed on his brakes and swore at him. Mallinson stepped back into a puddle which had collected in the gutter. He appeared to notice neither the state of his trousers nor the taxi-driver's language, but walked off along the pavement staring straight in front of him.

"One born every minute," said the taxi-driver.

When he got back to his office, Mallinson took the lift up to his office and went in and sat in front of the fire. Jennie found him there twenty minutes later.

She said, "What *have* you done to your trousers?"

"My trousers?" said Mallinson vaguely. "I must have stepped in a puddle on the way back from the bank. They're dry now."

"You look as if you've been paddling in the Serpentine. I'll get a brush. Put your foot up on that other chair."

While she was brushing off the mud, Jennie said, "You've been off-color lately. I should think you wanted a holiday."

"When this case is over I'll take one."

"I know it's nothing to do with me. You can tell me to shut up if you like, but don't you think it might be a good thing if you gave this case up?" When Mallinson said nothing, she said, "I know I'm speaking out of turn."

"No. Go on."

"Well, what I meant was, is it worth it? It's interfering with your business. I know that. You haven't done a decent day's work since it started. Always being interrupted to go and see those solicitors or make affy-what's-its or look up old papers for them. Honestly, they must think you haven't got anything better to do."

Mallinson grinned and said, "What do you suggest we do about it?"

"Well, you started it. Couldn't you stop it?"

"It's not as easy as that, Jennie. Litigation's a bit like poker. Do you know how to play poker?"

"I've seen it on the films."

"You think you've got a good hand, so you put your chips down. The other chap think's he's got a good hand, too, so he raises you, and you raise him. And by the time you come to the showdown you've both gone so far that you can't *afford* to back out. If I did, I'd have to pay their costs as well as my own, and I don't suppose they're a penny less than mine."

"What *would* it cost?"

"To stop now? Two or three thousand pounds."

"Wouldn't it be worth it?"

"You'd better ask Mr. Partridge about that," said Mallinson grimly.

"And if you win they have to pay back all the money you've spent?"

"That's right."

"And what happens if you go on and don't win? I've done that one. Put your other leg up."

"That's when it comes really expensive. Do you realize that every day in court is going to cost *both* of us a thousand pounds for our leading counsel, about six hundred for the junior counsel, to say nothing of the solicitor who sits behind twiddling his thumbs? That makes the running costs about four thousand pounds a day. Work out what it comes to if you spend four or five days in court."

Jennie, looking rather white, said, "Is what you're saying that you've *got* to win this?"

"That's it," said Mallinson, "and— What do *you* want?"

"Sorry to interrupt your teet-ah-teet," said Mr. Crake, "but I've got Wibberley here."

"All right. Show him in. I'd better see him alone. But you can bring us in some coffee, Jennie, just as soon as it's ready."

The Derek Wibberley who came into the room was no longer the self-confident young advertising executive of three years before. His clothes were as smart as ever— smarter than in the days when he had not had to worry so much about the impression a salesman made on an employer. His shoes were polished and his light-brown hair was carefully parted and smoothed down over his skull. But his eyes were deep set in a face which had grown ten years older.

Mallinson pushed a box of cigarettes across the desk and noted the speed with which Wibberley took one. Smoke it quick and grab another. If I get nothing else out of the interview, I'll be two fags to the good.

He said, "I won't beat about the bush, Wibberley. I think you've had a raw deal."

"Business is business, I suppose," said Wibberley cautiously. He wasn't sure how matters were going to develop.

"As a matter of fact, I wasn't thinking about your unfortunate difference of opinion with Mr. Jacobsen."

"Unfortunate difference of opinion" seemed to Wibberley a curious euphemism for being sacked from the agency and barred by the personal efforts of his head from getting any other job in the advertising field, and being forced to sell insurance on half commission. Still playing it carefully, he said, "What were you thinking of, then?"

"Not long ago I stumbled across an odd piece of information. It indicated to me, quite clearly, that someone known to both of us had played a dirty trick on you. It was not only that the trick was dirty in itself. It also lost you your job. I talked it over with Jacobsen—and we came to certain conclusions."

Wibberley had lost all pretense of disinterest. He was leaning forward, his mouth half open.

"What are you talking about?" he said.

"If I'm going to tell you this, I shall have to ask you to respect a confidence."

"Of course," said Wibberley impatiently.

"You'll promise anything," thought Mallinson, "and break the promise as soon as it suits you." He went on placidly with what he had to say. "A fellow-member of Brett's Club—he had drunk one double whiskey too many or he would not, I think, have said what he did—was talking to me about Oliver Nugent. He recalled passing Nugent on the steps of the club on one occasion when he appeared to be engaged in a slanging match with someone who was trying to stop him getting through the door."

"With me, you mean?"

"From the description it sounded like you. And the timing was about right. About three years ago, he thought."

"He can't be making a complaint about it now?"

"My dear fellow. It wasn't *your* conduct he was criticizing. It was Nugent's. What he said was 'I thought that fellow Nugent was something of a bruiser. Able to look after himself. The chap who was arguing with him was tight and about half his weight anyway. What did he need police protection for?' "

"What did he mean?"

"Apparently the first thing Nugent did when he got into the club was to ring up the police. The phone booth's in the hall. This other chap had stopped to have a word with the porter and couldn't help overhearing him. He got on to —the Wimbledon police I think it was."

"The *Wimbledon* police?"

"Yes. It wouldn't have meant anything to him, but it didn't take me long to work it out."

Wibberley was breathing hard through his nose. He said, in a choked voice, "They were waiting for me when I got home. Of course I was tight and I lashed out. That's what started all the trouble."

"It started more trouble than you know," said Mallinson. Now he was departing from the world of half truth to the world of untruth, and he picked his words carefully. "I expect you thought you lost your job because of the snarl-up over the Lucille advertising. That's only partly true. If it had been that alone, Jacobsen would have overlooked it. But the police court case coming on top of it—well! *You* know how careful top-class agencies have to be."

"Yes," said Wibberley. He was white round the mouth. "What I ought to do is break his neck."

"What you shall do," said Mallinson, "is have a cup of Jennie's excellent coffee. Put it down there, Jennie."

"I didn't know if Mr. Wibberley took sugar. I've put two lumps in his saucer."

"Fine," said Wibberley.

"While we drink it," said Mallinson with a smile, "we can turn our minds to thinking of something a great deal more painful and a great deal more lingering for Mr. Nugent than simply having his neck broken."

As Mallinson, after visiting his bankers, had walked north along Moorgate, Oliver had been walking along it in the opposite direction and on the other pavement. He was making for the offices on Coleman Street of the Westfälischer Group. The invitation to do so had arrived in a neatly typed and politely worded letter that morning.

"It's a trap," said Harrap. "They'll kidnap you."

"A shade obvious, don't you think?" said Oliver.

"It's because it's so obvious that you'll fall for it."

"Just exactly how would they set about kidnapping me in broad daylight in the City of London?"

"I once read a book," said Blackett. "There was this master criminal who wanted to kidnap the hero, and he asked him to the Ritz. What he did was he impregnated the back of one of the armchairs with dope, and when the hero leant the back of his neck against it he went out like a light."

"A bit farfetched," said Harrap.

"It seemed plausible when I read it," said Blackett. "I was only ten at the time."

Oliver was studying the letter. He said, "If they'd meant mischief, surely they'd have telephoned, not written. Anyway, I must go along and see what it's all about. I'll refuse the first two chairs they offer me, Bill. And if I'm not back by twelve, Wilfred, you can send in the Flying Squad."

The offices of the Westfälischer Group looked entirely unsinister. A large blond girl with glasses showed Oliver into a waiting room equipped with tubular steel furniture and a bookcase full of German and Italian pharmaceutical magazines, and reappeared three minutes later to lead him to the office of the Managing Director, Mr. Buchholtzer.

Mr. Buchholtzer was thin and sandy-haired. He got up as Oliver came in, shook hands with a surprisingly vise-like grip, motioned Oliver to a seat beside the desk, and returned to his own chair. He said, "It was kind of you to come, Mr. Nugent. The matters we had to discuss were, we considered, easier to talk about than to write about in the first instance. Do you find that chair uncomfortable?"

"Not at all," said Oliver. "When you say 'we,' do you mean you and me or you and someone else, if you follow me?"

"When I said 'we,' I was referring to our Board in Munich. Our Board has been following the development of Quinn & Nicholson in England under your chairmanship with close interest and attention."

"I have been conscious from time to time of your attention," said Oliver cautiously.

If Mr. Buchholtzer read anything into this remark, he gave no sign of having done so. He said, "We felt that the moment might be ripe for exploring the possibility of a somewhat closer community of operations. Our interests need not conflict. We manufacture in Germany and sell mainly on the Continent and a little in England. You manufacture in England and are beginning to sell on the Continent. It seemed to us that by agreeing on a certain division of territories, we might assist each other to expand."

Oliver lit a cigarette to give himself time to think about this. It was undoubtedly an attractive proposition: an alliance with their main European competitor, with a selling arrangement covering the Continent. Add an American firm and you would have a tripartite cartel of real power. On the other hand, dare he trust them? Might the whole thing be a trick? Having failed to nobble him in any other way, was the shadowy Steyr Engelbach now trying to cast a commercial noose round his neck, ready to jerk it tight at the most inconvenient moment?

Mr. Buchholtzer leaned forward over the desk and said, with a slight smile, "I must not attempt to influence your decision in any way, Mr. Nugent, but there is one item of information which might interest you. Our new Chairman, Rudolf Hartmann—I succeeded him here in London—he instigated this proposal."

"Your *new* Chairman. Then is—"

"Herr Engelbach is no longer with us."

"I see."

"Between you and me, Mr. Nugent, Herr Engelbach had conducted himself in a way which did not commend itself to the rest of the Board. He was a man of great personal force and character, and to such a man a degree of latitude is permitted. But there is a limit. When it became known that he had apparently been using his position and resources of the company to pursue a personal vendetta—"

"A most improper course of action," agreed Oliver. "You spoke of him in the past tense. Do I understand that he is dead?"

"Not dead. He has retired, I understand, to his estates in Austria."

"What you have told me certainly makes a difference. I shall have to think it over and discuss it with my Board. If they agree with me, then our solicitors and accountants should be put in touch with each other."

As he walked back down Cheapside and High Holborn, Oliver was conscious of a lightness of heart which he had not known for years. If this news was true—and there was little point in lying; it would be too easy to check up—if it was true, it meant the removal of the larger of his two worries. He had set eyes on Steyr Engelbach once, and once only, a fleeting figure, seen in the dusk of an Austrian forest. Yet he had been conscious of him for years, conscious of his hatred. The knowledge that someone hates you, and will lose no opportunity to harm you, touches a deep and primitive spring of fear.

So far, Engelbach had tried three times, and each time by chance he had failed. But Oliver had noted the increasing scale of his attacks. The first, the attempt to wreck his car, had been the simplest—probably carried out by a wartime comrade who owed him a good turn. The second had needed more money, and more connections. The third had been the most elaborate in proportion. As Steyr's power and position and resources had increased, so had the threat grown.

Now he had overreached himself. He had lost his position. The venom was still there, but not the power to extrude it. He would live, in retirement, in Austria, feeding on his hatred.

"I shall have to be jolly careful," said Oliver to himself, "about parcels with foreign postmarks."

As soon as he reached his office, he knew that something had happened. The other three directors were all there, and there was an air of crisis you could cut with a knife.

Harrap said, "We've just heard Mallinson's nobbled Wibberley. It's not clear just how he did it, but it's been done."

"Which means he'll give evidence for him," said Blackett, "and tell any damned lie he's told to tell."

"Are we certain?"

"Straight from the horse's mouth," said Taylor.

"In that case we've got no option, have we? If they're going to play it dirty, there's only one thing we can do."

The three of them looked at Taylor, who said nothing, his heavy face unusually grim.

Oliver said, "It's the only way, George. We've got to do it."

(iv)

I joined Quinn & Nicholson as company Secretary a week before the case started. Most of our routine work was suspended while it was on, so I had plenty of time to go along and listen in.

I'd been to that unhappy mixture of cathedral and government department which is known as the Law Courts a number of times before, twice to give evidence in compensation cases and on other occasions simply out of curiosity. The difference between watching a case and being involved in it was exactly the difference between being a happy, carefree Roman citizen and an early Christian.

As Wilfred Harrap and I walked in, by the Strand entrance, we noticed the little groups of press and agency photographers on the steps. I wondered which of the many cases starting that morning was attracting their attention, and had a shock when I realized that it was ours. The "Struggle of the Scents" or the "Battle of the Bottles," as the papers had begun to call it, had caught the fleeting fancy of readers.

"It's going to raise the stakes," said Harrap as we pushed

through the crowd. The photographers had caught sight of Oliver coming in behind us with Kendrick Starkey and Lewis Moffat, and the flashes began to explode.

"How so?"

"It's not just money now. It's reputation. This is going to be a damned bad case to lose."

"We're not going to lose," I said. But I wasn't sure. That's the blight of the Law Courts. You may be convinced of the rightness of your case and dead certain you're going to win, but the moment you get into court a damp depression centers round your middle. You see every flaw in your own case and every strength in the other side's and wonder how you could have been such a mug as to start the thing.

We were in Queen's Bench Four. The ecclesiastical motif was much in evidence here: lancet windows, oak pews with carved finials, and two galleries, one at the back for the choir and a tiny one on the cantoris side for the organist.

Fergus Campbell was there ahead of us with his litigation clerk and a cubic yard of documents. Mr. Justice Mee, a wizened monkey, bright eyes peeping mischievously out of a bundle of robes and wig, took his place at ten o'clock precisely, and Starkey turned to Fergus Campbell and said, in what I thought was an absolutely audible voice, "Crafty little bastard, but quite a sound lawyer."

James Snow, who further emphasized the liturgical nature of the proceedings by looking and sounding like a lay preacher, rose and opened his client's case with commendable brevity.

It had, he said, been no pleasure to businessmen like Mallinson's to waste their time and money, to say nothing of the valuable time of the court, in a case of this sort. Here he shot a quick look at Mr. Justice Mee, who stared blandly back as if to say, "You don't fool me. We're both getting paid for this."

His client's hand, said Mr. Snow, had been forced. They and their colleagues had devoted years of patient research, and a large sum of their shareholders' money, to perfecting and bringing out a new perfume, to be known as Lucille. The name had been chosen quite arbitrarily, being a girl's Christian name, of Anglo-French origin, but in common use in this country.

"Lux," said the Judge.

"I beg your Lordship's pardon."

"Lux, lucis. The name is derived from the Latin word meaning 'light.' "

"I am obliged to your Lordship."

"There's a school of thought that connects it with the Roman satirist Lucilius."

"Shortly," said Mr. Snow hurriedly, "before this new perfume was due to be placed on the market, the defendants discovered, by means unknown to us but presumably by some form of industrial espionage, both the name of the product and the nature of the advertising campaign which was being launched in support of it. They thereupon set on foot a deliberate campaign to slander the name and cheapen and vilify the product. I do not propose at this point to go into the details of what they did. All that will appear fully from the evidence I propose to call. But I would like to say one word first. My clients are not bringing this action out of any motives of personal spite or vindictiveness. In many ways it is an action they would much rather have not have brought at all. But they felt that their good name and the ethical standards of the business in which they are engaged forced them to do so."

"My housemaster used to talk like that before he beat you," said Starkey. *"He* always did it against his will and for highly moral reasons. He was a bloody clergyman, too."

Mr. Snow said, "I will now call Mr. Jacobsen."

Mr. Jacobsen did not occupy them long. He gave some impressive details of the care, forethought, artistic endeavor, and money which had been spent on the promotion of Lucille, was mildly cross-examined by Lewis Moffat, and was allowed to escape.

Mr. Crake came next. He presented the same picture from the company's point of view, confirmed the costings produced by Mr. Jacobsen, and gave an estimate of the loss which they had suffered by having to cancel their advertising campaign, withdraw the complete stock, relabel and repack it, and mount the same campaign six months later.

Mr. Starkey said, "Tell us, Mr. Crake. If it cost you such a lot of money to cancel your original campaign, why did you do it?"

"I've already explained."

"Explain it again."

"Because three days before we were due to start, Quinn's brought out this lavatory cleaner. Practically the same name, same format, same adverts."

"And you thought that people might *confuse* the two products?"

"That was the whole idea."

"Whose idea?"

"Quinn's, of course."

"You don't think that their advertisements appearing three days before yours might have been a coincidence."

"I'm bloody sure it wasn't."

"When answering questions in this court," said Mr. Justice Mee, "you will not employ the language of the barroom or the barrack square."

"I'm sorry, sir—my Lord."

"This is not a B.B.C. television program."

"No, my Lord."

"Tell me, Mr. Crake," said Starkey, "did you have any reason to suspect that a campagin of this sort might be launched by your rivals?"

"No. Why should we?"

"I don't *know* why you should. The maneuvers of the advertising industry are a closed book to me. I was simply asking you a question. Did you think that your campaign might be anticipated?"

"No. We didn't."

"Then why"—here Mr. Starkey rustled through the pages of his brief like a snake approaching through the dry grass—"why, at about that time, did you get one of your subordinates to make special inquiries about the bookings of advertising space on the days in question?"

"On what days?" said Mr. Crake, playing for time.

"On Thursday and Friday, July 1st and 2nd."

"Have I got to answer that? It seems to me to be irrelevant."

"If you're addressing me," said the Judge, "I shall rule that the matter is entirely relevant. In answer to an earlier question, you said that you made *no* inquiries about other bookings. It is now suggested that you *did* make certain inquiries. If you did, your earlier answer is incorrect."

"Well, Mr. Crake?"

"Now that you remind me," said Mr. Crake, "it is true that I did make some inquiries about the bookings on July 1st and 2nd. It was a routine matter and it had slipped my memory."

"I see," said Mr. Starkey. "Yes. I see. It slipped your memory. Although you caused one of your subordinates to make two *special* trips to the City to check up on those bookings."

"I've told you. I'd forgotten all about it."

"Yes," said Mr. Starkey. "You told us that." He referred again to the papers in front of him, and said, "Would you call the advertising business an ethical one?"

"As ethical as most."

"What does that mean?"

"It's as ethical as its clients allow it to be."

"And you were one of its clients?"

"Certainly."

Mr. Starkey resumed his seat. The Judge looked at Mr. Snow, who shook his head. He said, "Counsel has no more questions for you, Mr. Crake. You may stand down."

Mr. Crake left the box unwillingly. He may have felt he had not done justice to himself. While all this was going on, I had been watching Victor Mallinson and Wibberley. They were sitting in front with their solicitors. The revelation that the opposition knew a good deal of what had gone on inside their own offices had hit them hard. I wondered if this was the object of Starkey's tactics. A succession of scribbled notes had passed between them. Victor Mallinson was looking grim. Derek Wibberley was reading the note which had been handed to him, and he had turned round to have a word with his solicitor. He jumped when his name was called, scrambled to his feet, and made his way to the box.

His own counsel handled him very skillfully, I thought. The story he told wasn't designed to make him look like a hero. In fact, it made him look rather a fool. But a comparatively honest fool. He went through the whole of his association with Bargulder's, the work he did on Quinn & Nicholson's account, the growth of that account, the launching of the Tendresse campaign.

"It was about that time, I believe, that you suggested to

your employers that they might consider giving you a seat on the Board."

"Yes. I did."

"Because of the importance of this particular account?"

"That was the main reason. Yes."

"Looking back, Mr. Wibberley, do you think your request was justified?"

"Looking back, I think I'd got a bit too big for my boots."

There is nothing more ensnaring than a man who admits having made a fool of himself. I could see the jury's sympathy going out to Wibberley.

"When you were forced to leave Bargulder's, can you tell me why you applied for a job in Mr. Jacobsen's firm?"

"There really are only three or four firms of that sort of size and standing. I did approach one of the others but they hadn't any vacancies."

"And Jacobsen's offered you a job?"

"They did. And I took it."

"Had you any *particular* reason for going to Jacobsen's?"

"No particular reason. Jobs aren't all that easy to get in my line."

"In fact, I believe, after leaving Jacobsen's you were actually out of advertising for nearly three years."

"That's right. I've just got back."

"With the same firm?"

"Yes."

"Why did you leave them?"

"I didn't leave them." Wibberley paused, then added, "There was trouble over a driving offense."

"You needn't go into all that if it isn't relevant," said Mr. Justice Mee kindly. "You can just tell us the facts. That you left them and are now working for them again."

He, too, seemed to be brimming over with sympathy. Wibberley said, "Thank you, sir," and smiled faintly.

"Now, I want you to listen most particularly to this question," said Mr. Snow. "When you left the Bargulder agency and joined Jacobsen's, did you take away with you any documents or drawings relating to the Quinn & Nicholson account which you had been looking after?"

"Well—"

"You'll remember that you're on oath and I'm sure that you'll answer the question honestly."

"Yes, I did."

"What were they?"

"They were some layouts that I'd made. Suggested layouts of the Tendresse advertisements."

"Why did you take them?"

"It was a silly thing to do. But I'd done a lot of work on them. I was rather pleased with them. And since I'd been kicked out—well—to be honest I didn't see why Barguider's should have them."

"Wrong, as you say," said Mr. Snow. "Understandable, perhaps. Did you show these advertising layouts to your new employers?"

"It crossed my mind. I may even have suggested it to them."

"But you didn't?"

"I didn't because they wouldn't let me. They didn't think it would be playing the game."

By this time Wibberley was everybody's favorite. The Judge was twinkling at him, the jury had taken him to their heart, and Mr. Snow was brooding over him with the benevolence of an Inquisitor over a repentant heretic.

Speaking impartially, it seemed to me that they had steered round the dangerous corners very skillfully. Mr. Starkey had been spending most of his time talking to his junior and had not, I thought, been listening to the proceedings at all. However, I was wrong.

He said, "Since you raised the point yourself, Mr. Wibberley, perhaps you'll allow me to pursue it for a moment. Why did you part company with Jacobsen's agency three years ago?"

Mr. Snow slid swiftly to his feet.

"I think your Lordship has already ruled that that particular matter is irrelevant."

The Judge said, "I told the witness that if it embarrassed him he need not pursue the matter, but since he volunteered the information, counsel is entitled to cross-examine him on it."

Mr. Snow sat down again. I found it difficult to explain. There was nothing to warrant it, but the atmosphere in court had suddenly changed. It was as though someone had opened a window and the temperature had dropped ten degrees.

"Well, Mr. Wibberley?"

"I don't mind telling you, though it all seems rather pointless. I was involved—unfortunately involved—in a brush with the police. I hit one of them and I went to jail for thirty days."

"And you mean to tell us that for this misdemeanor, which had nothing to do with your job, you were dismissed without notice?"

"Agencies don't like their staff getting mixed up with things like that. I bear them no grudge. They've given me my job back again. A better one, actually."

"Perhaps that's because they have a guilty conscience," suggested Mr. Starkey.

"I don't follow."

"For dismissing you for something you hadn't yet done."

Wibberley stared at him.

"You were dismissed by Jacobsen's agency on Thursday, July 1st. Your cards were stamped down to the end of that week. That's right, isn't it?"

"I—I really can't remember."

"We can recall Mr. Jacobsen if you wish. He will have his firm's records."

"I'll take your word for it," muttered Wibberley.

"And your brush with the police occurred on Thursday, July 8th?"

"If you say so."

"Yes or no?"

"It was about then."

"A remarkable piece of clairvoyance on the part of Mr. Jacobsen, don't you think? To dismiss you for something that was *going* to happen in a week's time."

"What really happened," said Wibberley, "is that we had a difference of opinion over a professional matter. Mr. Jacobsen did threaten to sack me. I'm quite sure he'd have thought better of it if it hadn't been for the other matter— the things were cumulative."

Neat, I thought. Not quite neat enough, though.

"You'll remember when you entered the box," said Mr.

Starkey, "that you undertook to tell the truth, the whole truth, and nothing but the truth?"

"Certainly. You asked me about something that happened three years ago. For the moment I'd forgotten the exact sequence of events."

"Then think carefully about my next question. You told my learned friend that when you left the Bargulder agency you took certain drawings—layouts, I think you called them—with you. You admitted that it had crossed your mind to show them to Mr. Jacobsen, but that he wouldn't let you."

"I said that, yes."

"You said it, but is it true?"

"Perfectly true."

"You're sure of that? This isn't another matter that happened three years ago and may have slipped your memory?"

"I am quite certain," said Wibberley.

"And you agree with Mr. Jacobsen's ethical view on the matter? He said, I think, that it wouldn't be playing the game."

"That's right."

"In fact, to come over from one agency to another with a client's confidential documents and to show them to a new employer would be an extremely dirty trick, wouldn't it?"

"I agree."

"And if a man was capable of a dirty trick like that, you wouldn't place much reliance on his word, would you?"

I think Wibberley said "No," but it was almost inaudible.

(v)

Victor Mallinson's examination-in-chief opened the proceedings on the second day. What he had to say was not in itself of great importance. Most of it had been said before by Jacobsen and Crake. What mattered was the impression he made on the jury. This was the man they had been waiting to hear, the man who had made the complaint, who said he had been unfairly treated, who was asking for their sympathy—and their verdict.

I had to admit that he did very well. His easy, courteous,

slightly self-deprecating manner, coupled with his quick reflexes, made him a formidable witness.

He repeated the sequence we had heard three times before—briefly from Jacobsen, bluntly from Crake, and effusively from Wibberley. The conception of Lucille, the care and attention lavished on it in the antenatal period, the expectations of its proud parents, all rudely shattered by the brutal, unwarranted, unethical last-minute attack which had caused the infant to be stillborn.

It occurred to me to wonder how Mr. Starkey was going to deal with this witness. I was pretty sure that rudeness wouldn't pay off. Mallinson was too quick on his feet for the bludgeon. I could visualize counsel trying it and failing and the strong reaction of the jury in favor of a witness who succeeds in getting the better of a bullying counsel.

I needn't have worried. Mr. Starkey was far too old a hand to fall into any such trap. His manner, when he rose to cross-examine, was as courteous as Mallinson's own.

He said, "Your partner, Mr. Crake, told us that the advertising profession was as ethical as its clients allowed it to be. Would you go along with that?"

"I should need notice of that question. It covers rather a wide field."

"I'll be more specific. If the client wanted to pursue a course which was—I won't say criminal—unethical, would the advertising agency feel impelled to stop him, or would it say, 'you're the boss. You're paying us. We don't like it but we'll do what you tell us'?"

"It's a theoretical question," said Mallinson cautiously, "but I should say that if the course was clearly unethical, a good advertising agency would refuse to act."

"What sort of conduct would you describe as 'clearly unethical'?"

"I can't think of examples on the spur of the moment."

"Would you include industrial espionage?"

"Oddly enough, no."

"Then you approve of it?"

"I neither approve nor disapprove. Business is war. Both sides employ spies without necessarily approving of spying."

It was a good debating answer, but I don't think the jury liked it very much. Mr. Starkey said, "Have *you* ever installed a spy in your enemy's camp?"

"Personally, no."

Now, this was a lie and Mr. Starkey knew it was a lie, because Oliver had told him about Philippa. Also Oliver had refused to let him use the information so that Mallinson was, in fact, quite safe. But he was not to know this, and Mr. Starkey, who was watching him with close attention out of his heavy-lidded eyes, noted the very slight wariness in the witness's eyes, the tensing at the corners of his mouth which betrayed him. It is always of interest to counsel to see how a witness behaves when he is forced to tell a lie.

He said softly, *"Never, Mr. Mallinson?"*

"Never."

Mr. Starkey let the word hang. Then he returned to his brief, shuffled through the papers, and said, "Your partner, Mr. Crake, was telling us about the first Lucille campaign. The one which had to be postponed. He said that you mounted the *same* campaign six months later. Was it, in fact, the same?"

"Not word for word, no. Advertising's a very topical matter."

"But broadly the same?"

"In broad terms, yes."

"Then your second campaign was also directed to making fun of Quinn & Nicholson's Tendresse advertising?"

"I'm afraid I don't follow that at all."

"You said that both campaigns were broadly similar. My instructions are that your first campaign—the one you had to abandon—was designed almost exclusively to taking the wind out of your rival's sails."

"That's ridiculous."

"My instructions are that you knew—or thought you knew—that Quinn & Nicholson were running a line of 'snob' advertising and that your original campaign was designed to crab this."

"Our original campaign was designed to sell Lucille. And for no other purpose at all."

"My instructions are that you actually had in your office three proofs of Quinn & Nicholson's advertisements side by side with your own and that yours were purposely set out in the same type and format."

"If those are your instructions, they're wrong."

"You deny having seen any of your competitor's proposed advertisements?"

"I deny it emphatically."

Again Mr. Starkey noted with satisfaction that slight tensing of the jaw muscles. He said, "Then I have no more questions."

Mr. Snow said, "That concludes the plaintiff's case."

Victor Mallinson left the box and walked back to his seat. Mr. Starkey had been engaged in a whispered conversation with Lewis Moffat, in the row behind him. Moffat now spoke to Fergus Campbell, who squeezed out of his place and left the court. Mr. Starkey said, "Before calling my first witness, I should like to say something. My learned friend"—here he bared his teeth briefly in the direction of Mr. Snow—"in opening his case, made an observation which many of you must have found curious. He said that the plaintiff *regretted* having to bring the case. It may have occurred to you that he could easily have spared himself such a painful duty. He is the aggressor. It is a simple matter for an aggressor not to start an attack. For the man who is attacked, it is not so easy. He has to defend himself. And he has to defend himself in the best way he can. For myself, I would much have preferred that the truth in this unfortunate case—and I am in hearty agreement with my learned friend that it is a case which should never have been brought—had been elicited out of the mouths of his own witnesses. In view of certain of their replies, the defense is forced to take a course which I, personally, regret. It is never pleasant to have to ask a man's private secretary to give evidence against him."

In the light of Mr. Starkey's questions, and by the process of elimination, I think Mallinson's must already have arrived at the truth. I could almost signpost, from the expression on his face, the stages by which he had got there. The first glimmer of suspicion, dismissed as an impossibility. The returning nagging doubt. The final growth of certainty that this unthinkable thing *must* be, because it was the only answer to an otherwise unanswerable conundrum.

(In fact, it had not been difficult. Oliver had taken two precautions. He had set Jennie up in a flat, apart from her family. And he had seen that she got her references from the typing school. In a sense, even these precautions were unnecessary. It was the bridge game over again. Mallinson had been too confident in his own tricks to suspect that others might play them back on him.)

When Jennie came into court, I saw him go white as paper, and thought for a moment that he was going to pass out. Then the blood rushed back, and his face was as scarlet as if it had been slapped.

Jennie had been outside in the corridor, and Mrs. Comrie had been holding her hand. "I could hear the poor girl's teeth chattering in her head," she said. "If I hadna' been there, she'd have run away long syn."

That I could believe. I had been there the previous evening when the decision had been made, and have rarely seen anything more distressing. I think Oliver had asked me to be there to ease the tension and make it seem a bit more official, but it was still a girl having her arm twisted by two men.

Jennie had started by refusing, point-blank, to give evidence in court.

"I've told *you* about it," she said. "You know exactly what happened."

Her father said, "That's not good enough."

"I'm afraid we can't give evidence about what you've told us," said Oliver.

"I suppose not. But—"

"For God's sake!" George Taylor looked as baffled as if a newly joined recruit were defying him on the parade ground. "What's come over you, girl? Didn't we wangle your job so you could keep an eye on Mallinson?"

"I know."

"Then what's the snag? All you've got to do is to stand up in court and answer a few questions. They can't eat you."

Jennie said, "It's difficult to explain. He's treated me right. I just don't want to do it, that's all."

"You're not soft about him, I suppose?"

"Don't be daft."

"Then what the hell's wrong with you?"

"Stop shouting at me."

Oliver gave Taylor a look which would have stopped a tank. He could see that he was simply putting Jennie's back up. He said, "Don't bully the girl, George. Look here,

Jennie. You'll have to make up your own mind about this, but I'd just like you to know how important it is. If we lose this case, we lose more than money. We lose reputation. And when that's gone, a business might as well put up the shutters. We'll all be out of a job."

"It can't all depend on me, surely."

Oliver said, very gently, "I don't know, Jennie. You never know what's going to happen when you get into a court of law. It depends a good deal on what they say. I'll promise you this. Unless it's absolutely essential for you to give evidence, we'll keep you out of the box."

Jennie said, "Oh dear," and started crying.

Of course, in the end she promised to do what they wanted.

"Now, Miss Taylor," said Mr. Starkey after the preliminaries were over. "I'd like you to tell us about an occasion —I don't know the exact date, but you'll probably remember it because I believe it was the first time Mr. Wibberley came to your offices."

"Yes, I remember Mr. Wibberley coming."

"Who was there?"

"There was Mr. Mallinson and Mr. Crake and the advertising man, Mr. Jacobsen."

"And you?"

"Yes. I was there."

"Good. Now, would you mind telling us, in your own words, exactly what happened?"

"It was some time ago," said Jennie faintly. I felt George Taylor stir angrily in his seat beside me. If he'd been a tiger, it would have been the moment when the tip of his tail would have started twitching. Oliver, next to him, looked bored.

"I don't want you to remember actual things that were said." Mr. Starkey's voice was soft as silk. "You could hardly be expected to do that after all this time. Just see if you can tell us what happened."

"Well, Mr. Wibberley had these three pictures."

"Can you remember what they were?"

"They were sort of posters. Roughs, I think he called them. They were advertising a new perfume Quinn & Nicholson were doing."

"Tendresse?"

"That's right."

"And what did they do with these posters?"

"They had them side by side on the table and they were comparing them and saying how much better their lot were."

"Was anything else said?"

"There was something about their lot being in the same type as Quinn's. I gathered they'd been got up to look like them only better. And would they get away with it, and Mr. Jacobsen said he'd talked to his lawyer and his lawyer had said they would."

"I'm getting confused," said Mr. Justice Mee. "Which lawyer said what to whom?"

"I gather, my Lord, that Mr. Jacobsen had consulted his own lawyer as to whether they would be in danger of legal process if their Lucille advertisements were markedly similar to the Tendresse advertisements."

"And those were the Lucille advertisements which *didn't* come out?"

"That is so."

"Because of the Loo-Seal advertisements which came out looking like *them?*"

"That is correct."

Mr. Justice Mee said, "Thank you, Mr. Starkey," and made a lengthy note.

Mr. Starkey said, "Now, Miss Taylor. I'd like you to turn your mind to a much more recent incident. Can you recall Mr. Wibberley visiting your office again in the last few weeks?"

"Yes, it was about ten days ago."

"Were you present at his interview with your employer?"

"I was in and out."

"Can you remember anything that was said when you were in the room?"

"The second time—when I came back with the coffee—Mr. Wibberley was saying how he'd like to break Mr. Nugent's neck, and Mr. Mallinson said he could think of a better way of doing him down."

"He didn't explain what that way was?"

"Not while I was there."

"I expect we can guess what he had in mind," said Mr. Starkey, and sat down.

It was plain to Mr. Snow—as it was to everyone else in court—that he had to break Jennie's evidence or go down. There were two roads open to him. He could suggest she was honestly mistaken; that it had all happened a long time ago; that she had forgotten exactly what was said and done; that in an honest but misguided attempt to help her father's firm (it was clear from the flurry of notes which had attended her appearance that her relationship to George Taylor was known) she had misconstrued certain words and actions.

If he had taken this course, I think he might have had a chance. Instead he set out to break her down entirely and show that she was a liar.

In a vicious cross-examination, which lasted the whole of that afternoon, he accused her of being a spy and a cheat; of having wormed her way into the confidence of her employer, who had trusted her implicitly, with the intention of telling lies about him, lies which would serve the purpose of her real employers.

Now, such an assault is a two-edged weapon. If it succeeds, it succeeds completely. If it fails, it can turn in the hand of the user and wound him mortally. Under sympathetic questioning and probing, Jennie might easily have been led into such a maze of qualifications and contradictions that the jury would hardly have known whom to believe. Under bullying, she showed a surprising streak of native toughness. It certainly surprised Mr. Snow. It also annoyed him. And when counsel gets annoyed his client's case suffers.

When he used the word "treachery" in a question, Mr. Justice Mee leaned forward from the bench and said, "I think, Mr. Snow, that you ought to reconsider the form of that question. We are here to discover the facts, not to dissect this witness's character."

After that it was a walkover.

When Jennie left the witness box, Mr. Starkey said, "It had been my intention to call further witnesses, but in the circumstances I see no point in doing so. The evidence we have just heard will have made it abundantly clear that what happened in this case was that the plaintiff attempted to discredit the defendant's product and was out-maneuvered. The biter can hardly complain if he gets bitten."

Mr. Justice Mee felt it to be his duty to sum up at length, but no one paid much attention to him. The jury had made up its collective mind before Jennie left the witness box. They found for the defendant with costs.

My last impression was of Victor Mallinson's eyes, in a very white face, following Jennie as she walked out of court with her father and Oliver.

(vi)

We had not planned any particular celebration. It was the sort of party which develops spontaneously. Oliver said, "It's ten past five. By the time we get there the bar'll be open at Brett's. If it isn't we'll damned well open it. Come along, all of you."

The invitation was clearly intended to include not only the lawyers but Jennie, who was standing close to her father. She wasn't actually holding on to him, but she looked as if she was glad to have him there.

George Taylor said, "I think I'd better take Jennie home first. She's got a rotten headache. No wonder after being slanged by that prime bastard in a wig. I felt like wringing his neck for him."

"He wrung his own neck," said Oliver. "If Jennie won't come with us we'll send her home in style. That's the least we can do." He never seemed to have any difficulty in attracting taxis, and three of them were already lined up along the pavement in front of the Law Courts. He put Jennie into the first one. As he did so, I caught a glimpse of her face. It was twisted up like a rolled handkerchief and almost as white as Mallinson's had been. I think it was only then that I fully realized how much we had hurt her.

The rest of us got into the other two taxis and went round to Brett's. We were a silent crowd to start with. The directors had been living under the shadow of litigation for so long that they could hardly realize that they were not only out of the wood but successfully out of it. However, a round of drinks quickly thawed us out. Mr. Starkey obliged with his celebrated but unrepeatable story of the male litigant with a cleft palate and a delusion that he was pregnant. After that the party warmed up nicely. The third round of drinks was bought by Jacob Naumann, who looked in with Saul Feinberg to congratulate Oliver and attached himself to the crowd round the bar. Other members, who had been following the progress of the case and had heard the result, came in to tell Oliver that they'd always been quite sure he was going to win, and the thing gradually became a Roman triumph.

I knew very few of the people personally and was happy to sit in a corner drinking the glass of whiskey which was thrust into my hand at regular intervals and watching Oliver.

I had seen him drinking before but never with quite the steady ferocity that he showed that evening. I lost count of the singles and doubles that went down, but on any computation he must have drunk between half and three-quarters of a bottle before the calls of dinner began to thin the party out.

Taylor had been one of the first to go. In the general excitement I think I was the only person who noticed his defection. Normally it was the sort of impromptu party that would have suited him down to the ground, with an added attraction that he was doing his drinking in one of the most exclusive clubs in London. But he had been uneasy from the first, and it wasn't hard to guess why.

Three whiskies later I had forgotten all about him.

Jennie shared a small flat with two other girls in a converted house in that honeycomb of converted houses which lies south of Kensington High Street. One of the girls worked a late shift at a security printing plant, and the other had aspirations to be an actress and spent most of her evenings hanging round Television Centre chatting up producers and script editors. It was the knowledge that both of them were likely to be out and that Jennie would be on her own that had pulled an uneasy Taylor away from the party and put him into a taxi heading west.

He stopped twice—the first time at a delicatessen store in Soho, where he bought a veal-and-ham pie and a carton of cold potato salad, and the second time at a pub, where

he got hold of half a bottle of gin and a bottle of sweet
white wine.

A considerable experience of dealing with homesick re-
cruits had convinced him that food and drink were the
answer to most human problems. He could be wrong, in
which case he would have to eat and drink the stuff himself. As the taxi trundled slowly along Knightsbridge, it
occurred to him that he had never known much about his
daughter even when she was at home. Now that she was
living on her own, he knew nothing at all. Might it be possible that she had, in fact, fallen for that bearded pansy
who employed her? He hoped not, but girls of her age
did the strangest things. Or had Mallinson taken the initia-
tive? Had he taken advantage of his position and superior
education and money to seduce her? If he had, he deserved
to have his bloody neck broken.

The taxi came to a halt in a traffic block outside Har-
rods. Taylor was suddenly conscious of being furiously
hungry. He thought of starting on the veal-and-ham pie,
but realized that he had nothing to eat it with. As he was
trying to work this out, the taxi jerked forward again.

"What do you think he's going to do?" asked Blackett.

"He's bust to the wide," said Oliver. "Don't you agree,
Wilfred?"

"I think he must be," said Harrap. "I had it on good authority that the bank was clamping down on his overdraft.
When he's finished paying both sets of costs, he won't
have any credit left."

"He hasn't got much credit left now," said Oliver. He
was looking at the late editions of the evening papers that
Naumann had brought along with him. In his summing
up, Mr. Justice Mee had worked in a few caustic com-
ments about pots calling kettles black, and since nothing
more important was occupying the public mind just then,
these had won a headline and a half share of the front
page.

"What can the bank do?" said Blackett. "They can squeal
for their money, but if it isn't there they can't get it. They
could put them into liquidation but that wouldn't do
them a lot of good, either."

Oliver said, "What they'll do is look for a purchaser. And they won't have very far to look."

I could see Blackett almost licking his lips. "You mean us?" he said. "Do you think we're big enough to do that?"

"In business," said Oliver, and he suddenly sounded completely sober, "you're big enough to do anything you dare to do."

As soon as Jennie was safely back in her flat, she had had the good cry which had been threatening for the last few hours, then washed her face and restored her make-up as carefully as if she were going out for the evening, boiled a kettle, and made herself a cup of Nescafé. Then she switched on the hired television set in the corner of the communal living room, but it was suffering from a fit of the staggers, so she switched it off and put on a record of Marlene Dietrich singing "Where Have All the Flowers Gone?" This was so sad that it made her cry again so she switched it off, decided to change into pajamas, and while she was undressing put on a saucepan of water to boil herself an egg.

When the bell rang, she knew it would be her father. She shouted out "Hold on a moment," flung on a dressing gown, and opened the front door.

Victor Mallinson was standing outside.

The hall was so dark that, for a moment, she didn't recognize him. Then she stood staring at him.

Mallinson said, "I'm sorry to startle you. Can I come in?" His voice sounded high and unnatural.

Jennie said, "Well, I don't know—"

"I won't keep you long."

"There's no one else here."

Mallinson said "No?" in a disinterested way, and walked past her into the tiny hallway of the flat and through into the living room. Jennie was about to close the front door, but thought better of it. She left it a few inches ajar and then turned round and followed Mallinson, closing the living-room door behind her.

He was standing in front of the fireplace with his back to her. As she came in, he swung round and she saw his face clearly for the first time. Its pallor was emphasized by the tiny, livid patches under the eyes. Her first thought had been that he might be drunk. Something was working powerfully in him but it wasn't alcohol.

He said in the same high, flat voice, "I'm sorry to force my way in like this but I couldn't go to bed tonight until I'd seen you. I had to find out why you did it."

"What—"

"I didn't think I'd treated you badly. Perhaps I'd annoyed you? Upset you in some way without knowing it?"

"Of course you hadn't. It was simply—"

"If I had, I can assure you it was quite unintentional." Jennie realized that he wasn't listening to her at all. He wasn't even talking to her. He was arguing with himself. Arguing with his own hurt pride. She thought, "If I say anything nice to him, he's going to burst into tears. What he really needs is a doctor and a sleeping dose, or something like that. I wonder if a cup of coffee—"

She said, "Would you like me to make you a cup of coffee," and started toward the kitchen. The move brought her closer to him than she had intended.

He put a hand up and grabbed her, not roughly, but very firmly by the arm. He said, "Jennie, how *could* you?"

Jennie tried to pull her arm away, found that she couldn't, and gave an involuntary scream.

It was not loud, but her father heard it at the moment when he reached the front door. He kicked it open, dropped the food and drink that he was holding, put his shoulder to the door of the living room, and went through it like an enraged bull carrying a locked gate on its horns.

Then he hit Mallinson.

The first blow, a clumsy right-hander, landed in the small of Mallinson's back, to one side, and swung him round. The second, with the left hand, hit him in the bottom of the stomach and doubled him up. Jennie had just time to gasp out "Stop!" when the third blow, an uppercut with all the strength of George Taylor's shoulders behind it and all the weight of his body under it, hit Mallinson full in the throat.

This was the blow that killed him.

"When I was a boy at school," said Oliver, "they used to make us go to chapel every morning. A brisk, no-nonsense fifteen-minute service. It was like cleaning your teeth.

Some of the boys used to finish off the prep they hadn't had time to do the night before. Others used to spend the time gooping at whichever of the smaller boys in the choir they happened to be in love with at the time. One boy used to shave with an electric razor which he worked off a pocket battery. If you'd had any true religious feelings, a course of those morning services would have killed them dead."

"*Did* you ever have any religious feelings?" asked Wilfred Harrap.

The four of us were alone in the bar. Even the barman had left us to attend to the members in the cardroom.

"At the age of ten," said Oliver, "I believed firmly in God. I confused him with my father sometimes, but that was all right because I believed in my father, too."

Bill Blackett said, with genuine curiosity in his voice, "Do you believe in anything now?"

"Of course I do," said Oliver. "I believe in success."

As he said this, he slid off the stool on which he was half perched, screwed up his face in a way which suggested that he was trying very hard to think out the answer to an insoluble problem, and folded forward onto his knees on the floor. Our discussion on religion was still running in my head, and I thought for a moment that this was a grotesque parody of prayer. Then I realized that the look on Oliver's face was pain. He heeled slowly over, holding his chest in both hands and fighting for breath.

Blackett started to say something about never expecting to see Oliver pass out, but Harrap was already down beside him, tearing open his coat and shirt. He said, over his shoulder, to me, "Get downstairs quick. Frank Collet is having dinner here. With any luck he won't have left." And to Blackett, who was still staring stupidly, "Ring the Middlesex Hospital Emergency Service. Tell them it's a bad heart case. They'll know what to bring."

The shock seemed to have driven the drink out of me. I found Collet, the heart surgeon, finishing his coffee and blurted out the news. He put down his coffee cup carefully, rose to his feet, and said, "If it's as bad as that, I can't do much without drugs."

"We've rung the Middlesex."

"Right. In the upstairs bar you say?"

As I turned to follow him, one of the club porters stopped me. He seemed to be as nearly upset about something as a good club porter can ever get. He said, "Are you with Mr. Nugent's party?"

I thought for a moment that the ambulance might have arrived in record time, then realized that this was absurd.

The porter said, "There's a message for him."

"He can't attend to anything now."

"Then perhaps you'd better take it for him, sir. It's very urgent." I stared at him stupidly. "It's the police."

(vii)

Two things combined to save Oliver's life. The fact that Collet was on the spot and the fact that Oliver's system was chock-full of whiskey. In some odd way the alcohol in the blood neutralized the blockage sufficiently to keep the heart fed until they could get him under the proper drugs.

It was touch and go for the whole of that night. It would have been the longest and most miserable in my life if I hadn't had too much to do to stop and think.

I went round to the Kensington flat. I assumed that the police would be looking after George Taylor, but I might be able to help Jennie. I needn't have worried about her. She'd been taken care of by the lady who owned the house, a big gray-haired woman who treated everyone with contempt. She had given Jennie a powerful sleeping pill and refused to let anyone into her bedroom.

The C.I.D. Inspector turned out to be quite a sympathetic character. He had got George's story from him. I think George expected to be arrested there and then, and was quite prepared to be led off in handcuffs. The Inspector thought differently. He solemnly inspected the broken wine bottle and veal-and-ham pie and potato salad, which were still lying messed up together in the hall where George had dropped them, and the small table which he had kicked to pieces in his whirlwind entry. He concluded that it was all pretty strong evidence that George was speaking the truth and that he really had broken in and found his daughter being assaulted. He warned George that he would be needed for inquiries and sent him home in a taxi. I think he sent one of his men to keep an eye on him, but

I'm not sure. The police never react the way you think they're going to.

Then I went back to the hospital but wasn't allowed to do anything sensible. It was five o'clock and a morning like a dirty shirt was spreading itself over the roofs of London when I crawled into bed. I didn't sleep much.

That afternoon we had an emergency Board meeting and started to clear up the mess. Wilfred Harrap took over as Chairman. With his City connections he was the obvious man for the job. One of the first things he did was to promote my understudy to be Secretary and ask me to join the Board. We then set about looking after George Taylor. He reserved his defense in the police court and was committed to the Old Bailey charged with manslaughter, with half a dozen other felonious-homicide and grievous bodily-harm charges slung in for good luck.

Fergus Campbell briefed Starkey and we came up in front of Mr. Justice Crawley, who seemed to take an instant dislike to all of us and summed up dead against George. I thought he was booked for two years at least.

I had underestimated the British jury. We had ten men and two women, all of them middle-class and nine of them married. If Mr. Justice Crawley thought they were going to let a father suffer for protecting his daughter from the lascivious attentions of her employer, then Mr. Justice Crawley could think again. They closed their ears to every word of his summing up, retired long enough for a quick cigarette, and came back and found the prisoner not guilty on all charges. Several of them made a point of congratulating him afterward.

One of the side results of the publicity attending the case was that Jennie got about forty proposals of marriage. One of the proposers, a very nice boy who played regularly at fullback for West Ham, was so persistent that she eventually said yes. The directors of Quinn & Nicholson gave them a canteen of cutlery.

The next thing we had to worry about was Oliver's stake in the company. The doctors were quite clear that he had to retire. The trouble was that although he was now a rich man, practically the whole of his fortune was in his large shareholding in Quinn & Nicholson. We talked about buying them ourselves, but it was going to stretch our resources to breaking point.

While we were still trying to work this out, Jacob Naumann called on us. He brought us a piece of information, and a proposition.

The information was that he had just bought a controlling interest in Mallinson's. They had been mortally hit, first by the lawsuit going against them, then by the death of their Chairman, and finally by the bank withdrawing all support, a thing which banks do automatically when you need it most. I imagine that Naumann had bought Victor Mallinson's entire holding and had then picked up other parcels of shares on the cheap until he had the whole thing in his pocket.

His proposition was to purchase Oliver's shares in Quinn & Nicholson at a full and proper price, of course, and then to amalgamate the two companies. He'd already formed Pharmaceutical & Galenical Properties, Ltd., to act as holding company.

I don't think that any of us was really surprised at the suggestion. It seemed an entirely logical step. When he added that he was prepared to undertake that the two companies would continue to operate separately with only financial control at the top, I could see that it was going to go through.

Naumann asked Wilfred Harrap to come onto the parent company and offered me the secretaryship of the whole group. Since this would leave the Quinn & Nicholson management a bit thin on the ground, he suggested that we invite Dumbo to come back. We were all glad to say yes to that.

Then the lawyers got in on the act and we seemed to spend the next six months signing papers.

I visited Oliver quite often while he was in hospital and afterward when he was in a convalescent home out in Hertfordshire. To start with, he asked a lot of questions about the firm and how the various changes were working, but his interest soon cooled off. I had noticed the same thing about the war. He didn't look back. I never once knew him to attend a regimental reunion. When a thing was over, it was over. It was the same with business. As soon as he realized that the curtain was down on Act II, he started planning Act III.

There were a good many loose ends to be cleared up. One of them was the girl Oliver had installed in his flat and had been living with since Philippa left. She was a society prostitute. I'll leave her name out of it, because you'll see her face often enough in the glossies. Oliver deputed me to make her a small capital payment, and an affair which had had only financial roots withered as quickly and as quietly as it had flourished.

It was while I was doing this job for him that Oliver made a remark that stuck in my mind. He said, "It's an odd thing, when you come to think of it, that the only really satisfactory relationship I've had with a woman was when I couldn't get her into bed with me."

I guessed he was thinking about Serena Strickland.

When Oliver was fit to move, he started planning the Villa Korngold. In a way I was responsible for this. I had spotted the site on one of my skiing holidays, and had mentioned what a beautiful spot it would make for a house, without thinking that anyone would be mad enough to try.

The challenge appealed to Oliver. He had a long wrangle with the Bank of England over getting the money out, and a fight with the Swiss authorities to get permission to build. And what with one thing and another it was nearly two years before everything was ready and Wilfred Harrap, Bill Blackett, and George Taylor went with me to Heath Row to see him off. We promised to keep in touch, but I knew, really, that it would be occasional visits, at longer and longer intervals. He was flying out of our lives.

POSTSCRIPT:

Continued and Concluded

It took the newcomer, wheeling his bicycle, a further ten minutes to reach the Villa Korngold. We had identified him by his uniform as a member of the Felden-Gendarmerie, and by his badges, as he came closer, as a senior sergeant.

He paused for a moment below the veranda, on which the three of us were breakfasting, to wipe the sweat from his broad red forehead with a blue handkerchief and to straighten his uniform cap. Then he came clumping up the steps.

At the sight of Professor Lindt, he stiffened to attention and his hand went up in a salute.

The Professor said, "At ease, Sergeant, and tell us what brings you up this hot, steep hill."

The Sergeant fumbled in the leather pouch which he carried on his belt beside his automatic pistol (and very much in the way if he had had to use it, I should have thought) and brought out a buff form. He said, "A complaint has been laid before the Superior Court at Vienna affecting Herr Nugent. This complaint, coupled with a formal request for extradition, has come before the Federal Court at Bern. It was doubted to start with whether the complaint was in order, but the court decided that, being a criminal charge deposed to by independent witnesses, it must be investigated."

"The charge being?"

The Sergeant managed to look both official and embarrassed at the same time. He said, "It is a charge of murder."

"Indeed. And whom has he murdered?"

"And when?" asked Dr. Hartfeldt dryly.

"It related to an incident which took place in the month of June, 1945, when Herr Nugent, then in the Army, was in charge of a prisoner-of-war camp near Klagenfurt."

"So? A war crime?"

"The court suggested that it was a war crime, but the complainant, Herr Engelbach, whose brother and the other man were alleged to have been killed, pointed out that the incident occurred after the armistice and the men concerned had reverted to civilian status. The charge was therefore one of murder of civilians and would not ·be affected by the amnesty for crimes committed in the course of operations of war which was promulgated last year."

The Sergeant said all this respectfully but firmly. Personally I was feeling sorry for him. It had been a hot and dusty clumb up that hill.

"I very much fear," said the Professor, "that the case of Herr Nugent has been removed to a higher court than either the Superior Court at Vienna or the Federal Court at Bern." He looked at Dr. Hartfeldt, who said, "It is true, Sergeant. Herr Nugent died last night. To be precise, at three o'clock this morning. I at once reported the matter to Professor Lindt, as coroner for the City and District of Oberthal."

The Sergeant saluted again and turned on his heel. Professor Lindt said, "It is courteous of you to accept my word, Sergeant. Nevertheless, I think your superiors would wish you to satisfy yourself. You may go in."

We all went in. Oliver was looking remarkably peaceful. Indeed, although it is always difficult to tell in such cases, I could have sworn that there was a smile of satisfaction on his face.

Incidentally, the sudden death of a company chairman— even an ex-chairmen—always upsets the delicate nerves of the Stock Exchange, and I imagine that when the news reaches England, Pharmaceutical & Galenical Properties will dip a few points. I have asked my brokers to buy a hundred for Rupert Strickland. I thought Oliver would have approved of that.

FINE MYSTERY AND SUSPENSE
TITLES FROM CARROLL & GRAF

- [ ] Bentley, E.C./TRENT'S OWN CASE $3.95
- [ ] Blake, Nicholas/MURDER WITH MALICE $3.95
- [ ] Blake, Nicholas/A TANGLED WEB $3.50
- [ ] Brand, Christianna/FOG OF DOUBT $3.50
- [ ] Browne, Howard/THIN AIR $3.50
- [ ] Boucher, Anthony/THE CASE OF THE BAKER STREET IRREGULARS $3.95
- [ ] Boucher, Anthony (ed.)/FOUR AND TWENTY BLOODHOUNDS $3.95
- [ ] Burnett, W.R./LITTLE CAESAR $3.50
- [ ] Butler, Gerald/KISS THE BLOOD OFF MY HANDS $3.95
- [ ] Carr, John Dickson/DARK OF THE MOON $3.50
- [ ] Carr, John Dickson/THE DEVIL IN VELVET $3.95
- [ ] Carr, John Dickson/THE EMPEROR'S SNUFF-BOX $3.50
- [ ] Carr, John Dickson/FIREBURN $3.50
- [ ] Carr, John Dickson/THE BRIDE OF NEWGATE $3.95
- [ ] Carr, John Dickson/IN SPITE OF THUNDER $3.50
- [ ] Carr, John Dickson/LOST GALLOWS $3.50
- [ ] Carr, John Dickson/NINE WRONG ANSWERS $3.50
- [ ] Chesterton, G.K./THE MAN WHO KNEW TOO MUCH $3.95
- [ ] Chesterton, G.K./THE CLUB OF QUEER TRADES $3.95
- [ ] Chesterton, G.K./THE MAN WHO WAS THURSDAY $3.50
- [ ] Coles, Manning/ALL THAT GLITTERS $3.50
- [ ] Coles, Manning/GREEN HAZARD $3.95
- [ ] Coles, Manning/NO ENTRY $3.50
- [ ] Coles, Manning/THE MAN IN THE GREEN HAT $3.50

☐ Wallace, Edgar/THE FOUR JUST MEN   **$2.95**
☐ Woolrich, Cornell/VAMPIRE'S HONEYMOON **$3.50**

Available from fine bookstores everywhere or use this coupon for ordering: